THE FAMILY WAY

"So, are we getting married?"

She smiled, though it was a shaky attempt. "If you're absolutely sure this is the right thing to do."

"I think it's the *only* thing to do, Dana."

"All right, then. We'll do it." She moistened her lips again. Cody wished she would stop doing that. Before he gave in to the urge to do it for her.

Oh, God, he was a quivering, nervous wreck, terrified that he was doing the wrong thing. But he was also feeling a strange, inexplicable excitement—ever since Dana had said yes.

"So..." Dana said slowly.

"So..." he repeated, smiling a little.

Their eyes met. Cody held out his hand. "We should probably shake or something," he suggested.

Hesitantly, she placed her hand in his. "Or something," she agreed.

THE FAMILY WAY:
When their beloved Granny Fran begins to play matchmaker, four cousins find love!

Dear Reader,

Silhouette Special Edition welcomes you to a new year filled with romance! Our Celebration 1000! continues in 1996, and where better to begin the new year than with Debbie Macomber's *Just Married*. Marriage and a baby await a mercenary in the latest tale from this bestselling author.

Next we have our HOLIDAY ELOPEMENTS title for the month, Lisa Jackson's *New Year's Daddy*, where a widowed single mom and a single dad benefit from a little matchmaking. Concluding this month is MORGAN'S MERCENARIES: LOVE AND DANGER. Lindsay McKenna brings her newest series to a close with *Morgan's Marriage*.

But wait, there's more—other favorites making an appearance in January include *Cody's Fiancée*, the latest in THE FAMILY WAY series from Gina Ferris Wilkins. And Sherryl Woods's book, *Natural Born Daddy*, is part of her brand-new series called AND BABY MAKES THREE, about the Adams men of Texas. Finally this month, don't miss a wonderful opposites-attract story from Susan Mallery, *The Bodyguard & Ms. Jones*.

Hope this New Year shapes up to be the best year ever! Enjoy this book and all the books to come!

Sincerely,

Tara Gavin
Senior Editor

GINA FERRIS WILKINS

CODY'S FIANCÉE

Published by Silhouette Books
America's Publisher of Contemporary Romance

ISBN 0-373-24006-6

CODY'S FIANCÉE

This edition published by arrangement with Harlequin Books S.A.

Printed in U.S.A.

Books by Gina Ferris Wilkins

Silhouette Special Edition

**A Man for Mom* #955
**A Match for Celia* #967
**A Home for Adam* #980
**Cody's Fiancée* #1006

*The Family Way

Previously published by Gina Ferris

Silhouette Special Edition

Healing Sympathy #496
Lady Beware #549
In from the Rain #677
Prodigal Father #711
†Full of Grace #793
†Hardworking Man #806
†Fair and Wise #819
†Far To Go #862
†Loving and Giving #879
Babies on Board #913

†Family Found

GINA FERRIS WILKINS

This award-winning author published her first Silhouette Special Edition in 1988, using the pseudonym Gina Ferris. Since then she's won many awards, including the Reviewer's Choice Award for Best All-Around Series Author from *Romantic Times* magazine. Her books have been translated into twenty languages and are sold in more than one hundred countries.

THE CARSON FAMILY

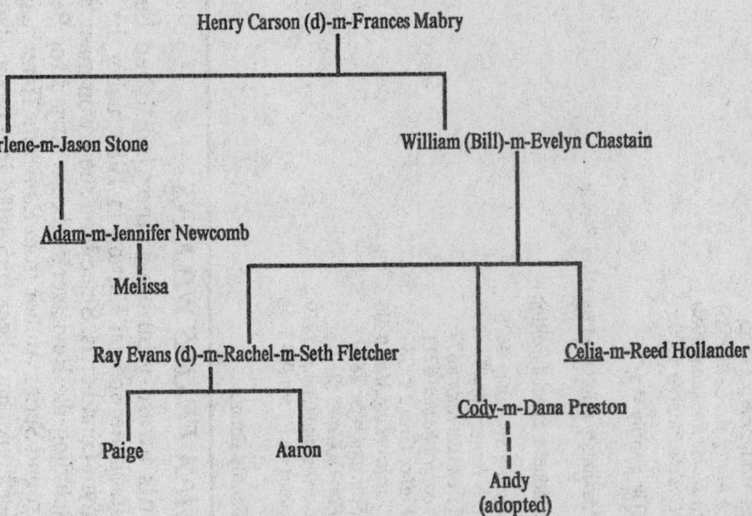

Chapter One

Standing behind the massive antique bar of his restaurant, Cody Carson hung up the phone with a hefty sigh. *Family,* he thought ruefully. *God love 'em, they'll be the death of me yet.*

The man and woman who'd been chatting quietly on the other side of the bar looked up curiously in response to Cody's gusty exhale. Country Straight wouldn't open for another hour, so they had the place to themselves except for the crew they could hear working behind the swinging doors that led into the kitchen.

"Problem, Cody?" Jake Dennehy, Cody's business partner, asked in concern.

Cody made a face. "Not really. That was my grandmother. She closed the call by reminding me of the family gathering for her birthday at the end of next month. It's six weeks away, but she talked as though it were tomorrow."

Jake chuckled. "She didn't really think you'd forget it?"

"Of course not. She just had to point out that the family hasn't seen much of me lately. I think she's convinced I'm up to something because I haven't been around much."

"You make her sound like my wife," Jake said, grinning. "Every time the kids disappear into another room and get quiet, Nancy just knows they're into mischief."

Cody winced. "Yeah, I guess that pretty much sums up the way the family feels about me. If I'm too quiet, there must be a reason."

Petite, red-haired Dana Preston, who worked for Cody and Jake as a waitress five evenings a week, looked puzzled. "I thought you were close to your family," she said to Cody.

He nodded. "I am."

"Then what's the problem with the family reunion? Why do you sound as though you're dreading it?"

Jake spoke up before Cody had a chance to say anything. "I can answer that. He's the only single adult left in the Carson family, and he's just had his thirtieth birthday. He knows good and well what's in store for him when the family gathers next month."

"Matchmaking," Cody agreed ruefully. "Granny Fran's already started. She told me a couple of her friends have granddaughters with 'very nice personalities.' She wants me to meet them. *All* of them."

Jake groaned in sympathy. "'Nice personalities,' huh? You, my friend, are in deep trouble."

"Don't I know it. Granny's married off the rest of her grandkids and now she's gunning for me. Somewhere out there is a gold band with my name on it—and I've got a big red *X* painted right on my forehead."

Jake laughed.

Dana turned to him in exasperation. "What's so funny?" she demanded. "Why are you both acting like marriage is such a horrible prospect? Especially you, Jake. You're happily married and have two adorable children. How would Nancy feel if she heard you talking like this, hmm?"

"Hey, I've got nothing against marriage," Jake protested. "Personally, I think it's great. But Cody—well, he doesn't exactly share my view of the institution."

Dana gave Cody a once-over that had him bristling. "I guess I can understand that," she murmured. "Marriage probably involves too much hard work and commitment to appeal to someone like Cody."

Stung, Cody almost argued with her. Instead, he resorted to his usual defense—lazy concurrence.

Leaning against the bar, he shrugged. "You got that right, darlin'," he drawled. "Just the thought of all that effort makes me tired."

Satisfied that he'd confirmed her accusation, Dana nodded smugly. "That's what I thought."

Jake, who knew Cody better than Dana—or almost anyone else, for that matter—frowned, but didn't bother to protest. Jake knew it would be a waste of time to defend his friend's honor when Cody wouldn't make an effort to back him up. Instead, Jake returned to his teasing, obviously trying to keep the conversation light.

"So what are you going to do about it?" he asked Cody in challenge. "Fake the flu or something and miss the reunion altogether?"

"And get cut out of Granny's will?" Cody asked in exaggerated dismay. "I wouldn't want to risk that."

Dana eyed him as though she wasn't quite sure whether he was serious or not. Cody didn't bother to enlighten her.

"You could always get engaged before the reunion," Jake suggested, tongue in cheek.

Cody shuddered dramatically. "No, thanks. I thought I'd made myself clear. I'm not ready to get married!"

"Did I say anything about getting married?" Jake pulled thoughtfully at his lower lip, his dark eyes gleaming with an expression Cody recognized.

Cody straightened slowly, watching his partner closely. "What?" he asked, intrigued.

"I was just thinking that it's sure been a long time since you've pulled one of your great practical jokes. You've gotten downright boring lately, Cody. Staid, even."

Cody scowled. "Staid? *Staid?* Me? Them's fightin' words, partner."

"I've got an idea for one of your scams—if you're interested. If you still remember how to pull one off, of course," Jake taunted.

Challenged, Cody lifted his chin and tossed his heavy golden hair off his forehead. "What's your idea?"

"Take a fiancée to your family reunion."

"A fiancée? Are you nuts? Didn't I just say that I—oh." Cody suddenly understood. He frowned, then slowly began to smile. "Oh, man," he murmured. "This could be great."

Jake was grinning broadly now. "I thought you'd catch on."

Dana was shaking her head. "You two are impossible. What a terrible idea!"

Cody ignored her. "It would be especially funny if she managed to convince everyone she's all wrong for me. Someone totally unsuitable. Granny Fran would be appalled, thinking she'd pushed me into an entanglement that was going to end in disaster."

Jake sobered at the sound of that. "I don't know, Cody, maybe this isn't right, after all. You've got a nice family. They don't—"

"No," Cody cut in, shaking his head, caught up now in his scheming. "Every one of them has made some comment lately about how I need to settle down and get married now that I'm thirty. Even my old buddy, Seth, has gotten carried away with the subject since he's married my sister. They all deserve this. I'll lead them on, make them sweat and then I'll come clean and make them admit they've been meddling. And then I'll have every one of them swear they won't say another word about the subject in the future."

"It'll never work," Dana muttered. "You'll be sorry."

"She's probably right—"

"C'mon, Jake, it was your idea," Cody protested. "And it's a great one. Back me up here."

"Okay," Jake conceded with a rueful shake of his head. "So who are you going to get to help you out? How about Mitzi?" he asked, naming a woman who'd been hanging around the club quite a lot lately, doing everything but throwing herself at Cody's feet to get his attention.

"No way," Cody said fervently. "Pretending to be engaged to Mitzi is likely to get me in more trouble than I'm looking for."

"So who?"

Cody rubbed his chin, eyes unfocused as he ran through a mental list of women acquaintances, none of whom seemed quite right for this particular assignment. Jake leaned against the other side of the bar, tugging at his lower lip again, obviously trying to help.

"You are both certifiably insane," Dana pronounced, throwing up her hands, which loosened her yellow Country Straight T-shirt from the waistband of her slim-fitting jeans. "Who in the world would agree to go along with something this crazy?"

Jake suddenly straightened, staring at Dana with a new gleam in his eyes. "I know someone," he said.

Cody narrowed his own eyes, looking from his partner to their employee. Surely Jake wasn't suggesting... "You're kidding."

Dana Preston had worked for them for almost a year now, but he had to admit that he still knew very little about her. She was extremely private about her personal life. An excellent waitress, hardworking, punctual, dependable—but almost obsessively reserved. Which didn't mean that she had ever been shy about expressing her opinions—particularly where Cody was concerned.

Cody had made a few attempts at getting the pretty redhead's personal attention at the beginning, but she'd made it clear early on that she wasn't interested. In fact, he'd realized soon enough that she had a rather sizable chip on her shoulder when it came to him. Someone had burned her, he'd figured. Burned her badly. He'd quickly backed off. He'd never been interested in picking up the pieces of some other guy's mistakes. He'd made enough mistakes of his own to last a lifetime.

He and Dana had maintained a careful, co-worker relationship ever since, chatting easily, sometimes teasing and bantering, occasionally squabbling, but definitely platonic.

He wasn't at all sure that Dana was the right person to help him with his practical joke on his family. He opened his mouth to tell Jake so, but his partner was already speaking again.

Leaning toward Dana with a companionable smile, Jake asked, "How would you feel about getting engaged to Cody?"

Eyes wide with disbelief, Dana hastily backed a few steps away. "Now wait a minute—"

"Think about it before you say no," Jake said quickly. "You'd be perfect, Dana. Most of the family have met you, so Cody wouldn't be showing up with a suspicious stranger.

You and Cody usually end up bristling like a cat and a dog when you spend too much time together, so it would be easy enough to convince them that you'd be making a mistake getting married—"

"You've got *that* right," Dana muttered.

Cody held both hands up to halt Jake's enthusiastic arguments. "It wouldn't work," he said flatly.

"Why not?" Jake demanded. "If you really want to teach your family a lesson, Dana's just the one to help you do it."

"Look, I've known Dana for a year and, as you pointed out yourself, most of the family knows she works here. They're aware that there's never been anything personal between us—not even a date. Why would they believe I'd suddenly gotten engaged to her?"

Jake didn't seem concerned. "You can come up with a story they'd believe," he insisted. "Say the two of you were—oh, I don't know—trapped here overnight by a bad storm or something. Only then did you realize you'd been harboring a secret passion for each other all these months."

Dana groaned loudly and rolled her eyes. "Didn't I *warn* you that watching all those soap operas would warp your brain? Of all the crazy, harebrained, totally unbelievable stories I've ever heard, this one has to take the cake."

Cody sighed regretfully. "Face it, Jake, the joke was a great idea, but this just isn't going to work. My family's never going to believe I've fallen head over heels for Dana, of all people."

Dana stiffened. She planted her fists on her slender hips. "Excuse me?"

"Nothing personal," he assured her hastily, hiding a grin at the genuine affront on her pretty face. "It's just that you aren't my type."

A spark kindled in her emerald eyes. "That's true," she admitted silkily. "I'm not your usual type. I, after all, have a brain. And I'm not afraid to use it."

Cody scowled. "That was a particularly catty remark," he muttered.

She flushed a bit, but met his eyes steadily. "Maybe," she admitted. "But you're not exactly Prince Charming yourself, Cody Carson."

"I never claimed to be."

She tossed her head, her chin-length cinnamon hair swirling around her face. "Right."

Jake sighed wistfully. "It really could be a great gag," he mused. "If only the two of you had the talent to carry it off."

"Hey!" Cody protested, his pride piqued. "I can pull off *any* gag. Even this one, if I wanted to. Of course, Dana..."

Dana's chin rose another inch. "Are you implying that *I* couldn't pull it off?"

He shrugged. "Well, as Jake said, it takes talent to really work a practical joke. It's a highly refined skill. Not many people can handle it."

"I could," Dana said confidently. "If I wanted to, of course. Which," she added bluntly, "I don't."

"Not even for a week off—with pay?" Jake asked enticingly.

She shook her head. "Thanks, but no. And speaking of work, we'll be opening soon. I'd better get ready for my shift." She started to move away, toward the employee lounge.

"Cody will pay you," Jake said quickly, apparently reluctant to give up his clever idea. "Five hundred dollars."

Cody choked. No one had said anything about this costing him—especially not that much!

"Er, Jake—"

Dana looked over her shoulder, one eyebrow lifted. "What was that?"

"A thousand," Jake said promptly.

Cody pressed a hand to his heart.

Dana stumbled. She turned very slowly. "A thousand?" she repeated, gaping at Jake. "Dollars?"

"Of course." Jake glanced laughingly at Cody. "It would be worth it, wouldn't it? To have your family off your back forever?"

"A thousand dollars?" Cody whispered, staring at his partner as though he'd lost his mind. "Are you crazy?"

Dana suddenly laughed. "It would almost be worth saying yes just to watch Cody sweat for the rest of the evening. But the answer is still no."

Cody watched her as she turned away again. The snug T-shirt and well-worn jeans fit her nicely, emphasizing her slender curves. Almost too slender, he noted. She could stand to gain a few pounds. Her hair was a rich auburn shot with copper, thick and invitingly soft looking. Her face was a delicate oval, her large green eyes her most striking feature.

He didn't know what suddenly prompted him to speak. "You don't think I'll do it, do you? Well, tell you what—I'll pay the thousand dollars, Dana. All you have to do to earn it is pretend to be engaged to me for a few days. And make my family believe it."

Dana looked over her shoulder again, and her eyes met his. He wished he could read the expression in them. There seemed to be too many emotions to identify, some of them so strong that Cody was taken aback. There'd been times when he'd wondered if this woman *had* emotions. Now he realized that there was a great deal more to Dana Preston than she had allowed him to see.

This fleeting glimpse made him all the more curious to find out who she was, what she was really like.

Almost immediately, Dana's eyes grew shuttered, impenetrable. "I have to get ready for my shift now," she said.

"Think about it," Cody urged as she walked away.

She didn't answer.

"Think she'll do it?" Jake asked.

"I don't know," Cody said. "Maybe."

For some reason, he had decided that Dana was exactly the woman he wanted—for the joke he planned on his family, of course, he clarified hastily. He certainly wasn't interested in her for any other reason.

Dana's head seemed to be spinning as she stashed her purse in her locker. Maybe that accounted for her uncharacteristic clumsiness. She dropped the purse, spilling its contents on the floor at her feet.

Muttering imprecations, she knelt to scoop up her belongings. Lipstick, key ring, breath mints, loose change. And a crumpled handful of envelopes she'd just picked up from the post office on her way to work. She hadn't opened any of them yet, but she knew what they contained. Bills, most of them.

A thousand dollars would go a long way toward paying them.

She scowled and stuffed the purse into her locker, slamming the metal door closed with more force than necessary. *Forget it, Dana.*

Two other waitresses walked into the lounge at almost the same time, nineteen-year-old Kasey Lee and forty something Angela Hallbright, both wearing the standard uniform of Country Straight T-shirts and jeans. As always, Dana greeted them politely, a bit distantly. Though she liked a friendly working environment, she didn't make friends with her co-workers. To be quite honest, she didn't have time for friends right now.

Tying her tiny waitress apron around her waist, she reentered the restaurant and glanced across the large dining room, her gaze drawn involuntarily to the man behind the bar. Cody Carson. Golden haired, blue eyed, dimpled. In his red-and-black western shirt and black jeans, he looked like a cross between a long, lanky cowboy and a California lifeguard. The embodiment of a wide range of feminine fantasies.

Dana tried very hard not to have fantasies—particularly any that included a man like this one.

Dana wasn't looking for a relationship, and even if she had been, Cody would have been all wrong for her. The guy was a heartbreak waiting to happen. Nothing good could come from an involvement between them, no matter how fleeting.

Even if it were only a charade for a practical joke, she reminded herself sternly.

The restaurant opened at five, just in time to welcome patrons looking for a break after a day at work. Nothing stronger than beer was served from the antique bar, and the menu wasn't extensive or fancy—burgers and barbecue, mostly, with salads and grilled chicken dishes for diners who wanted something lighter.

Dana knew there'd been pessimistic predictions of an early bankruptcy when Cody and Jake had opened a couple of years ago. But the partners had proved those gloomy voices wrong. By providing a place where everyone could feel welcome, where conversation was as important as the food, where the customers could unwind, listen and dance to country music and spend time with their friends, Cody and Jake had hit upon the right combination.

Oh, she doubted they were getting rich. But they were making a good income, and they seemed content.

It was all she hoped to someday find for herself.

The first customers came in as soon as the door opened, making Dana suspect they'd been waiting outside on this Wednesday afternoon. They looked hot and tired and she knew exactly what they needed. She greeted them with a smile and an offer to bring them something cold to drink while they looked over the menu, an offer they accepted gratefully.

Dana was very good at her job.

It was a busy evening. Dana soon found herself almost running from table to table. She pocketed a dollar tip from a five-dollar drink bill, and she couldn't help thinking that she would have to serve a hell of a lot of drinks to earn a thousand dollars in tips.

Cody, Jake and a woman named Caroline rotated as bartenders during the week. Tonight, Cody was doing the honors, filling mugs with foaming beer, pouring sparkling waters and assorted juices and soft drinks. As usual, he talked almost as hard as he worked. Few customers came into the place without stopping by to swap jokes and lies with Cody.

He was leaning on the counter, telling a wildly improbable golf story, when Dana approached an hour or so after opening.

"I'll tell you the rest in a minute," he promised the prominent doctor with whom he'd been talking.

"Take your time," Dr. Bakerman said dryly. "I'm sure the story only gets better with age."

Chuckling, Cody turned to Dana. "What do you need?"

"One light beer, two diet colas and an iced tea."

"Coming right up," he said cheerfully.

A moment later, he slid the tray across the bar to Dana. He held on when she would have immediately scooped it up and carried it away. She lifted an eyebrow. "What's the problem?"

"No problem," he assured her. "I just wondered if you've been thinking about the gag."

"I thought we'd already settled that."

He shook his head. The stained-glass light fixtures above him streaked his thick golden hair with intriguing highlights, displayed to perfection the lean planes of his tanned face, added intriguing shadows to his devilish dimples. Dana tightened her grip on the tray as he spoke.

"This could be a lot of fun, Dana. And I'll make it worth your while."

She hardened herself against the warm entreaty in his eyes. She'd almost forgotten for a moment that he wanted something from her, and he was willing to pay for it. He wasn't the first to make a similar offer. She didn't find it any more flattering this time.

"I'm really busy, Cody. I have to get these drinks to table four and take food orders from table six."

He obligingly released the tray. "Maybe you don't really think you *could* pull it off," he needled her.

She walked away without responding.

It was after eight when the call came for Dana. She was already tired, though she hid her fatigue from the customers behind airy banter as she served their food and drinks. Taking college classes in the mornings and working nights at the club, followed by late hours of studying, was exacting a heavy toll from her. She couldn't remember the last time she'd managed a full eight hours of sleep.

"Telephone for you, Dana," Angela said, appearing at her side with an order pad in hand. "I'll take care of this table—you go ahead."

"Thank you." Dana went into the back to take the call.

"Dana?" a young voice said eagerly as soon as she answered. "It's me. Andy."

Dana's weariness vanished immediately. "Hi. What's up?"

"I won first prize on my school math project. I know you're working and you can't talk long, but I thought you might want to know, since you helped me so much with it."

"Andy, I'm so proud of you! I didn't help you that much. You did it mostly on your own. Thank you for calling to tell me your good news. I'll have a special treat for you when I come to visit this weekend."

"That's okay," her ten-year-old half brother said, sounding a bit embarrassed. "You don't have to do that."

"No," she agreed with a smile. "But I will, anyway. You deserve a reward for working so hard. I know your mom must be thrilled."

The boy hesitated only a moment before saying, "Yeah. She seemed pleased."

Dana bit her lip. "Bad day?" she asked, trying to sound casual.

"Yeah. She's not feeling so good today."

"I'm sure your good news made her feel better."

"Maybe. She smiled real big when I told her."

"I bet she did. I'm smiling, too."

"Yeah?"

"Yeah."

"I'd better let you go. Mom told me not to keep you long."

"You call me anytime you want, okay? And I'll see you in a few days."

"Okay. Love you, Dana."

"Love you, too, sweetie." She hung up the phone with a lump in her throat and a familiar moistness in her eyes. For a moment, she was almost overwhelmed with emotions—love, pride, worry. Fear.

He was so young, she thought sadly. So vulnerable. She couldn't bear the thought of what he had to face soon—what they both had to face. And she simply couldn't accept the very real possibility that she would be losing Andy as well as the stepmother she had grown so fond of.

A burst of laughter from the dining room reminded her that she had a job to do. With a weary sigh, she straightened and smoothed her apron, telling herself she would think about her personal problems later, in the privacy of her tiny apartment.

She had just stepped back into the main room when it occurred to her that a possible solution to one of her problems had already been presented that evening, quite by coincidence.

Her eyes widened. One hand rose to cover her mouth as her heart began to thud. Why hadn't she thought of this sooner?

And then she shook her head. No, she told herself firmly. It wouldn't work. It was a crazy idea, just as she'd told Jake when *he* had proposed it for another reason altogether.

But even as she tried to talk herself out of it, she found herself wondering why she hadn't come up with it herself.

A fake engagement. It's perfect, Dana.

"It's insane," she muttered aloud. "I'd never get away with it."

"Dana?" Kasey Lee spoke curiously, passing her with a heavy tray of food in her hands. "You okay?"

"Hmm? Oh, yes, I'm fine, Kasey."

"You look sort of funny."

Dana pushed a trembling hand through her hair. "Just tired, I guess. Is that the order for table six?"

"Yeah. Table four's getting impatient. Can you take care of them?"

"I'm on my way."

Dana hurried toward table four, her thoughts lingering on the wild idea Jake had inspired in her. Even as she politely jotted down food orders from the couple at table four, she found herself glancing surreptitiously toward the golden-haired cowboy behind the bar.

"I'll make it worth your while," Cody had told her enticingly.

He couldn't have known that the only payment she needed had nothing to do with money—not even the thousand dollars his partner had impulsively offered her.

It just might work, she thought tentatively. *If Cody would go along with it, it just might work.*

Now if only she could find the nerve to ask.

Chapter Two

A half hour after the restaurant closed, Cody was in the office, staring blindly at paperwork and thinking about Dana. He'd been thinking about Dana quite a bit lately—even before Jake's crazy idea about having her pose as Cody's fiancée as a practical joke on the Carson family.

Part of his reluctant fascination with her probably had to do with her being such a mystery to him. She'd come to the club with few references and little personal history. Cody and Jake had hired her because she'd made a favorable first impression, and because she'd offered to work cheap.

She'd explained that she was working her way through an education degree at Percy Teacher's College, and needed an evening job to help finance her schooling. Since they'd been relatively new in business then and still uncertain of their earning potential, they had hired her immediately.

The club had done well enough since then that they'd given her two raises. Cody suspected that Dana was part of the reason for the club's success. The customers liked her. She was efficient, courteous, quietly competent. When approached with personal overtures, she rebuffed them politely, good-naturedly—but always firmly.

Cody still found her attractive, and even though he'd long since abandoned any thought of an intimate involvement with her, he was intensely curious about her. Where did she go when she wasn't working or attending classes? Who did she spend her leisure time with? Who had hurt her so badly that she held everyone at arm's length now—or *was* that the reason she did so?

Especially during the past few weeks, he had begun to suspect that something had been preying heavily on her. Even when she smiled, as she so often did in the performance of her job, there had been a growing sadness in her eyes that had bothered him. Jake had commented on it, though neither of them had presumed to ask her personal questions.

Cody wouldn't exactly call Dana a friend. She annoyed him a bit too often for him to term their relationship friendly. It irked him that she always seemed ready, even eager, to believe the worst of him. He knew his weaknesses, and his failings, but he paid his taxes, took care of his employees and tried never to deliberately hurt anyone.

Maybe his way of working was different from Dana's, more laid back. And maybe he didn't regard life with the same seriousness that she did—but that didn't mean she should treat him with such cool disdain. Who did she think she was, anyway?

A tap on the office door made him look up, distracted from his thoughts. "Come in."

As though he'd summoned her only by thinking of her, Dana stepped into the office. She was still wearing her apron, wringing it nervously between her hands. She looked tired, worried and... something else. Embarrassed? But why?

"What is it?" he asked, hoping she wasn't there to lecture him about the evils of practical jokes. He could accept her refusal to help him with it—expected her to do so, in fact—but he'd be damned if he'd let her tell him what he should or shouldn't do with his own family.

"I've, um, been thinking about your offer," she said. "You know—for me to act as your fiancée for a couple of days as a practical joke?"

"I remember the conversation," Cody said dryly.

She nodded, her cheeks a bit pink. "Yeah. Well, anyway, I might be willing to go along with you. If you're still interested, of course."

For a price. She didn't actually say the words, but they seemed to hang in the air.

Thinking of the thousand dollars Jake had rashly offered her, Cody mentally gulped at the thought of the money he really couldn't afford to spend frivolously. Funny. He wouldn't have thought Dana was the type who'd do anything for cash.

But he *had* gone along with Jake's offer, and he wouldn't go back on his word now. "I'll pay you the money," he assured her.

Her chin lifted in obvious pride. Her flush deepened. "I don't want your money," she told him coolly. "Please don't mention it again."

Startled, Cody blinked. "Then what *do* you want?"

"A return favor—something very much along the lines of the favor you've asked me," she explained. "I want you to pretend to be my fiancé this weekend for *my* family. I'm expected for the long Labor Day weekend—and I'd like for you to go with me."

Cody searched her face again, looking for a sign of humor in her eyes. Finding none. "Is this another practical joke?" he asked, thinking she was awfully grim about it if it was.

Again, she shook her head, her cinnamon hair swaying around her jawline. "Not—not exactly. No one can know we aren't really engaged. I want them to believe that we're perfect for each other, that we're genuinely committed. Can you do that? *Will* you do it?"

Piqued at what sounded like doubt in his acting abilities, Cody almost repeated adamantly that he could pull off any role she gave him—but he wasn't so sure he wanted to.

"What game is this?" he asked warily. "Is someone going to be hurt by this?"

"No one will be hurt," she assured him quickly. "Just the opposite, in fact. I promise, I'll tell you all the details when you need to know them. If you'll go along with me on this, I'll do whatever you want to pull off your big joke on your family."

Cody liked the sound of her offering to do anything he wanted. He was still more than a bit concerned about her counterproposal, though. She looked so damned serious about it.

Cody wasn't comfortable when anyone depended on him too much for help. He was a self-admitted clown, a joker by nature. Lots of fun to be around, but not one to come through in a crunch, he reminded himself with a touch of old regret. He'd let too many people down over the years.

He started to tell Dana not to look at him so hopefully, that he would only disappoint her—but something held him back.

Maybe it was the sadness he saw in her eyes again.

When his silence had stretched too long, Dana sighed and started to turn away. "Never mind. It was a stupid idea, anyway."

"Okay," Cody heard himself saying. "What, exactly, do you want me to do?"

Dana stumbled, then quickly righted herself as she turned to face him again. "You'll do it?"

"Yeah. Sure. Why not? I'll help you with your scheme if you'll help me pull off my practical joke and object lesson on my own well-intentioned but meddlesome family," he added with a wry smile.

Dana took a deep breath. "Okay," she said. "It's a deal." She held out her hand.

Cody still hoped she wasn't as serious as she looked, that all she wanted him to help her with was a lighthearted charade. He wasn't comfortable with the seriousness in her eyes when she offered her hand.

Impulsively, he stood, took her hand and used it to tug her forward. And then he planted a smacking kiss right on her surprise-parted lips.

He'd kissed her as a joke—a way of shaking her up a bit. He hadn't expected to like it quite as much as he did.

Dana didn't seem to share his reaction. After only a momentary hesitation, she pulled back abruptly. "Don't do that," she said, sounding cross, her cheeks flaming.

"You said we have to make your family believe we're really in love," he reminded her with an impudent grin. "Shouldn't we practice?"

Shoving her hands into her jeans pockets, she backed several steps away from him. "I don't think you're in need of any practice," she muttered. "We'll save the performances until we have an audience. This is a business deal. I have absolutely no interest in turning it into anything else."

And then she turned and all but bolted from the office.

Watching after her, Cody realized that she had pricked his pride. Again. And he found himself wondering if he could make her eat those words....

Two days later, Cody paced restlessly in the deserted parking lot outside Country Straight. Forgoing his usual jeans, boots and western shirts, he was neatly dressed in navy chinos and a navy-and-burgundy-striped cotton shirt. He'd had his hair trimmed, and had buffed the dust off his soft leather shoes. His Jeep Cherokee, freshly washed, sat nearby, packed and ready.

He'd made arrangements to be away for the rest of the long weekend, announcing that he would return to work on Tuesday afternoon. The club was closed on Mondays, anyway, so his and Dana's absence wouldn't be too much of a problem for the rest of the staff.

It was a beautiful Saturday morning. The sky was cloudless, a deep, rich blue that hinted of the autumn to come. The air was warm, but not too hot. A great day for a leisurely drive.

All that was holding him up now was Dana. She was supposed to have met him here fifteen minutes ago.

Surely she hadn't changed her mind. This trip had been her idea, after all.

He'd offered to pick her up at her home, but she'd refused, saying she would meet him here, instead. Cody didn't even know where she lived. The only address she'd listed on her employment records was a post-office box in nearby Parkerville. She'd mentioned a time or two that she lived in an apartment, but that was the extent of his knowledge about her personal life.

He glanced at his watch again, then at the empty streets. Seventeen minutes late...twenty minutes. *Had* she changed her mind?

At exactly thirty minutes past the time they were to have met, Dana pulled into the parking lot in an aging sedan and climbed hastily out from behind the wheel. Wearing a short-sleeved green silk blouse and loosely pleated taupe slacks, she was more formally dressed than Cody was accustomed to seeing her.

"I'm sorry I'm late. I couldn't get my car started," she explained. "It needs a new battery, I think. I had to get a neighbor to jump-start it for me this morning."

"I was beginning to think you'd changed your mind."

"I told you I'd be here," she said, as though that should have been enough to belay any doubts. She sounded annoyed that he'd even questioned her word.

"Yeah. Sorry. Here, let me help you with your bags."

"I've got them," she said, clutching a bag in each hand. She stubbornly insisted on loading them into the back of his Jeep herself. And then she walked around the vehicle, opened the passenger door, climbed into the seat and snapped the seat belt.

She looked, Cody thought wryly, as though she'd just stepped onto a tumbril headed for the guillotine.

Oh, yeah, he thought with a sigh. This was just going to be loads of fun.

Shaking his head, he climbed behind the wheel and fastened his seat belt before starting the engine. "How long does it take to get to your stepmother's house in Memphis?" he asked as he backed out of the parking space. All he'd been told about the upcoming weekend was that they would be staying overnight with her stepmother, for whose benefit they were putting on the charade of an engagement.

"An hour and a half," Dana replied, looking out the window.

Cody couldn't help noticing that she twisted her hands in her lap as though she were nervous. He knew the feeling. He loved pulling over a joke as much as anyone, but there was something really strange about this escapade. He got the feeling that there was a lot riding on the outcome, and that made him nervous, too. Especially since he didn't have a clue what it was all about.

Glancing at her hands again, he suddenly remembered something. He reached into his shirt pocket, pulled out a small velvet-covered box and tossed it into her lap. "You'll probably want to wear this," he said, keeping his tone casual.

She looked at him quickly, then turned her gaze slowly toward the box. "What is it?" she asked, sounding wary.

"Open it and see."

She opened the little box as carefully as though she'd been warned that it might blow up in her face. One look at the contents had her snapping the lid shut in a hurry.

"I can't wear this!" she said, pushing it back in his direction.

"You're the one who wants your family to believe we're engaged," Cody said with a shrug, ignoring her attempt to hand him the box. "Won't they expect you to have a ring?"

"Not necessarily. Not everyone wears an engagement ring."

"Still, it does make the story more believable. Try it on."

Dana still didn't reopen the box. "Where did you get it?"

Cody sighed. "Lighten up," he advised her. "I didn't steal it or anything. It's sort of on loan."

"On loan?" she repeated, surprised. "From whom?"

"Bennigan's Jewelry Store. Bob Bennigan's a buddy of mine. Owes me a few favors."

"Your friend let you borrow a diamond engagement ring? What did you tell him? What if it gets lost or stolen or something?"

"Dana, relax. It's a nice ring, but it's hardly the Hope diamond. And I didn't tell Bob anything except that I needed to borrow an engagement ring for a few days. He handed me this one and said to keep it as long as I needed it."

Cody smiled then. "He said he'd make me a good deal on it if I decide to keep it. He's probably hoping he'll make a sale as well as pay off a favor. Two birds with one stone, so to speak."

Dana still looked dazed. Cody nodded toward the box in her hand. "Try it on. It might not even fit."

With visible reluctance, she opened the lid again and lifted out the ring. A round diamond in a plain gold setting sparkled in the sunlight streaming through the windshield. Dana slid the ring carefully onto the third finger of her left hand.

It appeared to fit perfectly.

"It's lovely," she said quietly.

"Not very fancy."

"No, but I've never liked gaudy jewelry. This is beautiful. Tastefully elegant."

Cody liked that description. Reminded him of Dana herself. "You're going to wear it, then?"

"I, um, I guess so. As you said, it does make our story more convincing. You thought of everything, didn't you?"

He grinned, relieved that the tense moment had passed. "I've orchestrated some pretty elaborate hoaxes in my time. I'll have to tell you about some of the stunts my university buddies talked me into pulling. There was one in particular. It involved a goat, a parachute and a particularly pompous history professor."

"I didn't know you went to college," Dana commented, stashing the ring box in her purse.

Cody winced. "University of Arkansas. But I didn't finish," he admitted. "I washed out during my sophomore year—found out they wouldn't let me major in partying."

Evading unpleasant memories, he quickly changed the subject. "Tell me about your family. If we're going to pull this scam off, I really need a few more details than you've given me so far."

Dana drew a deep breath, as though wondering how to begin. Cody sensed that she was still reluctant to talk about her personal business, even though it had been her idea to involve him this weekend.

"You said we'll be staying at your stepmother's house," he said promptingly. "Is your father still living?"

"No. He died five years ago."

There was grief behind the quiet statement. "I'm sorry," Cody said.

Dana looked out the side window, her face averted from him.

Though he was tempted to shut up, Cody pressed on, needing to know more about the circumstances he'd impulsively fallen into. "What about your mother?"

"She died when I was eight. My dad and I moved in with his parents after that. He met Barbara, my stepmother, when I was eleven. She was a divorcée, with a daughter who's almost three years older than I am. They married when I was twelve, and had my half brother almost two years later. Dad was forty-three when Andy was born, and Barbara was thirty-nine. They were both delighted to have a son together."

"How did you feel about it?"

Dana glanced at him with a faint smile. "I'd grown very fond of Barbara, and I'd always wanted a little brother. I fell in love with Andy the first time I saw him. Daddy called me Andy's 'other mother.'"

"What about your stepsister? Was she as pleased?"

Dana's smile faded. "Lynette had a harder time adjusting to the new family. Her father was still living, and she was close to him. She never really got over her parents' divorce, though Barbara once told me the marriage had been a mistake from the beginning. Barbara and Daddy were so happy together, and I think it hurt Lynette that Barbara loved my father in a way she'd never been able to love Lynette's."

"I guess I can sympathize with that," Cody murmured.

Dana nodded. "So can I, now that I'm older. Lynette and I weren't close—she wouldn't allow us to be. But there was never any real conflict between us while we were young."

Something in Dana's voice made Cody wonder if there *had* been conflict more recently. Not that it was any of his business, of course, he reminded himself.

"You weren't very old when your father died," he said instead.

"I'd just graduated from high school," Dana explained. "I'd planned to start college in the fall. I've wanted to teach since I was in junior high. But Lynette had just married and moved away when Dad died, and poor Barbara had a terrible time dealing with his death. To be honest, she fell apart. I couldn't leave her and Andy like that, so I decided to postpone college for a while and stay at home to help out."

Cody couldn't help but be impressed by her sacrifice. It must have been difficult for a grief-stricken eighteen-year-old to put aside her own plans in order to take care of her widowed stepmother and baby brother, he thought. Had it been then that she'd become so cool and serious—or had she always been that way?

"Anyway," Dana continued briskly, obviously wanting to finish the story quickly, "I went to work in an insurance office, and Barbara went into grief counseling, and things got better. Andy started school, and Barbara became involved in volunteer work at the children's hospital. A little over a year ago, right after my twenty-third birthday, I decided it was time to concentrate on my own plans again.

"With Barbara's encouragement, I applied to several colleges. Percy Teacher's College offered me a scholarship. I looked it over, liked what I saw and signed up. Then I saw the ad in the local paper for a waitress position at Country Straight—and you know the rest.

"There you have it," she said flippantly. "The life story of Dana Marie Preston."

Cody suspected that several significant details had been left out of her so-called life story.

Men, for example.

Had Dana ever been involved in a serious relationship? With her looks, he found it hard to believe men hadn't noticed her. He certainly had, not that it had gotten him anywhere. Had she treated all men with chilly reserve, or had she saved that distinction for him?

Which brought him to another missing detail. "You still haven't told me why you need a phony fiancé this weekend," he reminded her. "I haven't got a clue what you want me to do—or why."

Dana twisted the diamond ring on her left hand and chewed her lower lip.

Watching her out of the corner of his eye, Cody couldn't help but remember how her lips had felt beneath his. It wasn't the first time he'd replayed the kiss in his mind. And he found himself wondering when he'd have a chance to kiss her again.

He told himself he wanted to do so only out of curiosity—would it feel as good to kiss her again as it had that first time?

He was beginning to think he would have to prod her to answer him when she finally drew a deep breath, looked up at him and said with devastating simplicity, "My stepmother is dying."

The Jeep swerved. Cody brought it quickly back under control. "She's...dying?" he repeated, uncertain that he'd heard her correctly.

Dana swallowed audibly and nodded. Her green eyes were moist. "Yes. Her fiftieth birthday isn't far away. It's very unlikely that she'll live to celebrate it."

Cody was stunned. "Are you sure?"

"I'm sure. Barbara knows it, too."

Cody shook his head, glanced into the rearview mirror and pulled the Jeep over to the shoulder of the road. Putting it into Park, he turned in his seat to face her, unable to concentrate on driving until he'd gotten this straight.

"Look, Dana, we've got to talk about this. I really thought you wanted to pull a practical joke on your family, something along the lines of what I planned for my own."

"I told you it wasn't a joke," she reminded him.

"I know you did, but..."

He shoved a hand through his shaggy blond hair. "Why do you want to lie to your dying stepmother?" he finally asked bluntly, unable to think of a more tactful way to phrase the question.

Dana winced. "It isn't as bad as you make it sound," she protested. "I have a good reason, believe me."

"I'm waiting to hear it."

She gave him a resentful look. "Stop sounding so critical. I wouldn't have even thought of this if you and Jake hadn't come up with the idea the other day."

"We were talking about a *joke,*" he reminded her. "A gag."

"Call it what you want, but you're still planning to deceive your family," she snapped. "And for a lot less of a reason than I have."

He folded his arms. "I'm still waiting."

She exhaled, pushed her hair away from her face, twisted the ring again, then looked at him. "Barbara was an only child and her parents have been dead for years. My father's people are all gone, too, except for a couple of distant cousins. Once Barbara is...gone, Lynette and I will be Andy's only family."

She seemed to choose her words very carefully. "Lynette is married and lives in New York with her husband, Alan, who does something in the stock market. I'm not sure what, exactly. Lynette's a commercial artist. They don't have children—by choice—and hadn't planned to start a family anytime soon."

Cody was beginning to understand. "Does this have something to do with your little brother?"

Dana nodded. "Lynette has told Barbara that she and Alan are willing to take Andy in, but I think that would be a terrible mistake. They're both so busy, so involved in their careers and their social activities. Lynette said she'd hire a nanny for Andy initially, and then make sure he receives a good education as he grows older."

"Boarding schools," Cody interpreted.

Dana bit her lip again. "I'm afraid so," she said after a moment. "She's never come right out and said so, but—"

Cody shrugged. "Sounds like a logical assumption. I've never thought New York City was a place to raise a child. Of course, growing up in small-town Arkansas myself, I find it hard to imagine raising kids in any big city."

Dana nodded. "I grew up near Memphis, but we always lived in quiet neighborhoods, always had a house with a big yard to play in, and safe places to ride our bikes and our roller skates and skateboards."

"I always had a big dog for a pet, and nearby woods to explore and creeks to splash through. I can't imagine growing up surrounded by concrete and skyscrapers," Cody mused.

"Neither can I," Dana agreed with a shudder. "Andy would be miserable in New York, Cody. I just know he would."

"How does he feel about your stepsister and her husband?"

"He's fond of them, I suppose," she said slowly. "He really doesn't know them very well. He was little more than a toddler when Lynette moved away. They don't get back to visit very often."

Cody still didn't quite understand. "Are you saying that you want to raise Andy yourself?"

"Yes," Dana whispered and there was so much longing in her eyes that Cody's throat tightened. "Oh, Cody, I couldn't bear to have Lynette and Alan take him away. He's so sweet and so open and loving—I just know they'd change him. I'd hardly ever get to see him, and we'd grow apart—that would break my heart."

Cody touched her shoulder consolingly. "You love him very much, don't you?"

"He's the only family I have," she murmured.

Cody thought of his own large, close-knit clan. His parents lived in Saint Louis, and his younger sister, Celia, had recently married and moved to New Mexico, and he knew how hard it was to be separated by so many miles. But he was lucky. His sister Rachel, her husband and her two children still lived in Percy, where Cody could see them anytime he liked. His beloved grandmother was only a couple of hours away, and the rest of the family gathered at every opportunity, so that they saw one another often.

He couldn't imagine being alone, without that close family bond he'd so often taken for granted. As exasperated as he became with them at times, he loved his family dearly. Losing any one of them would devastate him.

Dana interrupted his thoughts when she drew herself up straight in her seat and lifted her chin in that stubborn pose he was beginning to recognize. "I want to get custody of my little brother, Cody," she said quietly. "And I need your help to do it."

Cody swallowed a groan.

Dana had been right about one thing, he decided abruptly. Jake's brilliant idea of a pretend engagement had been a mistake from the start.

Chapter Three

A huge tractor-trailer rig zoomed past on the highway, buffeting Cody's Jeep in its wake. Roused by the noise and motion, Dana blinked and looked around. "We really should be on our way," she reminded Cody. "I told Barbara we'd be there in time for lunch and we did get a later start than we'd planned."

He frowned. "But—"

"I promise I'll tell you everything while you drive," she assured him.

He sighed, checked the mirrors and pulled back onto the highway, headed toward Memphis. "Okay," he said, certain he wasn't going to like this. "Shoot."

She drew a deep breath, turned her gaze to the summer-parched crop fields they were passing and began. "Barbara is a wonderful woman. Sweet, thoughtful, kind—but rather old-fashioned in many ways. She honestly believes that no woman is complete without a husband and a family. That's why she stayed in her unhappy first marriage for so long—she didn't want to be single again, even though her first husband was compulsively unfaithful to her. When she finally realized it was never going to work, she filed for divorce, but she has told me that she was miserable until she met my father."

"Some people are like that," Cody commented. "Just can't stand to live alone."

Dana nodded. "That's Barbara. And she can't stand to see anyone else living alone, either. She's been so afraid that I'll end up an old-maid schoolteacher—her words, not mine," she added quickly when Cody shot her a quizzical look.

"Yeah, that sounds about like my marriage-obsessed family. Granny Fran told me I wanted to be careful not to turn into one of those fussy old bachelors."

Dana managed a smile. "Then you *do* understand."

"I understand that part," he agreed. "But I'm still not sure how I come into this. Is this pretend engagement your way of reassuring your stepmother that you won't end up alone?"

"Partly. But that's not all."

Cody sighed. "I was afraid of that," he muttered.

Dana ignored him. "Since the extent of her illness became clear a few months ago, Barbara and I have talked about Andy, and she agrees that Andy would be happy living with me. But she doesn't think I can take care of him alone. She's afraid I wouldn't finish my education and that I wouldn't be able to have a social life or manage financially with a ten-year-old boy to raise. I wanted to quit and move back home to take care of her when we learned that she was ill, but she wouldn't hear of it. It upset her so badly that I had to drop the subject. She's determined that I'm going to finish college this time."

"She obviously has your best interests at heart."

"I know. But it's been very hard spending these past few months away from her."

"You should have told me, Dana. Jake and I would have given you all the time off you needed," Cody chided her gently.

She managed a weak smile. "Thanks, but I've been able to go home almost every Sunday, since it isn't very far. And you and Jake have both been very generous when I've needed time off."

Cody remembered a couple of occasions during the past few months when Dana had asked for time off to be with a sick family member. She'd never been specific, but he'd never doubted her excuses, instinctively trusting her honesty.

Now he realized that she must have been spending those days off with her stepmother. He wondered how she'd managed to keep up with her schoolwork and put on such a cheerful face for her customers, even with this burden weighing so heavily on her.

He couldn't help but admire her spirit. No wonder he'd thought her so serious and humorless at times. She'd had little reason to laugh.

"It isn't only my education that concerns her," Dana continued. "Barbara isn't sure a single young woman can provide the proper upbringing for a spirited little boy. She knows Alan has never really wanted children, but since he's agreed to give Andy a home, Barbara thinks it might be good for both of them. She says a boy should have a man around to give him guidance." Dana sounded disgruntled at the admission.

Cody cleared his throat and focused on the license plate of the old black Cadillac traveling ahead of them. Tact had never been his strong point, but he made an effort to phrase his words carefully. "You have to admit that some of her points are valid, Dana. You *are* a single young woman—a college student working evenings as a waitress. It wouldn't be easy for you to take on the responsibility of a small boy."

She started to protest, but he quieted her by raising one hand. "I didn't say you *couldn't* do it," he emphasized. "I just said it wouldn't be easy. Your stepsister, on the other hand, is married, established in a career and is apparently willing to take the boy in. I can see why your stepmother would be torn by the decision."

"She knows I love Andy, and that he loves me," Dana said, her voice low, throbbing with emotion. "She knows there isn't anything I wouldn't do to make him happy, even if it means quitting school and finding a better-paying daytime job. I'm prepared to do that."

"And she doesn't want you to have to," Cody surmised.

"It wouldn't be a sacrifice this time," Dana insisted. "Not if it means I can keep Andy."

Cody admired her dedication to her little brother. She obviously loved the kid—so much so that it was blinding her to reality. Knowing it wouldn't do any good, he wouldn't argue with her about it now, but he suspected her stepmother was right to be hesitant about leaving her son in Dana's custody.

It took more than love to raise a kid, Cody thought with the airy wisdom of a childless bachelor. A lot more.

As though to forestall him if he did intend to argue, Dana turned toward him and spoke quickly. "When you and Jake started kidding around about a pretend engagement as a practical joke on your family, I started thinking about my own problems. That's when it occurred to me that Jake might have stumbled on to a solution. If Barbara believes that I'm happily engaged to a man with a steady job and a secure future, she'll see that I can provide a good home for

Andy. She won't be so worried about naming me as his guardian."

"But—"

"She's commented several times that Lynette and Alan don't seem to have a very warm or demonstrative marriage," Dana rushed on before he could finish. "She worries that they aren't terribly happy together. You and I can convince her that we're crazy about each other, that we can provide Andy with a home full of love and laughter. You're good with kids—I've seen you with your niece and nephew. You'll like Andy, and I know he'll like you. Can't you see? It's the perfect solution."

Cody was getting seriously worried now. The almost feverishly enthusiastic look in Dana's eyes was new to him; he'd never seen her quite so passionate about anything. He wasn't sure she was thinking clearly about this—in fact, he was darned sure she *wasn't.*

"Dana, you haven't thought this through," he suggested. "Even if we do convince your stepmother that we're a happily engaged couple—then what?"

She frowned. "What do you mean?"

"How long do you expect us to keep up the charade? Do you plan for me to accompany you as your fiancé every time you come home to visit?"

"Of course not. I'm sure Barbara would understand that you're a busy man, that you have your own business to run and can't take time away very often."

"Still, she would probably expect to see me a few more times, at least. Holidays, family gatherings, that sort of thing."

Dana's lower lip quivered. "The next big holiday is Thanksgiving, which is three months away. Barbara... Barbara won't make it until then."

Cody's hands tightened on the wheel. "It's that close?"

"Yes." Her anguish was unmistakable.

"I'm sorry."

Dana only nodded.

Cody was growing more frustrated with every revelation she made to him. She was obviously acting impetuously, motivated by her grief and her fear of losing both her stepmother and her little brother. She wasn't thinking ahead, wasn't considering all the consequences.

Oddly enough, he was the one who was usually accused of being overly impulsive, of acting without thinking, of rushing in where angels feared to tread...but this scheme of Dana's sounded like a mistake even to him.

How had he managed to get himself into *this* mess?

"So what you're saying is," he said, trying to sound logical, "you want us to announce our engagement to your stepmother, spend the weekend convincing her that we're madly in love, talk her into naming you the guardian of her son, then go back to Percy and I'm out of the picture. From then on, you'll continue the charade of an engagement for Barbara, making excuses for my absences, assuring her that everything's just fine and that Andy will have a home with us. Then, after everything is settled and Andy has moved in with you, you'll announce to whomever is interested that you weren't really engaged, after all, and that you'll be raising the boy alone."

Dana nervously twisted the ring. "You make it sound..."

"What?" he prodded when she hesitated.

"Deceitful," she muttered.

He thought that pretty well summed it up.

Dana pushed a strand of hair away from her face and looked at him beseechingly. It was all Cody could do not to pull the Jeep over again and take her in his arms. Something about the look in her eyes made him ache to comfort her. The way a friend would, he assured himself. That was all it was.

"I don't know what else to do," she said, her voice breaking.

"Maybe..." He swallowed. "Maybe you should forget this idea," he suggested carefully. "Introduce me as a friend, nothing more. Let Andy go live with Lynette and her husband, at least until you earn your degree and get established in your teaching career. Maybe then Andy could come live with you for a while and..."

But Dana was shaking her head, her chin set stubbornly, her wet eyes glinting. "No," she said.

"Dana..."

She laid a hand on his arm. "Cody, please. Listen for one more minute, okay?"

He sighed and nodded. Something told him he was going to regret this.

"I know this all sounds crazy to you. Trust me," she added wryly, "this isn't at all the way I usually behave. I know there's a chance it will all fall apart, that it won't turn out the way I've planned—but I honestly don't know what else to do. I could fight legally for Andy's custody, but that would upset Barbara, and I just can't bear to do that to her. And, besides, there's always a chance I wouldn't win."

Cody thought there was more than a chance. He couldn't imagine a judge granting custody of the boy to Dana, not under the circumstances she'd described to him. But, having promised to hear her out, he kept his opinion to himself.

"I know what you're thinking," Dana said. "I know I haven't explained this very well, that you think maybe Andy *would* be better off with Lynette and Alan. I can't help resenting that you doubt I can raise my brother just because I'm single—"

"Hey!" Cody interrupted. "I never said that."

"No, but you implied it."

She went on before he could argue. "Still, I realize that you haven't met my family, so you don't have a full picture of the situation. All I'm asking you to do is to play along with me for today—meet Barbara and Andy, spend some time with them. Lynette and Alan are supposed to arrive tomorrow morning. I want you to meet them, too. I want you to judge for yourself whether Andy would be happy living with them."

Cody was startled. "Me? Dana, I'm not the one to make that decision. This really isn't—"

"Just meet them, Cody. That's all I'm asking."

He hesitated a minute, then asked, "And if I decide that Andy *would* be better off with them?"

"I'll listen to your reasoning," Dana said curtly. "Just as you've listened to mine."

"And how are you going to introduce me?" he asked warily.

"I would still like to introduce you as my fiancé," she replied, her cheeks a bit flushed, but her voice steady. "I think that would make Barbara happy. If you're still willing to cooperate, of course."

Cody lifted one hand from the steering wheel to shove it through his hair. "This is nuts."

There was a weak ripple of amusement in her reply. "I know. It was your idea, remember?"

He shook his head. "Oh, no. This isn't anything like what I had planned for my family."

"But you'll go along with me?"

He took his eyes from the road ahead long enough to search her face. She looked nervous, worried, a little tired and only faintly hopeful. And suddenly he knew he would do almost anything she asked. He exhaled deeply. "I'll do it."

"You'll pretend to be engaged to me? Act like you're in love with me?" she asked, as though to make absolutely sure he knew what he was agreeing to.

He nodded. "Yeah. But I'm not getting involved with your family business. I won't pressure your stepmother into naming you as Andy's guardian. I'm not going to do anything to influence her decision, is that clear? She's the boy's mother. It's her right to decide what is best for him."

He started to add that the decision shouldn't be influenced by belief in a nonexistent engagement between him and Dana, but he'd already given his word that he would go along with that. He wouldn't back out on her now.

Dana seemed a bit taken aback by his vehemence, but she finally nodded. "All right. We'll keep the focus on us, and leave Andy out of it this weekend. I'll talk to Barbara in private about his future."

"Just don't use me as an argument in your favor," Cody reminded her. "That wouldn't be right, Dana. If you honestly believe you can provide the best home for your little brother, it's up to you to convince your stepmother. Remember, Andy's whole future is at stake here."

"I'm well aware of that," Dana muttered a bit resentfully.

He nodded. "I hope so," he said, his own voice grim.

They were well over halfway to Memphis by the time Cody was satisfied that he'd heard the whole story. Neither of them said much after that. Dana seemed lost in her own thoughts, and Cody was busy chewing himself out for letting his impulsive nature get him into another awkward situation.

He knew something was going to go wrong this weekend, that he'd somehow let Dana down. She wanted him to convince everyone that he was the stable, responsible, dependable type—and he just wasn't sure he was that talented an actor.

He was still surprised that she'd asked him to meet her family and form an opinion about who should be responsible for Andy. He wouldn't have thought she'd have cared about his judgment one way or the other.

He idly scanned the Memphis skyline as he drove across the bridge that spanned the Mississippi River, connecting Arkansas and Tennessee. It had been a while since he'd been to Memphis. The gleaming aluminum pyramid just on the other side of the river caught his eye. The oddly shaped coliseum was utilized for concerts, sporting events and other large gatherings. Cody had seen Billy Joel perform there a few years ago; it had been a hell of a concert.

Dana broke her silence to give him concise directions to her stepmother's house on the east side of Memphis, in Germantown. Cody knew the area. He navigated carefully through the Saturday-morning traffic. An internationally familiar face loomed on a billboard ahead. Trying to establish conversation, Cody asked lightly, "Ever been to Graceland?"

"Hasn't everyone?" Dana asked wryly.

"Well—no."

"You haven't taken the tour?"

He shook his head. "I wasn't really an Elvis fan. I mean, he was okay, but a little before my time. I was just a kid when he died."

"So was I, of course. But it's hard to grow up in Memphis without becoming an Elvis fan. Odd as he was in some ways, the man had something . . . special."

"Okay, I'll grant that. There's never been anyone else quite like him."

Which exhausted *that* subject. Searching for another one, Cody noticed a proliferation of glittery billboards advertising the riverboat casinos in nearby Tunica, Mississippi. "I suppose you've been to Tunica a few times."

She shook her head. "No. I've never had enough extra money to risk on the turn of a card or the roll of a die."

He chuckled dryly. "Smart move. I've been twice with friends, and I came home busted both times. I'm afraid I have no luck as a gambler."

"'Unlucky at cards...'" she murmured.

He winced when he recognized the allusion. Cody had been no more lucky at love than he had been at games of fortune—maybe because he'd spent so many years avoiding that particular risk.

"What do you do in your spare time?" he asked, quickly changing that subject. "When you aren't going to school or waiting tables."

Dana shrugged. "I haven't had a lot of free time the past year," she admitted. "When I'm not in class or at work, I'm usually studying."

"What did you like to do before you started school last year?"

"Before that, I worked long hours for the insurance company and helped Barbara with Andy in the evenings."

Exasperated, Cody turned his head to look at her. "Surely there's something you like to do just for fun. No one can work all the time."

Cody, himself, had a passion for golf. When he wasn't at the club, he could usually be found hanging out with his buddies at the golf course. He'd always considered it one of the few things he was really good at, frivolous as that one talent might be, since he'd never even attempted to turn it into a paying career. As far as he was concerned, doing so would have taken away from the pure pleasure of the game.

Dana didn't seem to have a similar passion. She was quiet for a while, then she made a face and lifted one hand in a gesture of bewilderment.

"I guess I don't have what you would call a hobby," she admitted. "I used to play tennis in high school, but I haven't held a racket in years. I like to read, but for the past few months I haven't had time to read anything but college textbooks. I can't remember the last movie I saw that wasn't animated—I've seen a few of those on weekends with Andy."

Which only reinforced Cody's doubt that Dana should try to raise her little brother. Dana needed a life of her own, and she had little enough of that now.

Oh, sure, maybe if she had a husband...and, no, it wasn't a sexist thought, he assured himself sanctimoniously. He simply meant that if she had someone to share the burden of child raising, it would be easier for her to pursue her own goals. But with that overachieving nature of hers, she was more likely to give up everything else to take care of Andy. What would that leave her after her brother had gone off on his own? No family of her own, no degree in the career she'd always wanted, no hobbies... He almost shuddered at the thought of the emptiness the boy would unintentionally leave behind.

Though he knew Dana would vehemently disagree, Cody still wondered if it wouldn't be better for Andy to live with his other sister, the one who'd already established a home and a career.

"You, uh, aren't dating anyone?" he asked without even realizing his thoughts had taken that turn.

Dana sighed. "If I were, would I have had to ask you to pretend to be my fiancé?" she asked logically.

"No," he had to admit. "So you haven't ever been, uh—?"

"Involved with anyone?" She looked disconcerted for a moment, but answered evenly enough. "There was someone once. Three years ago. Charming, funny, great looking. I was . . . infatuated with him for a while."

Cody sensed that she'd been hurt. Though he knew it was none of his business, he couldn't help asking, "What happened?"

"Nothing happened. I learned quickly enough that *fun* was the only serious word in his vocabulary. Turned out he didn't believe in responsibilities, compromises—or commitments. When my family obligations got in the way of his 'fun,' he simply found someone else to play with. Anyone else would do."

Cody winced at the underlying bitterness in the words—and the barbed innuendo. Was she suggesting that he was like the guy she'd once fancied? The guy she made sound so shallow and worthless? Was that why she'd been so cool to him from the beginning—because he reminded her of the man who'd hurt her?

Was she that far off the mark in her comparison? Cody scowled at the errant thought.

"Turn left at the next street," Dana said abruptly. "Barbara's house is the second on the right."

Relieved to have a distraction from his sudden discomfort, Cody turned left.

He was a bit startled by the size of the house Dana pointed out as her stepmother's. Dana always seemed so strapped for money—yet her stepmother's house was a big, expensive-looking place in a decidedly upscale neighborhood. A circular driveway branched off to a three-car garage at the right of the house; the landscaping looked to have been professionally done.

"Nice place," he commented.

"It was Barbara's when she and Dad married," Dana explained. "She received a sizable inheritance from her parents—they owned a profitable chain of department stores in the sixties. Though she's never quite said so, I've suspected that her first husband married her for her money."

Cody fought a brief, all-too-familiar battle between discreet silence and rampant curiosity. As it usually did with him, curiosity won. "If your stepmother is wealthy, why are you working at Country Straight to put yourself through college?" he asked bluntly.

Dana looked at him incredulously. "You really are as tactless as Jake says, aren't you?"

He didn't bother to disagree.

Dana sighed. "My father was a police officer who lived on a cop's salary. He never touched Barbara's money, for himself or for me. I suppose I inherited his independence. Since I've moved out, I've made my own way. Barbara's illness has been very expensive, and anything left over after...afterward should go in trust for Andy's education. Any other personal questions you want to ask before we go in?" she added a bit waspishly. "The balance of my checking account, maybe?"

He cleared his throat. "Sorry if I was out of line," he said gruffly. "I was just curious."

She nodded and opened her door. "Let's go in," she suggested. "We can come back out for the bags later."

They climbed the four steps to the double front doors. Dana hesitated at the threshold.

She turned to Cody and took a deep breath. "If we're going to do this," she said, suddenly looking nervous, "we have to do it right. Barbara has to believe that we're really in love, that we have a real commitment. If you don't think you can do it, please say so now. Before we go in."

Cody looked into her beseeching eyes and felt something twist inside him. What a position she'd put him into! Not only did he have to hide his own doubts about her plans for her little brother's future, not only did he have to spend a weekend in a home with total strangers, one of whom was very ill, but she also expected him to pretend to be madly in love with her. To pretend he wanted to marry her.

He almost told her right then that he couldn't do it. And then his gaze fell on her slightly unsteady lower lip. And he remembered the way she'd tasted, the way she'd felt in his arms. And he heard himself saying, "I can do it."

He immediately told himself that he meant only that he was a talented enough actor to handle the role she'd assigned him. He certainly didn't intend to get carried away with the charade. He wouldn't let himself forget that he wasn't the type to make commitments. And he wouldn't allow Dana to forget that he wasn't the type of man to depend on in the long run.

She was probably right to compare him to her ex-boyfriend. Cody had let too many people down—himself included. He'd long since decided the best way to avoid hurting anyone in the future would be to make no promises, no guarantees.

If no one really expected him to come through for them, no one would be disappointed—or disillusioned—when he blew it.

He would get through this weekend somehow, no matter how difficult it would prove to be. And then, he told himself in determination, he was never going to allow his impulsiveness to get him into a weird situation like this again!

Chapter Four

Dana had just led Cody through the front door when her name was shouted with enthusiasm from somewhere above. Looking up, Cody spotted a boy at the top of a staircase leading up from the spacious, marble-floored entryway.

"Hi, Dana!" The boy pelted down the stairs, his shaggy red hair tousled around a Rockwell-cute freckled face. Obviously, this was Andy. The reason Cody was here.

Dana was at the foot of the stairs to catch her brother as he threw himself down the last three steps. Laughing, she hugged him tightly.

"It's only been a couple of weeks since I was here last," she admonished him lovingly. "You act as though it's been months."

"It seems like a long time," her little brother said ingenuously. "I've missed you."

"I've missed you, too," Dana replied with a smile that made Cody's chest go tight again.

Oh, hell, he thought. *How could I—or anyone—expect her to willingly walk away from a bond like this?*

He was just grateful that it wouldn't be his decision to make. He was here only for the weekend, and had he known all the details before he'd begun the trip, he wouldn't even have come this far.

The boy noticed Cody then. Without self-consciousness, he pulled out of his sister's arms and gave Cody a thorough once-over. "Hi," he said. "I'm Andy. Mom said Dana was bringing a friend for the weekend. Are you her boyfriend?"

Cody gulped. Dana's cheeks pinkened.

"Yes," she said, looking at Cody as though daring him to argue. "Andy, this is Cody Carson. My boyfriend."

"Yeah?" Andy cocked his head, studied Cody a moment longer, then shrugged. "Cool."

He turned away. "Benji Nesterman fell off his bike and broke his arm," he announced to his sister. "I got to be the first to sign his cast."

Cody had been around his niece and nephew enough not to be overly surprised by Andy's matter-of-fact acceptance of Cody's presence. Dana chuckled and tousled her brother's copper hair. "That's quite an honor," she teased him.

Andy grinned and nodded. "I drew a smiley face under my name. Did you ever break your arm, Cody?"

"Yeah," Cody answered, unconsciously flexing his left arm. "My leg, too. In a car accident."

He knew his light tone belied the horror of the memories. Nor was he inclined to elaborate on the single most devastating experience in his lifetime.

"Did you wear a cast?"

"From my wrist to my shoulder, and from my ankle to my hip," Cody replied with a shrug. "There was room for everyone I knew to sign them. And they did."

"Cool," Andy pronounced, his all-purpose word apparently.

A stocky, gray-haired woman in a brightly-colored windsuit appeared at one end of the foyer. "I thought I heard your voice," she said to Dana, smiling in welcome. "Your stepmom's getting impatient to see you and meet your young man." She glanced curiously at Cody as she spoke.

Dana greeted the woman with a warm hug, then turned to gesture toward Cody. "Cody Carson, this is Hilda DeWitt. She's been with us a long time. I don't know what we'd have done without her these past few months," she added.

Cody assumed Hilda was a housekeeper. He responded to the introduction politely, rather amused that the woman was giving him the same thorough scrutiny that young Andy had only minutes before. Like Andy, she seemed to approve of what she saw.

"Miss Barbara is waiting for you," she said, motioning toward the doorway behind her. "I'll be in the kitchen if you need me. I'll let you know when lunch is ready."

"Thanks, Hilda." Dana swallowed visibly, ran her hands down the legs of her slacks in a nervous gesture, then nodded toward Cody. "Ready to meet my stepmother?" she asked, her eyes searching his face.

Her display of nervousness fueled his own. One wrong move, he thought...one wrong word, and Dana would never forgive him.

One last time he wished he'd never agreed to this, had never listened to Jake's crazy idea in the first place. But then he reminded himself of the pledge he'd made to Dana, and he nodded somewhat curtly. "Ready."

She held out her hand to him, and he noticed that her fingers weren't quite steady. "Let's go, then."

He took her hand. Leaving Andy with Hilda, Dana and Cody walked into a hallway lined with framed portraits. Cody noticed that several of them were of Dana at various ages; he would have liked to stop and examine them, but she tugged at his hand to keep him moving.

He made a mental note to study the photographs later during the weekend—just for curiosity, of course.

Dana paused in an open doorway. Looking past her, Cody saw that it led into a large bedroom decorated in rose and white frills and lace. A four-poster bed rested in the center of the ultrafeminine room. Propped against a mound of pillows lay a woman Cody knew must be Barbara Preston, Dana's stepmother. At his first glance, he realized that Dana hadn't exaggerated the extent of Barbara's illness.

Barbara's gaunt face brightened when she saw Dana. She smiled, and Cody saw that she had once been beautiful. He knew she wasn't quite fifty, but her disease had aged her beyond her years, digging lines of pain into her pale skin, hollowing her cheeks and eye sockets.

"Dana," she said, her voice weak but still musical. "I'm so happy to see you."

Dana dropped Cody's hand and rushed forward to hug her stepmother. "Hi, Mom," she murmured as she drew back. "How are you feeling?"

"Not bad at all," Barbara assured her.

Even Cody could see that she was lying.

Barbara was already looking at him, an eagerness in her eyes she made no effort to hide. "You must be Cody."

He smiled and stepped forward. "Yes, ma'am. It's a pleasure to meet you. Dana's told me a lot about you."

Barbara reached out to take his hand. Hers was cold, and so frail it almost broke Cody's heart. He cradled it gently.

"She's told me a lot about you, too," she said, taking him completely by surprise with the archly teasing look that accompanied the words.

"Has she?" he murmured, glancing from Barbara to Dana.

"Oh, yes. From the day she started working for you and your partner, I always suspected Dana was more fond of you than she'd let me know."

Dana shifted restlessly. Intrigued, Cody leaned closer to Barbara. "What makes you say that?" he asked encouragingly.

Still holding his hand, Barbara patted the bed beside her. Cody perched there gently, touched by her pleasure in meeting him.

"Why did I suspect that she was interested in you?" Barbara's eyes suddenly filled with mischief that belied her obvious pain. "For one thing, when she first described you, she mentioned that you were very handsome, with thick blond hair, deep blue eyes and a wicked smile."

"Um, Barbara," Dana murmured, her cheeks suspiciously pink.

"She told me that you have a wonderful sense of humor and that you're an excellent golfer. She told me you've lived in Percy a long time and that you're very close to your family. And she told me that you're good to your employees, always ready to lend a helping hand. I thought it was sweet that you changed Dana's flat tire for her one night when it was pouring rain, even though she says she tried to talk you out of it. She said you got drenched. I knew from the way she talked that you were someone special."

"Barbara, I've told you about all the people I work with," Dana said hastily, carefully avoiding Cody's quizzical eyes.

Barbara smiled gently at her stepdaughter. "Yes, I know. But there was something different in your voice when you talked of Cody. I always suspected you were especially fond of him—and I was right, wasn't I?"

Cody swallowed a chuckle at the look on Dana's face. He could tell her first instinct was to deny that she held any special feelings for him—and he, better than anyone, knew she didn't. But Barbara was so eagerly waiting to hear Dana agree.

Dana had no choice but to smile and say, "Of course you were right, Barbara. Aren't you always?"

Barbara laughed softly, and Cody understood Dana's reluctance to disappoint the woman.

Barbara squeezed Cody's hand. "I'm just so happy to hear that you've been dating. I've been so concerned about Dana. I've told her many times that she works too hard. I've worried about her being alone after..." Her voice faded.

Cody could have groaned at the expression in the woman's eyes. He was torn between remorse at deceiving her and sympathy with Dana's desire to assuage Barbara's worry. "She won't be alone," he said quietly, reaching for Dana's left hand.

Her eyes following the gesture, Barbara suddenly stiffened. "Is that... an engagement ring?" she asked in an excited whisper.

Dana and Cody exchanged a quick half guilty, half rueful glance.

It was Dana who answered. "Yes," she said. "It is an engagement ring."

It wasn't a lie, Cody mused. It *was* an engagement ring. He and Dana just didn't happen to be engaged.

But Barbara was blissfully unaware of that technicality. She caught her breath in delight and drew Dana down for a fervent hug. And then she reached for Cody.

Patting her thin, bony back, Cody shot Dana a look of reproach over her stepmother's head for getting him into this painfully awkward situation.

She had the grace to look penitent.

Barbara's eyes were filled with tears when she drew back. "I'm so happy for you." She sniffed, reaching for the tissue Dana had quickly pulled from a nearby dispenser. "So relieved. . . ."

She blew her nose, then managed a watery smile. "I knew something was up when you called to tell me Cody was coming with you this weekend," she told Dana. "When did this happen?"

"Very recently," Dana replied, looking determinedly away from Cody.

"My little girl's getting married." Barbara sighed. She laughed a bit self-consciously. "I suppose you think I'm being ridiculously sentimental, Cody."

He smiled. "Not at all. My own family is obsessed with the topic of marriage. Especially this year. Both my sisters and my cousin have married within the past twelve months."

"I want to hear all about your family," Barbara assured him eagerly.

He agreed to tell her everything she wanted to know.

Looking a bit tired, she settled back against the pillows, holding Dana's hand in her left, Cody's in her right. "When are you planning to get married?" she asked.

"Um, we haven't really set a date yet," Dana hedged.

Barbara's expression grew wistful. "I would so love to be there to see it for myself."

A heavy silence fell between them. Barbara shook it off. "You can tell me all the details later. I'm sure you'd like to unpack before lunch. Dana, you'll show Cody to his room?"

"Of course." Dana kissed her stepmother's cheek and stepped back. "Cody?"

On an impulse, he followed her example, fleetingly pressing his lips to Barbara's cool, thin cheek. "I'm looking forward to getting to know you better this weekend," he told her, and it was the truth. He'd liked Barbara from the moment he'd seen her.

Her smile was radiant, if weary. "So am I," she murmured.

Andy wandered into the room then. "I want to tell Mom about Benji's cast while you and Cody unpack," he said, moving to his mother's bedside.

Dana nodded. "All right. We'll see you at lunch, then."

"She looks worn out," Cody murmured as soon as he and Dana were out of hearing range.

Dana nodded. "Yes. Andy knows not to overtire her. He'll sit with her and talk quietly for a little while. They both treasure their time together."

Cody cleared his throat. "Does Andy know . . . ?"

"How little time she has left?" Dana nodded. "He knows. I'm not sure he's fully accepted it, but she thought it best for him to be prepared."

Cody sighed. "Damn."

She didn't ask him to explain, didn't need to. She slipped her hand beneath his arm. "You were very sweet to her," she said softly. "Thank you."

Cody covered Dana's hand with his own, a gesture of sympathy and understanding. "I like her."

Her smile trembled. "Everyone does."

Uncomfortable with the hint of tears in her voice, Cody decided to lighten the mood. And he knew just how to do it. "So I have a wicked smile, hmm?" he murmured tauntingly.

Dana immediately tugged her hand from his arm and moved a step away from him.

"She was exaggerating," she said coolly. "I've told Barbara all about my life in Percy. But I haven't talked about you any more than I have Jake...or Kasey or Angela or Caroline or..."

Cody chuckled. "Okay, I get the picture. You haven't exactly raved about me."

"Hardly." She sniffed.

"Mmm. Still..."

Dana tossed her head and moved ahead of him. "Let's get our bags."

Smiling at her obvious annoyance, he tagged obediently at her heels, much the way her little brother had earlier.

After they retrieved their bags from the Jeep, Dana led Cody upstairs. She pointed out Andy's room, then escorted him down the hall to two opposite doors. "You take the bedroom on the right," she said. "Mine is this one on the left."

"Does Hilda live in?" Cody asked.

"She has a room over the garage. The stairs to her room lead straight down to the hallway in front of Barbara's room, so Hilda can get to her quickly, if necessary. We've set up a monitor system in both rooms so Mom can summon Hilda if she needs her during the night."

"I've noticed that you call her Barbara at times and Mom at others," Cody commented.

Dana nodded. "I always have," she said. She didn't add that Lynette had never really liked it when Dana called Barbara Mom. On more than one occasion, Lynette had made a point to not so subtly remind Dana later whose mother Barbara really was.

Cody opened the door to his bedroom. "I'll get unpacked. Let me know when you're ready to go back down."

She nodded and opened her own door. It was with a deep sense of relief that she stepped in and closed the door behind her. She sagged against the cool wood for a moment, eyes closed, nerves stretched to the breaking point.

She had made a terrible mistake.

It had sounded so simple when she'd come up with the idea—or, rather, had modified Jake's idea for her own use. Convince the family she was engaged, produce a fiancé, reassure Barbara that Dana wouldn't be left lonely and miserable. Easy, right?

Wrong.

She'd known that Barbara had been genuinely troubled about Dana's rather solitary existence. Dana had never been able to convince Barbara that it was by choice she'd lived that way, that it just seemed easier in the long run. Barbara had always believed, instead, that Dana had been more hurt by her disastrous relationship with Linc Roberts than she was willing to admit.

Oh, sure, Linc had hurt her, Dana admitted now. But only because she'd been naive and foolish, imagining him to be something he wasn't. It hadn't been Linc she'd missed after it was over; it was the mythical lover she'd created in her own mind. Dana had the sense to see that now. And she'd been very careful not to make that mistake again. She saw people the way they were now, not the way she wanted them to be. Yet they still managed to surprise her occasionally.

Cody had surprised her today.

The way he'd acted when she'd told him exactly why they were doing this, for example. She hadn't expected him to express such disapproval and misgiving. He'd thought it was a great idea when Jake had first suggested it. He'd shown no qualms at all about pulling the scam on *his* family. Dana hadn't anticipated that he would have serious doubts about fibbing to her.

Of course, he hadn't realized when he'd agreed that her reasons for doing this were all too serious. Dana supposed she should have known how Cody would feel about that; Cody didn't like anything serious. The man seemed determined to turn everything into a spoof.

His clowning made him extremely popular with the bar customers, of course, but Dana had never particularly admired that part of him. She took life too seriously herself to have patience with anyone who considered it all a big joke.

Shaking her head, she laid her suitcase on the bed and opened it. As she unpacked, she continued to think about Cody, and the many reasons he was all wrong for her. She'd always admired his devotion to his family, his thoughtfulness as an employer and his skill at running the club, but just about everything else about him had rubbed her the wrong way.

She knew how he felt about commitment, for example. During the year she'd known him, he hadn't dated a lot that she knew of—for one thing, he worked late every night at the club—but it hadn't been for lack of trying on the women's part. Dana had seen them practically throw themselves into the lanky blonde's arms. In return, he had teased them, flirted with them, occasionally taken them out, but there'd never been even a hint of a serious relationship.

Cody liked women, Dana had long since decided. He just didn't like the thought of making a serious commitment to one.

Like Linc, she couldn't help thinking. Except, of course, that Linc had been more aggressive in his own pursuit. Linc rarely let an evening go by without a beautiful woman at his side; he never seemed content with his own company, as

Cody seemed to be. Nor would he have enjoyed the hours Cody spent with his family, playing with his niece and nephew, visiting with his grandmother, sharing Sunday dinners with his sister and brother-in-law.

Dana pulled a thick textbook out of the bottom of her bag. She'd thought she might have a chance to study this weekend, maybe at night when everyone else had gone to bed.

She thought of Cody's admission to her that he'd "washed out" during his second year of college. And all because he hadn't been allowed to major in partying, according to his account.

She thought of those years she'd spent working in a job that bored her, longing to finish her education. How hard she'd worked to get good grades since she'd started at Percy Teacher's College. As determined as she was to gain custody of Andy when it became necessary, she knew she wouldn't be able to continue with her studies and raise and support him at the same time. Though she considered the sacrifice well worth making, it hurt to think of walking away from her career dreams a second time.

And Cody had thrown his own educational opportunities away.

It was obvious that she and he couldn't be more different in their outlook on life.

And yet...

She thought of the tenderness in his face when he'd sat with Barbara. The melting sympathy in his eyes when he'd looked at Dana and silently acknowledged how grave her stepmother's condition really was. His apparently genuine concern about Andy's future.

It was that particular reaction that had Dana worrying that she'd made a mistake asking Cody to help her this weekend. She certainly hadn't expected Cody to agree with

Barbara that a single woman couldn't provide a stable home for a child.

Cody's own sister, Rachel, had been widowed young and left with two small children to raise. Dana had often heard Cody brag about what a good job his sister had done with her children. Rachel had recently remarried, but Dana had never gotten the impression Cody thought Rachel particularly needed a man to make her family complete.

So why didn't he think Dana could handle it alone?

She hadn't liked it at all when Cody had suggested that she let Andy go to New York to live with Lynette and Alan. She knew he'd thought he was suggesting the best solution for everyone—Dana included—but he didn't understand. He hadn't yet met Lynette and Alan, didn't know how strong the bond was between Dana and Andy.

At least he'd agreed to meet everyone involved before he expressed his final opinion. He'd promised not to interfere with her plans, though he'd refused to actively campaign for her. She supposed that was all she could ask of him.

She shouldn't have brought him along, she fretted now, beginning to pace the room where she'd spent so many happy hours of her adolescence. Something was going to go wrong, she just knew it. Her impulsively brilliant idea was unraveling right in front of her, and there was nothing she could think of to do about it.

All she knew was that she couldn't give Andy up. Couldn't lose him, no matter what she had to do to keep him with her. And if Cody wouldn't help her, then Dana would find a way on her own.

She had no other choice.

Chapter Five

"Tell me more about your family, Cody. You said your sisters both married this past year?"

Cody swallowed a savory bite of spinach lasagna and turned to Barbara. He'd been surprised when she'd joined them for lunch, brought in a wheelchair by her solicitous housekeeper. Barbara had eaten very little of the excellent lunch Hilda had prepared, but she'd seemed to enjoy watching Andy, Dana and Cody share the meal.

She also seemed to enjoy asking questions. She'd been subtly pumping Cody for the past half hour, asking about his work, his hobbies, his family. It was more than obvious that she was making sure he was the right man for her step-daughter; Cody only hoped his answers were serving to set her mind at rest. As for him, he was so wracked with guilt that he was hardly able to taste the food.

Guilt was an emotion Cody had lived with for years, had finally learned to lock away somewhere deep in the recesses of his mind. He hadn't expected to find himself assailed with it this weekend.

But then, he hadn't expected to spend the weekend lying to a dying woman, either, he told himself grimly, resisting an urge to glare at Dana.

He only hoped she was having as difficult a time with this crazy scheme as he was.

And now Barbara was bringing the conversation around to marriage. Cody suspected he knew where it would lead next.

"Yes," he said, hiding his feelings behind a smile. "Both Rachel and Celia are married now. Blissfully so, according to them."

"Rachel's your older sister? The one who was widowed young and left with two small children?" Barbara asked, proving that she'd been listening carefully during her gentle inquisition.

Cody nodded. "She's a couple of years older than I am."

"Do you like her husband?"

"Actually, he's one of my best friends," Cody explained. "Seth Fletcher, an attorney. They met when Seth moved to Percy last year to open an office there. They were married last New Year's Eve, just four months after they met."

"Do the children like him?"

"Paige and Aaron? They're crazy about him. In fact," Cody added with a grin, "they picked him out for their mom before she'd admitted that she was even interested. He's equally fond of them. And now they're expecting another baby."

Dana looked up in surprise. "Are they? I hadn't heard."

"They just announced it last weekend," Cody explained. "The baby isn't due for another seven months." Cody was aware that Dana knew Rachel only casually, having served her when Rachel and Seth, and sometimes the kids, dined at the club.

"You have met Cody's family, haven't you, Dana?" Barbara asked, seeming a bit surprised that Dana hadn't heard the news.

"Of course," Dana answered quickly. "I've met all of them. His parents live in Saint Louis, so they don't get down to visit very often, but I always see them when they're in town."

Cody bit the inside of his lip against a smile. Dana was telling the truth, in her own way. Cody's family had all visited the club periodically and always took time to chat with Cody's partner and employees, Dana included.

"And what about your younger sister, Celia?" Barbara asked, directing the question to Cody again.

"As I mentioned, Celia lives in New Mexico now with her husband, Reed Hollander. Reed works for the Treasury Department, the Bureau of Alcohol, Tobacco and Firearms. Celia met him in Texas last November. He was working undercover at the time, and she almost got herself killed when she accidentally stumbled into the middle of his investigation."

Barbara gasped.

Andy looked up from his lunch with sudden interest, having drifted into his own thoughts during the adult conversation. "Your sister married an agent?" he asked in interest.

"She sure did," Cody answered. "He carries a gun and everything."

"Cool," Andy breathed.

Barbara was eager to hear the rest of the story. "What happened?"

"Reed and his partner—with Celia's help, she insists—exposed an illegal arms deal and put the ringleader behind bars. After he saved Celia's neck, Reed apparently decided it belonged to him. They were married only a week later."

Barbara's eyes were round. "How romantic," she murmured.

Cody made a face. "When I first heard that Celia had eloped with a guy she'd known only a couple of weeks, I thought she'd lost her mind. I was sure it would end up in disaster. But after I met Reed, I changed my opinion. He's a nice guy, and I think he's exactly what Celia needs. He'll keep her from getting bored—but he'll keep her out of trouble, too."

Dana snorted. "You make it sound as though she needs a keeper," she muttered. "Are you aware of how sexist that sounds?"

Cody only shrugged. "I've always said Celia needed a keeper," he reminded her. "Nothing to do with her gender. She's simply accident-prone. Just the opposite of Rachel, who was getting along very well by herself until she met Seth and decided she wanted to share her life with him."

Barbara seemed pleased with Cody's response. "You sound like a typical big brother," she said with a smile. "I think it's sweet that you were worried about Celia's welfare."

Cody chuckled. "You should have heard Adam's reaction when he heard that she'd eloped with a near stranger. He went ballistic. Granny Fran had to almost order him not to track them down on their honeymoon and interrogate the poor guy."

"Adam?"

"My cousin," he explained. "Adam's the oldest grandkid on my father's side and he's always considered himself the family protector, for some reason."

"Adam was recently married, too," Dana put in, obviously trying to sound as though Cody's family was quite familiar to her. "In the spring, wasn't it, Cody?"

He nodded and waited for her to continue, curious as to what she'd say. She'd met Adam and Jenny when they'd dined at Country Straight with Rachel and Seth a couple of months ago, but he didn't remember Dana spending any time chatting with them.

"Adam married a woman with a baby daughter, Melissa," Dana went on airily, the diamond glinting on her left hand as she reached for her iced tea. "The little girl's adorable. Big brown eyes, a mop of curly dark hair."

For a moment, Cody couldn't figure out how she could possibly know that. Adam and Jenny had never brought the baby into the club.

And then he grinned, remembering the photographs that lined the credenza in his office. Rachel, Seth and the kids dressed in Easter finery. Celia and Reed on their honeymoon in Hawaii. A posed portrait of Cody's parents. Another of Granny Fran. And a small, framed snapshot of Adam, Jenny and Melissa. Dana had been into his office dozens of times for one reason or another. Obviously, she was more observant than he'd realized.

"It sounds as though you're marrying into a very nice family," Barbara told Dana happily.

"They are a nice family," Dana agreed, flashing Cody a look he couldn't quite interpret. "Very nice."

Maybe she was implying that she liked his family better than she did *him*.

Telling himself he was being paranoid, he glanced at Andy, who was playing with the remains of his lunch and looking bored. "You haven't had a chance to get a word in edgewise, have you, partner?" he asked. "Anything exciting been happening in your life lately?"

Andy shrugged, though he looked pleased to have someone's attention. "Nah. Just school."

"Andy won first prize on a school math project this week," Dana announced proudly.

"Yeah? Hey, that's great. What did you do?"

"Oh, it was just a percentage project," Andy said, deliberately downplaying the achievement, his green eyes gleaming. "I tracked the accuracy of the three local weathercasters for a four-week period. You know, wrote down their five-day forecasts, then recorded the actual weather each day. Then I figured out which one had the highest percentage of accuracy."

"That sounds really interesting," Cody encouraged him. "What did you learn from it?"

Andy grinned. "That what they seem to be doing is mostly guesswork. All of them were pretty close a day or two in advance, but they weren't as good at predicting more than three days ahead."

Cody chuckled. "Even the national weather bureau admits three days is just about the reliable limit. That was clever of you to prove it."

"He produced some really wonderful charts and graphs to back up his findings," Barbara bragged. "Colorful and eye-catching—he even used little drawings of suns and clouds and raindrops. You'll have to show him the display you made, Andy."

"Aww, he wouldn't be interested in that," the boy disclaimed, looking embarrassed.

"No, I'd love to see it," Cody assured him. "Sounds fascinating. I've always liked statistics."

"Yeah?" Andy looked encouraged. "I want to be a sportscaster when I grow up—like Frank Gifford or Ahmad Rashad. They use a lot of statistics and stuff."

"Yeah, they do. You play any sports yourself?"

"I played baseball last summer. First base. And sometimes I go to the Boys and Girls Club and play basketball. I'm not very good at that, though. My shooting sucks."

"Andy," Barbara protested. "Please find a nicer way to phrase that."

Andy sighed, but obligingly reworded the statement. "I'm a lousy shot."

"Have you been practicing with the goal you got for your birthday?" Dana asked.

Andy nodded. "It's not helping much. I can't hit that one, either."

"You have a goal?" Cody asked.

"Yeah. It's on a pole at the back of the driveway. Regulation height."

"How about if you and I go out and shoot some hoops after lunch? I play with my friends most Saturday mornings. Maybe I can give you some pointers."

An eager grin spread across the boy's face. "Cool."

"Let Cody have his dessert first," Barbara instructed her son, though she looked pleased by Cody's interest in the boy. "Hilda's made blackberry cobbler."

"With ice cream?" Andy asked eagerly.

"Of course. Would you like to go tell her we're ready for it?"

Andy pushed away from the table, grabbing his lunch plate and reaching for his mother's. "Yes, *ma'am.*"

Dana gathered her own plate, as well as Cody's. "I'll help Hilda serve dessert," she said. "No, don't get up, Cody. I'll be right back."

"You like children, Cody?" Barbara asked the moment the two of them were alone at the table.

"Yeah, I like kids. I spend a lot of time with Paige and Aaron."

"I could tell from the way you talked to Andy that you're good with children. He's thrilled that you've offered to play with him, you know. He misses having a man around. He hardly remembers his father," she added regretfully.

Worried about what direction the conversation might take next, Cody tried gently to guide it. "Dana's good with Andy," he said. "The two of them seem unusually close."

"They are," Barbara agreed. "Very close. I know Dana worries. . . ."

She broke off, then shook her head and changed the subject. "She'll be a wonderful schoolteacher, won't she? It's what she's wanted to do for as long as I've known her. I wish she hadn't waited so long to pursue her education, but her father died just as she was prepared to enter college after high school. I know she thought we needed her here—and I suppose she was right. I don't know what I would have done. . . ."

Again, her voice faded, her eyes going distant. And then she looked at Cody, and her gaze was sharp again. "You will encourage her to complete her education this time, won't you, Cody? It would break my heart to think she'll never see her dream of teaching come true."

"I think it would be a shame if Dana didn't earn her degree," Cody replied, choosing his words carefully. "She's worked very hard at it this past year, and from everything I've heard, she excels in her studies. I would never do anything to stand in the way of her education."

"It won't bother you that your new bride will be busy pursuing her education?" Barbara persisted. "That there will be nights when she has to study for exams and won't have time to prepare an elaborate meal or give you personal attention?"

Cody couldn't help smiling then. Dana hadn't exaggerated about her stepmother's old-fashioned tendencies apparently.

"I would never expect my wife to sacrifice her own education or career to cater to me," he answered with total honesty. "I'm perfectly capable of making my own dinner, when necessary—or dining out. And I'm an adult with my own interests. I don't require a great deal of personal attention."

Unlike a child, he couldn't help thinking. He couldn't imagine how Dana would manage her education if she had a small boy to care for alone. He was sure other women had done it, but it had to be incredibly difficult.

Like Barbara, Cody was afraid Dana would feel obligated to give up her own dreams for Andy's sake. And, like Barbara, he was increasingly sure that would be a shame.

Maybe if she had someone to help her. Someone to give Andy attention while Dana was busy with her studies. Someone to help her financially so she wouldn't have to juggle work and school and child care. Someone to support her, encourage her, cheer her on....

Too bad she didn't have anyone like that.

But Dana was fully convinced she could handle everything alone. And maybe he *was* being sexist to think she couldn't.

He almost shook his head when the thought occurred to him. No, he decided. It wasn't sexist. He couldn't imagine anyone, male or female, successfully balancing a demanding college education, a job and the upbringing of a preadolescent child. There were only so many hours in a day, only so many priorities that could be competently fulfilled.

From all he'd heard, from his sister Rachel and others, it was difficult enough for a single mother to cope with a career and child rearing. He didn't see any way Rachel could have obtained an education for herself while struggling alone to support Paige and Aaron after Ray died.

He was willing to bet that Dana would quit school within weeks after she became responsible for Andy, even if Barbara left Andy well provided for financially. Dana was the nobly self-sacrificing type if he'd ever seen one. And though he admired her motives, he didn't like the thought of her throwing away her dreams.

Dana and Andy rejoined them then, each carrying two bowls of cobbler and ice cream. Though the others made short work of the treat, Cody noticed that Barbara hardly tasted her own. He could see that she was drooping in her chair, the luncheon conversation having visibly tired her.

"This meal was great," he said after swallowing the last bite of his dessert. "Now I really need to play basketball to work it off."

"I'm ready," Andy said, pushing his chair back.

Cody chuckled at the boy's eagerness. "Give me time to change into jeans and sneakers first, okay?"

"You should change into play clothes, too, Andy," Barbara instructed.

Hilda came into the dining room then to announce in a tone that brooked no argument from her employer that she was taking Barbara back to her room to rest.

"The rest of you leave the dishes on the table," she added. "I'll clear everything away."

Dana offered to help, but Hilda adamantly refused. "You visit with your brother and your young man," she ordered over her shoulder as she wheeled Barbara away. "It's not often we get to have company around here these days."

"How long will it take you to change?" Andy asked Cody, anticipation lighting his freckled face.

"Give me half an hour, okay, pal? I want to talk to your sister first."

Cody was watching Dana as he spoke, so he didn't miss the faint spasm that crossed her face. "I, er, I think I should help Hilda," she said quickly.

He held her gaze. "Hilda seemed to prefer to do her job without your assistance. I believe you have a few minutes to talk to me."

"I'll go change," Andy said, oblivious to the tension between the adults. "See you in half an hour, Cody."

"You bet," Cody murmured without looking away from Dana. He motioned toward the door through which Andy had already vanished. "Why don't we talk in my room?"

Dana twisted the diamond ring on her left hand. Cody thought absently that she seemed to have developed that habit rather quickly. "Maybe I should check on Barbara," she said.

Cody narrowed his eyes. "Barbara needs to rest. My room, Dana. Now."

Her chin lifted. "You aren't my employer here, Cody."

"No. I'm your *fiancé,* remember?"

She winced.

He motioned again toward the doorway. "Shall we?"

Dana released a short breath and nodded grudgingly. She turned without another word and left the dining room. Cody followed closely at her heels.

Dana swallowed when Cody made a point of closing his bedroom door behind them, guaranteeing their privacy. She shoved her hands into her pockets and turned to face him, determined not to show him that she found this new mood of his rather intimidating.

"All right, we're alone," she said bluntly. "What do you want to talk about?"

Cody propped his hip against one corner of the room's heavy dresser, crossing his arms over his chest. "Obviously, you know your stepmother better than I do. What do you think she would do if we told her the truth?''

"The truth?'' Dana moistened her lips. "You mean...?''

He nodded. "The truth about us. That we aren't really engaged. That we aren't even involved on a personal level.''

She gripped her hands tightly in front of her. The diamond on her left hand dug into her right palm. "Are you thinking of telling her?''

She couldn't read his expression. "I only asked how you think she'd react,'' he reminded her.

"I'm not sure,'' she admitted.

"Take a guess.''

"I suppose she would be disappointed. She obviously likes you. And you heard how relieved she is to think I've found someone,'' she added wryly. "I told you, she's been worrying a lot about it. She told me she's even woken nights imagining me all alone and unhappy. No matter how many times I've tried to reassure her that I'm perfectly fine on my own, I haven't been able to convince her.''

"Does she think you're still carrying a torch for that guy you used to date?''

"I'm afraid so.''

"Is she right?''

"No!''

Dana dropped her hands and met his gaze squarely. "No,'' she repeated more quietly. "It was my decision to break it off with Linc. I've never regretted doing so.''

Cody searched her face for a moment, then nodded. "So she's just afraid you'll be lonely.''

"Yes. As I've told you repeatedly, she thinks everyone needs someone to love, marriage, children—the traditional fairy tale. A successful career to her is just a nice sideline. She's been very supportive of my education and my desire to teach, but she doesn't want me to wait too long to start a family."

"You're only twenty-four," Cody stated. "You have plenty of time."

"Yes," Dana agreed quietly. "But she doesn't."

Cody looked pensive.

"I know you disapprove of lying to her—and you're right, of course," Dana murmured, torn between guilt and a need to justify her actions to him. "It *is* wrong. I just...well, I thought it would set her mind at ease. Coping with her disease and her worry about Andy is hard enough. I hate the thought of her fretting about me in addition to everything else."

"So you thought announcing your engagement to me would cheer her up."

Dana nodded. "I guess that's what I was thinking. And you have to admit it worked. She's been almost beaming ever since we told her. She really does seem to like you."

Cody winced. "That only makes it harder," he muttered.

Dana looked down at her hands. "I know. I'm sorry I got you into this. Maybe you were right. Maybe I didn't think it through enough."

He drew a deep breath. "Probably not. But we've started this thing, and I guess we have to see it through. I wouldn't know how to tell her the truth now."

"Neither would I."

"I still don't like it," he added.

Dana thought he'd made that clear enough. She scowled. "I don't like lying to her, either. But if it makes her happy..."

Cody pushed himself upright and moved to the suitcase lying open on the bed. He pulled out a pair of jeans and a T-shirt. "Want to shoot some hoops with us?"

"No, thanks. I have some paperwork to take care of for Barbara—bills to pay, that sort of thing. I've been handling most of that for her since she became ill."

Cody nodded and started unbuttoning his shirt. "Is there anything else I need to know to keep this charade of ours going? Any surprises waiting for me?"

Dana dragged her eyes away from the golden-tanned chest he revealed when he tugged off his navy-and-burgundy-striped sport shirt. Was he going to strip right here in front of her? That was taking the charade a bit *too* far!

She inched toward the door. "Uh, no, I can't think of anything else. I've filled you in pretty well on the family history."

Cody's head emerged from the opening of the blue T-shirt. He smoothed it over his flat stomach. "What about when your sister arrives tomorrow? Anything I need to know about her?"

"Stepsister," Dana corrected him automatically.

"Right." He reached for the snap of his slacks, his eyes glinting with sudden mischief, his uncharacteristically somber mood apparently having passed.

Dana spun around, turning her back to him. "You could at least wait until I'm out of the room to do that," she complained, heading toward the door.

"You're being awfully shy for an engaged woman," he teased. "One would think you'd never seen me naked before."

"I haven't! And that's not all," she added grimly. "I have no desire to see you naked."

"Are you sure? I've been told it's an awe-inspiring sight."

Dana jerked open the door. If only, just this once, she could come up with a great exit line, she thought wistfully. One that would put cocky Cody Carson firmly in his place.

Unfortunately, the best she could come up with was "Yeah, right."

She could hear him laughing when she closed the door behind her.

She never had developed a talent for great exit lines, darn it.

Chapter Six

An hour later, Dana licked and sealed the last envelope, then pushed herself out of the chair behind the antique writing desk in the small downstairs room that served as a home office. She stood, pressing both hands to the small of her back.

She'd been sitting in one position for too long, intent on the bills and paperwork that hadn't been touched since she'd last visited. The expenses of her stepmother's illness were staggering, despite insurance coverage, particularly since Barbara insisted on having as much care in her home as possible.

Barbara was fortunate to have such a sizable estate, Dana thought wearily. She could certainly see how catastrophic illness had bankrupted so many hardworking but underinsured Americans.

Spending so much time dealing with the realities of Barbara's condition had left Dana depressed and angry, as it usually did. She pushed her hands through her hair, massaging her temples against the dull ache that throbbed there.

She wondered if her life could get any more complicated, and how she would possibly handle it if it did.

On an impulse, she stopped to look out a window on her way to Barbara's room. She was curious to see if Cody and Andy were still playing outside.

She spotted them immediately. They stood in front of the basketball goal. Andy was holding a basketball, staring up at the hoop with a frown of fierce concentration on his face. Cody stood nearby, obviously giving instructions, lanky legs bent as he pantomimed a free throw. Andy bobbed a couple of times, then released the ball.

Dana held her breath as it flew upward, arched, then fell neatly through the basket.

Andy jumped and waved his arms. Though she couldn't hear him, Dana knew he was loudly cheering his accomplishment.

Cody pulled one fist downward in a gesture of satisfaction, then gave the boy a hearty high five. They looked like they were having a great time.

Dana could almost feel her lingering irritation with Cody slipping away. Darn it, why couldn't she stay mad at the guy? Heaven knew he could be a real jerk when he chose to be.

But he could also be very sweet, she thought with a sigh. Talk about a paradox!

Still thinking about Cody, she moved on down the hallway. She peeked into Barbara's room before entering, not wanting to disturb her if she was sleeping. Barbara was awake, sitting propped against the pillows, an open book in her lap.

She spotted Dana and smiled. "It's all right, sweetheart, I'm awake. Come on in."

"I thought you were going to rest," Dana said, walking to her stepmother's bedside.

Barbara made a face. "I couldn't sleep."

Studying the furrows around Barbara's eyes, Dana frowned. "Are you in pain?"

"A little," Barbara admitted with a dismissive wave of one frail hand. "I took one of my pills a few minutes ago. It should help soon."

"Is there anything I can do for you?"

"Just sit and talk with me," Barbara replied, closing the book and setting it aside. "Where's Cody?"

"He and Andy are still playing basketball. I just looked out at them. They seem to be having fun."

"I like him, Dana."

"He likes you, too."

Barbara took Dana's left hand and contentedly eyed the diamond that glinted there. "The two of you are perfect together," she said. "I can tell."

Dana forced a smile. "What makes you think so?"

"Oh, I don't know. Just something about the way he looks at you. It's obvious that he's crazy about you. And, of course, I've always known you were taken with him."

Dana couldn't imagine why Barbara kept saying that. Sure, she'd talked about Cody, along with the rest of her acquaintances in Percy. But she'd never implied that there was anything special about her feelings for him. Barbara must be fantasizing now that Dana had shown up with Cody's ring on her finger.

"So when are you getting married? Have you talked about it at all? You aren't going to try to earn your degree first, are you? That will be two or three more years yet—much too long for an engagement."

Dana moistened her lips. "We really haven't discussed it," she prevaricated. "As I said, we've only just gotten engaged."

"Cody looks like the impatient type to me," Barbara said. "I wouldn't think he'd want to wait very long once he'd made up his mind to do something."

Dana only smiled. Barbara didn't know, as Dana did, that Cody would go to almost any extreme to avoid getting married. A practical joke was as close to an engagement as he'd wanted to get, according to him.

Barbara was searching Dana's face again. "Dana? You *do* love him, don't you?"

Dana swallowed hard. It took all the willpower she possessed to keep her smile steady. "Of course I do. How could you even ask now that you've met him?"

Seeming to find reassurance in Dana's light tone, Barbara's smile returned. "You have a point there. With his looks and his charm—not to mention that wicked smile of his—he's probably had women falling in love with him since he started to shave."

"If not before," Dana agreed, resisting an impulse to roll her eyes. Good thing Cody hadn't heard that! she thought. His overinflated ego certainly didn't need any more encouragement.

"Well, no matter how attractive and charming he is, he's still a lucky man to have you," Barbara insisted loyally.

Dana chuckled and kissed her stepmother's pale cheek. "You're prejudiced."

"I'm entirely objective," Barbara argued, then laughed softly. "Or maybe not. I love you, Dana."

"I love you, too," Dana replied, dismayed when her voice broke on the words. Her smile faltered and she was forced to blink back a mist of tears.

Barbara's hand tightened on Dana's. "None of that now," she scolded gently. "This is a time for joy, not sadness."

Dana dashed impatiently at her eyes with her free hand. "I know."

"I'm so looking forward to tomorrow," Barbara said, determinedly cheerful. "It will be wonderful to have all my family together again."

Dana forced a smile. "Yes, it will be nice to see Lynette and Alan again."

"I'm sure you're looking forward to introducing them to Cody."

"Of course."

"If only they didn't live so far away," Barbara said with a faint sigh. "Andy hardly knows them. And you get to see them so rarely."

"They lead very busy lives in New York." *New York,* Dana thought with that familiar tightness in her chest. *So very far away.*

Barbara nodded, looking worried, though she didn't share her thoughts.

Dana was tempted to bring up Andy's guardianship, to repeat her wish to raise the boy, her doubts that Lynette and Alan could provide a happy home for him. She hesitated only because she was afraid Barbara would make a sudden connection between Dana's desire to get custody of Andy and her conveniently timed engagement.

She decided to wait. Surely an opportunity would arise during the weekend for her to argue that she could provide the best home for Andy. Maybe Lynette and Alan would suggest it themselves, particularly if they believed Dana was engaged now. She suspected that they would be relieved not to have the responsibility of a child thrust onto them—at least, she hoped they would. Dana had never been able to read Lynette well, and Alan was little more than a stranger to her, even though he and Lynette had been married for six years.

"Mom! Cody's been teaching me how to shoot baskets. I'm already a whole lot better!"

Both Barbara and Dana looked around when Andy burst into the room, still bouncing with excitement. Cody followed more sedately, looking a bit apologetic for their precipitous entrance. He hesitated in the doorway, but Barbara motioned him in.

"Come tell me all about it," she encouraged them.

Dana dragged her gaze away from Cody, chiding herself for noticing how very good he looked all windblown and disheveled from the game, his golden hair tumbling onto his forehead, his damp T-shirt stretched tightly across his muscular chest and arms. If she wasn't very careful, she was going to forget that this was all a charade for Barbara's benefit, she reminded herself sternly. That Cody was here only as a lark.

She had little doubt that getting lost in this particular fantasy would be the worst mistake she had ever made.

Barbara found it necessary to take another pain pill later that afternoon. It was obvious that she wouldn't be joining them for dinner that evening. Dana urged her to rest and recover her strength for the next day, when Lynette and Alan were to arrive.

"Cody and I will take Andy out for dinner and a movie or something," she added. "It'll be fun."

Barbara smiled wanly and closed her eyes, her face almost as white as her snowy pillowcase.

Her heart aching, Dana slipped quietly out of the room, closing the door soundlessly behind her.

Given a choice of entertainment, Andy immediately requested that Dana and Cody take him ice skating.

Dana groaned. She'd put in a long day already. She wasn't sure she was up to an evening of ice skating. "Wouldn't you rather see a movie?" she asked hopefully. "There's that new space adventure film."

"I saw it last weekend with Benji and his mom," Andy answered. "I've seen a lot of movies lately."

"Then maybe we could—"

"The kid wants to ice skate, Dana," Cody cut in. "Let's take him skating."

She sighed, looking from Cody's bland smile to Andy's eager expression. "Okay. Ice skating it is."

Andy cheered.

Cody slid an arm around Dana's shoulders. "Why don't you slip into one of those little skating dresses, darlin'? You know, the kind with the itty-bitty skirt and no back and a front cut down to—"

"I think not," she said coolly. Then, remembering her role, she gave Cody a saccharine smile. "I'm not sure your heart could take it, *darlin'*."

He pressed a hand to his chest. "You just might be right, honey."

Andy chuckled. "Dana usually just wears jeans and a shirt when she takes me skating. But some of the girls wear those little dresses, Cody. And some of them look *fine*."

Cody's eyebrows shot up with interest. "Yeah?"

Andy nodded enthusiastically, enjoying the male bonding. "There's this one—she's older, like fifteen or sixteen, maybe. And she has long hair and long legs. She looks kinda like Kristi Yamaguchi."

Stepping away from Cody's encircling arm, Dana looked at her little brother skeptically. "I thought you didn't like girls. You said they were yucky."

"I *don't* like girls," Andy answered gravely. And then grinned in sudden mischief. "I like *women.*"

Cody laughed and gave the boy a high five. "A young man after my own heart."

Dana gave him a repressive look. "He's too young to be turned into a sexist, playboy pig like—"

She stumbled to a halt.

"Like?" Cody inquired blandly.

"Like, er, some guys," she muttered, her eyes telling him exactly who she meant.

"When are we going to leave?" Andy asked, anxious to get started.

"I'll go change," Dana told him. "We'll plan on leaving in half an hour. Go wash you face and hands, okay? You, too, Cody," she added, making Andy giggle when Cody rolled his eyes.

Something told Dana that it was going to be an evening that would try her patience. The look in Cody's eyes as he moved away warned her that he'd had all the seriousness he could take for one day. He was in a mood for mischief—and she just happened to be the closest target.

The ice rink was in the center of the Mall of Memphis. Above it was the food court, a horseshoe-shaped grouping of fast-food counters with tables in the center, overlooking the ice.

Andy seemed to think it a great treat to have so many foods to choose from. He spent several minutes debating between pizza, tacos or a burger. He finally selected pizza.

Cody seconded that choice, and he and Andy got into line at the Italian counter while Dana slipped over to the Chinese establishment for a lighter stir-fry dish. She tried to give money to Andy first, but Cody imperiously sent her away, telling her that dinner was on him. She allowed him to buy Andy's pizza, but insisted on paying for her own food.

They selected a table next to the rail, so that Andy could easily watch the skaters below while they ate. He pointed out a few he thought were particularly good, laughed at the beginners and regaled Dana and Cody with tales of his previous adventures there.

Watching the pleasure in the boy's eyes, Cody thought of how difficult it must be for a lone child living in a house where sickness was a constant companion, death an inevitable guest. He was determined that Andy was going to have a good time for this one evening.

He pointed out an arcade, saying that it looked like a good place to digest their food for a while before going out on the ice. Andy quickly agreed.

Dana was watching Andy, too. During the evening, she saw the way Cody went all out to entertain the boy, from dinner to the arcade, to a toy store, to the skating rink and finally to an ice cream parlor for a late dessert. They were all tired when they returned to Barbara's house, Andy half-asleep from the short drive, but Dana didn't doubt that her little brother had enjoyed the evening more than he'd enjoyed anything in a long time.

For that alone, she could forgive Cody almost anything.

Oh, sure, Cody had teased and taunted her all evening. Spouted his usual annoying nonsense whenever she would listen. Made a few heavy-handed passes that she'd countered with a smile for Andy's benefit.

More than once during the evening, she'd longed to hit him right in his sexy mouth. But then she'd looked at the exhilaration shining in Andy's round green eyes, and she'd been more tempted to kiss Cody's sexy mouth just for making Andy smile.

That was, of course, the *only* reason she could possibly want to kiss him.

Hilda met them at the door when they walked into the house. "Barbara wants you to come up and tell her good-night," she said.

"She's awake?" Dana asked in surprise.

Hilda nodded. "Slept most of the evening, but she woke up a half hour or so ago. She ate a little soup, and now she's waiting to hear how your evening went."

Dana glanced at Andy and noted with a pang that part of the joy had already left his face. He'd gone from a fantasy evening to the grim reality of home, and it broke her heart that he was as aware of that fact as she was.

He was too young to deal with this, she thought angrily. Much too young to have to face the loss of a second parent in so short a time.

It was all so terribly unfair. And she intended to do everything she could to make up for his early misfortune. Even if it meant devoting the next ten years of her life—or more—to making him happy.

Barbara was sitting up in bed, waiting for them. She smiled when she saw them, and Dana thought the lines of pain had eased during her rest.

"Did you have a good time?" she asked, including them all in her question.

"Great!" Andy answered. "We played games at the arcade—look at the cool yo-yo I got with my prize tickets. It lights up when you spin it, see?"

"Yes, that's very cool," his mother assured him gravely. "What else did you do?"

"Cody bought me a football at the toy store. He said we could play touch tomorrow if the weather's nice. And then we ice skated. Cody's real good, Mom. He said he takes his niece and nephew skating in Little Rock. He can even do spins."

Cody grinned. "I'm not exactly Brian Boitano, Andy."

Andy shrugged, unfazed, his allegiance firmly established. "You're good," he repeated. "One lady said he should have gone professional."

Remembering the starry-eyed, miniskirted bleached blonde who'd managed to fall gracefully at Cody's feet on three occasions, Dana snorted. "Professional *what?*" she muttered just for Cody's benefit.

Cody poked her with his elbow.

"Cody kept trying to talk Dana into letting him pick her up and spin her around over his head like they do in pairs skating, but she wouldn't let him," Andy continued, to his mother's amusement. "He promised he wouldn't drop her, but I don't think she believed him."

"I didn't," Dana said flatly. "He isn't Christopher Dean, either, Andy."

"Who's that?" Andy asked.

"A champion pairs skater," Cody supplied helpfully.

"Oh. Well, anyway, we had fun. Cody taught me how to do a simple spin, and he said someday he might teach me how to do an easy jump."

"Did you do anything else?" Barbara inquired.

"We had ice cream sundaes, with hot fudge and whipped cream and nuts and a cherry on top. Cody said I needed the calcium," Andy said with a grin that showed he was in on the joke.

Barbara was smiling. "It sounds like you had a wonderful evening."

"Yeah," Andy said. "It was really—"

"Cool," all three adults finished in unison with him, then laughed.

Andy giggled.

"It's getting late," Barbara said a moment later. "You'd better get ready for bed, Andy."

"Okay." Dana thought that it was an indication of how tired he was that he didn't even attempt to delay his bedtime. He kissed his mother's cheek. "'Night, Mom."

"Good night, sweetheart. I love you."

"Love you, too." Andy turned to Dana and gave her a hug. "'Night, Dana. Thanks for taking me out tonight."

She held him tightly for as long as she thought he'd allow her to, then reluctantly released him. "Good night, Andy. And you're welcome. I'm glad you had a good time."

He'd already turned to Cody. He shuffled his feet as though unsure how to part from his new hero. "Uh, thanks, Cody."

Cody threw one arm around the boy for a rough, affectionate, utterly natural hug. "'Night, Andy. See you tomorrow, okay?"

Andy returned the hug eagerly. "You bet."

"It seems you have a new admirer," Barbara commented to Cody as soon as Andy had left the room.

"Andy's a great kid," he replied easily.

"Yes." Barbara's eyes gleamed—whether with pride or unshed tears, Dana couldn't quite tell. "Thank you both so much for taking him out tonight. I haven't seen him that excited in quite a while. It was obviously a special evening for him."

"I had a good time," Cody answered, wrapping an arm around Dana and pulling her close to his side. "Even if Dana wouldn't let me lift her over my head and spin her around," he added teasingly, looking meltingly into her upturned face.

It's only an act, Dana reminded herself quickly, steeling herself against the shivery reaction that coursed through her at his touch, his gruff, sexy tone. *Only an act.*

She slipped her arm around his taut, slim waist and smiled. "I'm afraid that would test my confidence in you just a bit too much for my peace of mind, darling."

His arm tightened and he dropped a light kiss on her mouth. "Oh, ye of little faith," he mocked her. "If I didn't know how much you love me, my ego would be hurt."

"Impossible," she assured him through a forced smile. "Your ego couldn't possibly be dented—sweetheart."

Barbara laughed and shook her head. "You two are impossible. Do you always carry on this way?"

"Always," Dana replied.

"One would think you almost disliked each other at times," Barbara chided, though she didn't look concerned.

"One would be wrong," Cody said, then kissed Dana again, a bit longer this time.

Only for Barbara's benefit, Dana told herself a bit more frantically. She sincerely hoped Cody would believe her suddenly glazed eyes were just part of the act.

Whatever his other failings might be, the man certainly knew how to kiss. She could only imagine how good he'd be if he *weren't* playacting.

Looking not so secretly delighted, Barbara waved them away. "I'm sure you're ready for some time alone this evening," she said without even pretending to be subtle. "Good night, both of you. I'll see you in the morning."

Bidding her good-night, Dana and Cody left the room.

Cody caught Dana's arm when she would have gone into her bedroom with only a cursory good-night for him. "Come into my room for a minute, will you?"

She looked at him suspiciously. "Why?"

He exhaled forcefully through his nose. "I just wanted to ask you something. I'm not going to ravish you."

Irked at his tone, she tossed her head. "I never thought you were," she lied, and brushed past him into his room. She turned to face him when he came in behind her and closed the door. "What did you want to ask?"

"Has Barbara made a will?"

Dana frowned. "Uh, why do you want to know that?"

"Humor me. Has she?"

Still watching Cody's face, Dana nodded. "Yes. She's had one since Daddy died."

"The will must name a guardian for Andy."

Dana winced. "Yes."

"And—?"

"It's Lynette," she admitted, then added hastily, "Of course, I was just eighteen when Daddy died, and Lynette was already twenty-one and married, so obviously—"

Cody silenced her with a raised hand. "You have no reason to believe Barbara has recently changed her will?"

Dana shook her head. "No."

"Then Lynette is the boy's guardian."

"Only after Barbara is gone," Dana returned. "And only if I haven't talked her into changing her mind in the meantime."

"Which you're going to try to do this weekend."

"Which I'm going to do soon," Dana corrected him. "Not necessarily this weekend. I'll wait until the time is right, though obviously it will have to be soon."

"You're still determined to start this fight?"

She set her jaw. "Yes. And just as determined to win."

Cody ran a hand through his hair. "He's a good kid, Dana. I can see that you love him."

"Almost as though he were my own son."

He nodded. "I know. It's in your eyes every time you look at him."

Sudden hope filled her heart. "Does this mean you agree now that I could give him a good home?"

Cody seemed to grope for words. "I know you could give him a lot of love."

She tried not to notice that he hadn't exactly answered her question.

"Then you'll help me?" she demanded. "You'll say something to Barbara to encourage her to leave Andy to me?"

Looking a bit regretful, Cody shook his head. "No. I told you I'm staying out of that. I haven't changed my mind."

Bitterly disappointed, Dana lashed out. "Then why the hell did you drag me in here and ask all these questions?"

"I guess I just wanted to know."

Dana whirled away, turning her back to him to hide her expression. "I'm so happy to satisfy your curiosity," she said cuttingly.

"Dana, don't—"

"You still think he'd be better off with *them,* don't you? You still think I'm not capable of raising him. Even after seeing us together, even after spending the whole day with us, you think I couldn't take care of him properly."

"I didn't say that."

"You didn't have to say it."

"I told you I'd meet your sister and her husband. Watch them with Andy—"

"Stepsister," Dana cut in. "Trust me, she'll make a point of correcting you if you get it wrong with her. She's never claimed me as a sister. And she's never referred to Andy as anything more than her half brother."

"Is she really such a terrible person? Will she abuse Andy? Harm him in any way?"

Impulsive words trembled on Dana's lips. And then the genuine concern in Cody's words got through to her. She sighed.

"No," she answered honestly. "She won't abuse him. She won't harm him. Regardless of our personal relationship—or lack of one—she isn't an evil person. But she won't make him happy, either. Not the way I can."

"Are you really so sure?"

She turned to him then, her eyes filled with hot, despairing tears. "Yes," she whispered. "Of that I *am* sure."

Cody searched her face for a moment, then reached a hand to her. "Look, honey, I—"

She flinched away from him. "I'm not your honey! You can drop the pretense now, there's no audience to perform for. You're here only because you want a return favor from me, not because you give a damn about what happens to Andy—or to me. Well, fine. We'll get through this weekend and then your part is done. I'll do whatever you want for your family, and then we're even. And you can forget all about my problems."

"Dana, you aren't being fair. I—"

She drew herself up with painful dignity, her chin lifted, her lower lip quivering despite her best efforts to hold it steady. "Didn't anyone ever tell you, Cody? Life isn't fair. If it was, I wouldn't be dealing with this now. Andy wouldn't be facing the loss of his mother, nor I the only family I have.

"But that's not your problem, is it? You're the golden boy. You have everything—your business, your friends, your looks, a family that adores you. You don't let anything spoil your fun—and it wouldn't be *fair* for me to interfere with your games, would it?"

He started to say something, but she didn't give him the chance. Within moments, she'd jerked open his door, thrown herself through it and closed it firmly behind her. A moment more, and she was locked in her own room, the tears streaming down her face, her fists clenched in impotent fury as waves of hopelessness washed over her.

She'd never felt so very much alone.

Chapter Seven

Lynette and Alan Manningly arrived late the next morning. Hilda opened the door; Dana, Cody and Andy stood nearby to greet them.

Leaving her husband outside to bring in the bags from the rental car they'd driven from the airport, Lynette swept in on a cloud of expensive perfume, her black designer outfit setting off her long, slender body, her artfully blond hair swirling around her striking face.

"There's my little sweetheart," she exclaimed, singling Andy out first. She held out scarlet-tipped hands to him. "Come give me a kiss, Andy," she crooned.

Andy gave Dana a speaking look before stepping forward slowly to greet his other sister. "Hi, Lynette," he murmured as she swooped down to give him a smacking kiss on the cheek that left a smear of crimson behind.

Turning to Dana, Lynette smiled brightly. "Dana," she said. "It's good to see you. You look lovely."

Conscious of her inexpensive sweater and slacks set, Dana forced an answering smile. "It's good to see you, too, Lynette."

"How is Mother?"

Dana phrased her answer carefully, aware of Andy standing so close by. "She's looking forward to seeing you."

"Is she in the den?" Lynette took a step in that direction.

"No," Dana said, detaining her. "She's in her bedroom. She's hoping to feel up to joining us for lunch."

Lynette frowned, then deliberately smoothed her expression as she turned to Cody. "And who is this? A friend of yours, Dana?"

Cody spared Dana the introduction by stepping forward. "I'm Cody Carson. Dana's fiancé. It's nice to meet you, Lynette."

"Dana's...fiancé?" Lynette was much too self-controlled to gape, but she did blink rapidly a time or two. "This is quite a surprise."

"We only announced it yesterday," Cody explained with his charming smile. He slipped an arm around Dana's shoulders. "Dana wanted her family to be the first to know."

Dana glanced up at Cody and smiled, some of her anger with him from the night before subsiding.

Lynette's gaze went straight to Dana's left hand. "Is that your ring? I'd love to see it."

Self-consciously, Dana held out her hand.

Lynette took Dana's hand in her left, her own massive diamond wedding set gleaming. She studied the unpretentious stone Cody had provided. "How sweet," she murmured. And then she kissed Dana's cheek again. "I'm so happy for you. When's the wedding?"

"We haven't set a date yet," Dana replied, avoiding Cody's eyes.

Lynette smiled at Cody. "Clinging to the single life?" she asked, obviously trying to make a slight joke.

Cody slipped his arm around Dana's waist. "I've found something better," he said, an affecting huskiness to his voice.

Dana couldn't help admiring his acting abilities. He should have been on a stage, she thought, wondering why she was suddenly feeling a bit wistful.

"What a nice thing to say." Lynette smiled at Dana. "You've found yourself a romantic one, Dana."

Dana returned the smile and murmured something noncommittal.

A suitcase beneath each arm and a very large leather attaché case in his left hand, Alan Manningly noisily entered the foyer, giving Dana an excuse to slip away from Cody's loose embrace.

"Gee, Lyn, you could have helped me with some of this," Alan complained, dumping the bags on the floor, but hanging on to the leather case. "Hello, Dana. Andy." His greeting was brusque, accompanied by a slight incline of his head.

At thirty-two, Alan was already balding, a fact his two-hundred-dollar haircut couldn't quite disguise and his post-trendy ponytail couldn't quite compensate for. He was tanning-salon brown, health-club fit, designer garbed.

Stuck in the eighties, Dana had always thought when she was around him.

He tapped the leather case. "Where can I set up my notebook and fax? Okay to use the office?"

"Alan, there's someone else here," Lynette chided, her voice resigned. "This is Cody Carlson. Dana's fiancé."

Alan looked Cody over, taking obvious note of Cody's black-and-purple western shirt, tight black jeans, and black fancy-stitched boots. He stuck out his hand.

"Nice to meet you, Carlson," he said, showing no surprise that Dana was engaged.

"Carson," Cody corrected. "Cody Carson." The handshake was brief.

"Uh, right. I'm Alan Manningly. But I guess you already know that."

He turned back to Dana. "I'm expecting a couple of faxes. I'll just go set this up now. Have Hilda take our bags up, will you?"

Dana set her teeth. She would take the bags up herself before she would ask Hilda to do so. And it hadn't escaped her notice that Alan hadn't even asked about his mother-in-law.

"I'll get the bags," Cody said, stepping forward. "Any more out in the car?"

"No, that's it. Thanks." Alan was already moving toward the office, his precious computer in hand.

At least, Dana thought seethingly, he hadn't tried to slip Cody a tip. "He's expecting faxes on the Sunday before Labor Day?" she asked Lynette.

"Oh, you know Alan. Work is his life. And his associates are all just like him. I'd like to see Mother now."

Assuming Lynette would appreciate some privacy, Dana nodded. "Just go on back. Her door is open."

Cody gave Dana a wry look when they were alone with Andy. She met his eyes and shrugged, knowing his first impression hadn't been particularly favorable. She thought it was an illuminating one, however. Alan consumed by work, Lynette graciously condescending. A fair assessment of the couple Dana knew.

Cody easily lifted the bags Alan had carried so awkwardly. "Where should I put these?"

"In the bedroom at the end of the upstairs hallway," Dana answered. "You'll show him, won't you, Andy?"

"Sure. Want me to carry one of those, Cody?"

Cody tightened his grip on the obviously heavy cases. "No, that's okay, pal. You can open doors for me, okay?"

"You bet," Andy replied. It was a phrase Dana knew he'd picked up from Cody.

Cody and Andy went out to toss the new football around after they carried the Manninglys' bags upstairs. Dana settled in the den with the Sunday newspaper, waiting for either her sister or brother-in-law to make a reappearance, or for Hilda to announce lunch, whichever came first.

Just over half an hour had passed when Lynette appeared in the doorway. She was obviously shaken as she made her way to a chair and fell heavily into it, her usual studied grace forgotten. "God," she whispered. "She looks... awful."

"You haven't seen her in a couple of months," Dana reminded her. "She's gone down quite a bit since you were here last."

"I didn't realize..." Lynette buried her face in her trembling hands.

Dana wanted to reach out to the other woman, but wasn't sure Lynette would welcome the gesture. Lynette had never seemed to like physical contact, other than those quick kisses she scattered upon arrival and departure.

Lynette took a deep, unsteady breath and lifted her head, her back straightening. "Mother said you've been here every weekend and occasionally on weekday mornings when you weren't in class. She said you've gone out of your way to make sure she's been comfortable and well cared for. For that, I thank you."

"I love her, Lynette. You know that. There's no need to thank me for anything."

Lynette's gaze slid away from Dana's. "You know, of course, that I would have been here more often if I could. But we live so far away, and our careers are so demanding. Neither Alan nor I could take any more time off without risking our jobs."

"Your mother wouldn't want you to lose your job because of her. When she needs you here, she'll call you."

"And I'll come."

Dana nodded. "Of course."

"What have the doctors said? I asked Mother, but she was very evasive."

Dana swallowed. "They've said there's nothing more to do for her, except keep her comfortable, try to manage her pain with medication...and wait. Hospitalization might become necessary soon, but for now home health care is sufficing."

"God." Wearily, Lynette brushed a blond strand away from her pale cheek. "How is Andy holding up?" she asked after a moment.

"Wonderfully. He's excelling in school—he's in the year-round program at St. Mark's, you know. He seems to show particular aptitude in math and science."

"And emotionally?"

Dana hesitated. "Emotionally...he's vulnerable. Scared. He's in denial, I think, about the true gravity of Barbara's condition, but deep inside he knows how serious it is. Still, he's being incredibly brave, at least outwardly. He's wonderful with her, seems content to spend hours just sitting with her and talking to her and making her smile. He's a very special little boy, Lynette."

"He seems to be quite fond of your Cody. I saw them playing on the back lawn as I came from Mother's room."

"Cody has a way with kids," Dana admitted. "They all seem to love him."

Lynette sighed. "Unfortunately, Alan and I don't elicit the same response from them. I don't think children like us much. I'm not even sure Andy likes us."

"Of course he does, Lynette. You're his sister. He loves you."

Dana took a deep breath then, sternly stifling a flicker of hope. She had to be cautious, she reminded herself. She didn't want to set Lynette on the defensive about Andy—and yet, this seemed like a good time to suggest that the boy would be better off with Dana.

She had just opened her mouth to do so when Alan wandered in. "When's lunch?" he asked. "I haven't eaten since six this morning, New York time."

"Hilda should be calling us soon," Dana assured him, cursing his timing.

"Mother will be joining us for lunch," Lynette said.

Alan took the chair nearest his wife. "How is your mother?" he asked belatedly. "Should I go see her now or wait awhile?"

"You'll see for yourself how she is at lunch," Lynette answered somberly. "Let her rest until then."

"I'd have gone back with you, but I knew you wanted to be alone with her first," he assured her—though Dana couldn't help wondering if the explanation was for her benefit, since Lynette didn't seem to be impressed.

She suspected that Alan had deliberately postponed seeing Barbara. He'd mentioned on his previous trip that sickrooms made him "antsy."

Cody and Andy came in a few moments later, both a bit disheveled from the stiff breeze that was blowing outside. Cody had rolled his sleeves up on his forearms.

He looked, Dana thought with complete objectivity, gorgeous.

"So, er, what business are you in, Carson?" Alan asked as Cody and Andy sat side by side on the couch near Dana.

"I'm part owner of a country-western club in Percy," Cody answered. "We call it Country Straight."

"Is that the bar where you work as a waitress, Dana?" Lynette inquired with a lifted eyebrow.

"It's not a bar, it's a restaurant and dance club," Dana corrected. "Nothing stronger than beer is served. And, yes, I do work there five evenings a week. That's how Cody and I met."

"Marrying the boss, hmm?" Alan asked jovially. "One sure way to get ahead."

The joke fell flat when no one laughed.

Andy cleared his throat. "Dana's going to college," he said proudly. "She's going to be a teacher."

"Yes, I know," Lynette said. "I think that's very admirable of her. She tells me that you're doing well in school, Andy."

Andy shrugged. "Yeah. Pretty good," he said, squirming on the couch.

He turned to Cody. "Want to go watch TV in my room till lunch is ready?" he asked. "The 'Bugs Bunny Hour' is on the Cartoon Network. Roadrunner's my favorite."

"You're allowed to have a television in your room?" Lynette asked with a frown. "But who monitors what you watch—or how much?"

Andy seemed surprised by the question. "I know not to watch the dirty stuff," he protested. "And Mama tells me to do all my homework before I turn it on. Mostly I like to watch cartoons."

"Most cartoons are violent and mindless," Lynette said with a curve of her lip. "Surely you can find something morc cdifying to watch if you must waste time staring at a television screen."

Andy looked distressed.

Cody came to the rescue. "Oh, I don't know," he murmured in his best cowboy drawl. "I like cartoons, myself. Especially Wile E. Coyote. How about you, Manningly? Didn't you ever wonder why the guy didn't just buy a hamburger or something if he had all that money to spend on Acme weaponry to trap the Roadrunner?"

Alan blinked, looking from Cody to Lynette and back. "I, er, hadn't really thought about it."

"I have," Andy said with a grin. "He's always ordering things like rocket-propelled roller skates and giant magnets and bazookas and stuff. How'd he pay for them, huh? Where would a coyote get a credit card?"

"What I could never understand," Dana piped in, "was how the coyote thought he was going to kill the Roadrunner. After all, the stunts usually backfired on him and *he* was never permanently injured. Even when boulders fell right on top of him, the coyote just walked around for a while with little birds and stars circling his head. Why'd he think the Roadrunner would be more seriously injured, hmm?"

Andy giggled.

Cody gave Dana a look of approval, which Lynette didn't share. "Honestly," she scolded. "All this talk of rockets and bazookas and killing and falling boulders only emphasizes my point. What sort of lessons are these to teach an impressionable child?"

"How about the value of a good laugh?" Cody suggested smoothly.

"If one is amused by that sort of thing." Lynette sniffed.

"Well, actually, I was always rather fond of that little yellow bird who was always seeing a 'puddy tat,'" Alan suggested hesitantly.

"Tweetie Bird," Andy supplied.

Lynette gave her husband a look that had him clearing his throat and quickly falling back into silence.

Fortunately, the conversation was interrupted when Hilda appeared in the doorway to announce that lunch was ready to be served in the dining room. She sent Andy to wash up and told the others she would be bringing Barbara in momentarily.

Cody held Dana back when Lynette and Alan left the room behind Andy. "You okay?" he asked quietly.

"Of course," she murmured. "Why?"

"No reason," he assured her, dropping a hand casually on her shoulder. "Just thought I'd ask."

"Thank you, but I'm fine."

Cody didn't seem convinced, but he let it go. He kept his arm around her shoulders as he escorted her into the dining room, and even though Dana suspected he was only playing his role, the contact felt pleasantly supportive.

She could almost believe he really was on her side.

Somehow Cody found himself alone in the den with Alan Manningly that afternoon. Andy was upstairs, Lynette and Dana in Barbara's room, Hilda puttering around in the kitchen. Cody sat at one end of the couch, trying to think of something to say and wishing he were somewhere else.

Alan didn't seem any more comfortable in Cody's presence. They'd already exhausted talk of Cody's restaurant, Alan's career plans and the weather. It was getting down to politics or religion, both of which Cody usually avoided in conversation with strangers.

He cleared his throat and tried to think of something innocuous to say. "Are you originally from New York?" he asked, aware of how bland the question sounded.

Alan seized on the gambit. "No, I grew up here in Memphis," he said. "Finished college here, married Lynette the weekend after I graduated and we moved to New York immediately afterward."

"You ever miss living here?"

Alan snorted. "You kidding? New York is alive, man. Fast. Moving. I couldn't slow back down to a Tennessee crawl now if I wanted to—which I don't."

Cody wondered how hard the guy had worked to lose his Southern accent. He'd noticed that both Alan and Lynette liberally sprinkled their speech with "Manhattanisms," carefully enunciating their artificially rapid speech.

For some reason, Cody had found himself exaggerating his own lazy drawl during the afternoon. Maybe because it irritated him that Alan and Lynette seemed to equate Southern with stupid now that they considered themselves Easterners.

He couldn't say he particularly liked either of them.

Not that he'd completely gone over to Dana's side on the custody issue, he reminded himself. He still thought she deserved a chance to finish her education, find a life for herself before she sacrificed her future for her half brother. Cody didn't have to like the Manninglys to accept that they could provide a decent home for the boy—though he was still reserving judgment.

Now it was Alan's turn to initiate a topic. He didn't seem to find it any easier than Cody had. "Er, Barbara looks pretty bad, doesn't she?"

"I only met her for the first time yesterday, but I can see that she's very ill," Cody replied somberly. "It's breaking Dana's heart."

Alan nodded, his expression glum. "Lynette's, too, of course. I know Dana's fond of Barbara, but Lynette is losing her mother."

"Dana thinks of Barbara as her mother," Cody felt compelled to point out. "She and Barbara are very close."

Alan frowned. "Well, yes, but...I guess you're aware that Dana's father was a Memphis cop. Nice guy, from what I remember, but not much money. The estate is Barbara's—and, of course, she will provide especially well for her *own* children. Lynette and Andy, you know. I'm sure she'll leave a nice little something for Dana, but—"

"It really isn't any of my business how Barbara chooses to distribute her estate," Cody cut in coldly, anger flickering inside him. It was all he could do not to add that it was no more Alan's business. "Knowing Dana as well as I do, I'm sure she couldn't care less about Barbara's money. She would willingly give everything she owns now just to keep her stepmother with her awhile longer."

Something in Cody's expression must have warned Alan that he'd irritated him. "I wasn't trying to imply, of course, that Dana has done anything for Barbara out of hope of monetary gain," he said quickly. "I know she loves her stepmother dearly."

"Yes, she does."

"She seems very fond of the boy, too."

"Dana adores Andy."

"Yeah. He's a good kid. I guess he'll be moving in with us after—er, afterward. I know Lynette's offered to take him."

Cody met Alan's eyes squarely. "How do you feel about that?"

Alan shrugged. "Never thought much about kids," he admitted. "But the boy doesn't seem like much trouble. Lynette says he's smart as a whip, so he shouldn't have too much trouble catching up to the New York kids in school."

"Catching up?" Cody murmured with a lifted eyebrow.

"Well, yeah. I mean, schools in Tennessee probably aren't as advanced as the ones in Manhattan. But we'll hire tutors, I guess, if necessary. There's a good prep school where most of my associates send their kids. If the boy works hard on his studies, maybe he'll be lucky enough to get in by the time he's twelve or thirteen."

"A boarding school?"

"They say they're best for adolescents," Alan said confidently. "Kids that age need discipline and supervision, you know. Boarding school programs keep them too busy to get into trouble."

"So do good parents."

"Well, yeah, sure." Alan quickly searched Cody's face as though trying to see if he were being criticized. "Parents who don't have demanding, full-time careers. That's why Lynette and I decided to wait to have a family of our own, if ever. Lynette's sharp as a tack, you know. Real talented. She has too much to offer to the work force to throw it away to stay home and change diapers."

"Well, at least Andy's beyond that stage."

Alan looked relieved that Cody seemed to understand. "Yeah. The boy's old enough to look after himself for the most part. We have a housekeeper, of course, though she's only part-time now. Guess we'll make her full-time when the boy moves in. His trust fund can cover the extra expense."

Okay, Cody had given Alan a fair chance. He still hated to see Dana miss out on her dreams. But the thought of Andy going to live with this guy who didn't even seem to know the child's name made Cody's blood run cold.

"Andy's going to need a lot more than a good education and paid supervision when he loses his mother," he said evenly, still holding Alan's gaze with his own. "He's going to need a lot of love. Someone to talk to. Someone who'll hold him when he cries. Family."

Alan squirmed in his chair. "Well, sure. We'll get him a good counselor, of course. Lynette's therapist doesn't treat children, but I'm sure she'll recommend someone who..."

He faltered beneath Cody's scornful expression.

"This really is family business, Carson," he said abruptly. "I'm sure Barbara and Lynette know what's best for the boy."

"Dana might have a few suggestions to make, as well," Cody added silkily. "He's as much her brother as he is Lynette's."

Alan was scowling now. "Just what's your interest in this, anyway? If you're thinking of the money, you should know that the kid's inheritance is going to be tied up plenty tight, with close supervision to make sure it's spent to benefit him."

Cody rose, his boots adding an inch to his already tall frame. He loomed over the seated man, who instinctively tensed.

"I have no more interest in Barbara's money than Dana does," he said quietly. "Whatever happens, you can bet I'll never touch a cent of it. But I *do* care about Andy. I've known him only a couple of days and I'm already very fond of him. You've known him most of his life. Can you say the same?"

"I—uh, you—er, damn it, Carson, this is none of your business!"

A taut moment of silence gripped them. It was broken by a quiet voice from the doorway. Dana's.

"There's a call for you, Alan," she said, though she was looking at Cody. "You can take it in the office."

Looking greatly relieved, Alan jumped to his feet. "While I'm gone, you might talk to this fiancé of yours," he muttered as he passed Dana. "He's a bit too inquisitive about our family business, if you ask me."

"But I didn't ask you, did I, Alan?" Dana inquired sweetly.

Alan snorted and stalked away.

Dana turned back to Cody. He shifted his feet on the carpet, wondering how much, if anything, she'd heard.

"Thank you," she said, proving that she'd heard more than he would have liked.

"I didn't do anything," he mumbled. "Just pointed out a couple of things he needed to know."

"I heard what you said. The last part, at least. You made Alan admit that he doesn't love Andy."

"He didn't say that," Cody felt compelled to say.

"No. But he couldn't say that he did, either."

"No." Cody slipped his hands into the pockets of his black jeans. "Your brother-in-law was right about one thing, though. This really is none of my business."

"Cody—"

Lynette wandered into the room then, rubbing at her temples with her well-manicured fingertips. "Has anyone seen Alan?"

"He's in the office," Dana answered, turning away from Cody. "On the phone."

Lynette grimaced. "Of course he's on the phone. He's always on the phone."

"Is Barbara resting?"

Lynette nodded. "She's asleep. I don't think she'll be getting back up today."

"No. Lunch seemed to wear her out. I think she really enjoyed sharing it with everyone, though."

"Yes, she did. By the way, Alan and I are taking Andy out for dinner this evening. I'm sure you and Cody will enjoy having some time to yourselves."

"Whatever you want to do," Dana said noncommittally.

Cody wondered if Dana, like him, suspected that Lynette had come up with this idea while Andy had raved about their ice-skating outing during lunch.

"Alan and I haven't been able to spend much time with Andy during the past couple of years," Lynette said, sounding a bit defensive. "We'd like to take him someplace nice, have a chance to visit quietly with him for a couple of hours."

"So Alan already knows about the plan?" Dana asked blandly.

"Um, no. That's why I was looking for him, actually."

"I see. If you like, I'll help Andy get ready. When would you like to leave?"

"Oh...an hour or so, I suppose. He does have a jacket and tie, doesn't he?"

"I'm sure he does," Dana replied through—Cody thought—gritted teeth.

He doubted that Lynette's plans for the evening included arcades or shopping malls. Or anything else particularly fun, for that matter.

Poor Andy.

Chapter Eight

Eating from TV trays, Dana and Cody joined Barbara in her bedroom for dinner that evening. Barbara had insisted that they needn't feel obligated to entertain her, but they'd refused to listen.

"This is fun," Cody assured her cheerily. "Like a picnic without the ants."

Barbara smiled, picking without interest at her own bland fare, served on a bed tray across her lap. "I'm really not very hungry," she murmured.

Dana encouraged her stepmother to eat a little of the meal. Cody kept up a running monologue of silliness that actually had Barbara laughing aloud a time or two, despite her obvious discomfort.

"It's no wonder Andy likes you so much," she commented after one of his more outrageous stories. "You're quite a clown, Cody Carson."

"I've told him that very same thing on numerous occasions," Dana commented.

Cody grinned, knowing that Dana had never meant the words as a compliment. She sent him a laughing look that told him she knew he'd caught her meaning. For a moment, their gazes held.

And Cody felt something kick him right in the chest.

During the past year, he had forced himself to ignore the attraction he'd initially felt for her. Hadn't allowed himself to notice the way her green eyes gleamed when she laughed, the way her auburn hair caressed her soft cheeks when she turned her head, the way her intriguing dimple flirted at him from the corner of her invitingly lush mouth. Hadn't allowed his gaze to dwell on her slender neck or full breasts, her tiny waist or sweetly curved hips.

He'd treated her as an employee, a casual acquaintance, occasionally as a friend—but nothing more.

He'd told himself he'd put that early fascination behind him.

He'd obviously been lying to himself.

He cleared his throat, reminding himself that now was no time to realize that he was still very deeply attracted to his faux fiancée.

He'd deal with that inconvenience later.

Barbara reclaimed his attention by sighing and pushing her tray away. "I'm sorry," she murmured. "Seems as though all I can do these days is sleep."

Dana immediately jumped up to clear away the dishes. She waved off Cody's offer of help, signaling him to talk to Barbara instead.

Less than fifteen minutes had passed when Cody judged that it was time to leave Barbara alone. Before he and Dana left the room, Barbara asked them to be sure and send Andy to say good-night when he came in. Dana promised not to forget.

Dana and Cody wandered into the den after leaving Barbara's room. Much too aware of the silence of the house around them, Cody cleared his throat and motioned toward the television cabinet. "Anything good on TV?"

Her expression was distant, pensive. She made a visible effort to respond to him as she sat at one end of the couch. "I don't know. Watch whatever you like."

"Is there something you'd rather do? We could go have dessert and coffee somewhere—get out of the house for a while."

Dana shook her head. "Thanks, but I don't think so. I don't really want to leave Barbara here alone tonight, even though I know Hilda checks on her often."

"I understand."

Leaving the television off, Cody moved to sit beside Dana. "The excitement of the weekend is probably tiring her," he suggested, sensing that Dana was rather depressed after their visit with Barbara.

Spearing her fingers through her hair, Dana sighed again. "It's not just the company," she said quietly. "She's getting worse. Weaker. I think... I think she's giving up."

Touched by the break in her voice, Cody laid a hand on her arm. "She doesn't strike me as a quitter. She just needs some rest."

"I wish that was all she needed," Dana whispered, looking away.

There was such misery in her voice that Cody put an arm around her and drew her toward him. She stiffened at first, resisted his efforts to pull her into his embrace. And then she shuddered and buried her face in his welcoming shoulder.

Cody wrapped both arms around her and held her close, his chest tight. Once again he cursed the lousy timing of his newly discovered attraction to her. She was suffering, obviously vulnerable, and he was a lowlife worm to notice how very good she felt in his arms when he should be concentrating on nothing but giving her comfort.

He rested his cheek on her hair, noticing how soft and fragrant it was even as he murmured soothingly to her. He knew she was crying from the dampness against his throat, and from the trembles that coursed through her, but she made no sound. Her tears were all the more heart-wrenching because of her silence.

How long had it been, Cody wondered, since she'd cried? Since anyone had been there to comfort her when she had?

He thought fleetingly of his own big, warm, loving, supportive family, and he made a mental promise never to take them for granted again.

Dana had been so very much alone this past year.

She wasn't alone now.

She allowed herself only a few minutes of weakness before she drew a deep, unsteady breath and lifted her head.

Cody resisted when she would have pulled away. "Are you sure you don't want to stay awhile longer?" he murmured, wiping her tear-streaked face with one thumb.

She looked at him a moment, then lowered her lashes, shading her eyes from him. "I'm sorry," she murmured. "I didn't mean to break down like that, or to cry all over you."

"Have you heard me complain?" he asked with a faint smile, keeping his arms around her.

She cleared her throat, toying self-consciously with a button on his shirt. "You're being very nice today."

He chuckled. "Why do you sound so suspicious? I can be a nice guy on occasion."

"Yes, I know," she admitted. "It's just—"

"Just not what you expect from Cody the clown, right?" he asked, unable to keep a touch of bitterness out of his voice.

She lifted an eyebrow, looking back up at him. "Did I strike a nerve?"

He forced a smile. "Never mind."

As though suddenly aware that she was still sitting in his arms, Dana pushed lightly against his chest. "I think I'll go check my makeup. I wouldn't want Barbara or Andy to see that I've been crying. Lynette, either, for that matter."

Cody didn't release her. "Your makeup is fine," he said, his voice husky again.

She went very still, as though something in his tone, or perhaps his expression, had sounded an alarm inside her. She tilted her head and frowned at him. "Cody—"

"Indulge me a minute," he murmured, his mouth hovering close to hers, his eyes holding her gaze. "Shouldn't your fiancé get a kiss every once in a while?"

"You're not—" she began, but he didn't give her a chance to finish.

He'd kissed her only a few times before, all but one of those kisses given in front of an audience.

This time it was only the two of them—and Cody wasn't pretending.

Dana's hands froze on his chest, as though in surprise. And then, very slowly, they crept upward, sliding around his neck. And she was kissing him back—for the very first time.

He could taste the faint saltiness of tears at the corners of her mouth. His kiss turned tender, his lips stroking, soothing, consoling. Beneath the tears he found the spice and sweetness that was Dana. The kiss deepened, grew hotter, hungrier.

And Cody felt himself start to shake.

He tore his mouth from hers with a gasp, and even he couldn't have said whether it was due to lack of oxygen or a sudden surge of panic.

He wanted too much, too powerfully, too suddenly. He ached with a depth of desire he hadn't allowed himself in years, a hunger made all the stronger by being suppressed for so long.

Unwilling to make promises he hadn't thought he could keep, he'd been very careful not to encourage anyone to lean on him, to depend on him, to want anything more from him than a good time and a few laughs. He hadn't allowed himself to want more.

Until now.

Until Dana.

For a year he'd been denying his feelings for her, ignoring his reactions to her, pushing thoughts of her away whenever they threatened to distract him. For a year he'd told himself she wasn't his type, that he didn't want her, that he had no interest in getting involved with a woman like Dana, who would expect—no, *demand*—so much more than he thought himself capable of giving.

He'd been wasting his time. He'd wanted her when he'd first met her. He wanted her still.

And she thought him a clown. A shallow, unreliable, self-indulgent joker.

The real hell of it was that she was right. And he would be a fool to try to convince her—or himself—otherwise.

Dana was staring at him, her emotion-darkened green eyes searching his face with an intensity that made him want to shut her out before she saw too much. She didn't seem to be aware that her arms were still locked around his neck. Cody was all too aware of them.

He reached up to gently free himself. "I think I'll go for a drive. Get some fresh air. Want me to pick up anything for you while I'm out?"

Her eyes dimmed. He could almost see her draw her emotions tight, lock them away. "No," she said, her voice expressionless. "I can't think of anything I need. But thank you for offering."

He almost winced at the bite in her politeness. "I'll, er, see you later, then," he said, pushing himself abruptly to his feet. "Um, just tell your family I'm visiting an old friend or something for a couple of hours."

She nodded.

He needed to get away quickly, before the sight of her trembling, kiss-smudged mouth and tousled, sexy cinnamon hair made him forget again that she was too vulnerable for him to take unfair advantage of her. He turned on one heel and left the room with more haste than dignity.

He was running as much from himself as from Dana.

Cody returned a couple of hours later. He couldn't have guaranteed that he had himself completely under control, but he couldn't risk staying away any longer. Dana shouldn't be forced into making awkward explanations because of his cowardice.

An unfamiliar car was parked in the driveway in front of the house. Eying it curiously, Cody mounted the steps and rang the bell. Hilda opened the door, her face pale, her hands wringing nervously at her waist.

"What's wrong?" Cody asked sharply, moving to step past her. "Where's Dana?"

Hilda stalled him with a hand on his forearm. "She and Lynette are with Barbara and the doctor."

"The doctor? What's happened?"

"Barbara had a bad spell. Couldn't breathe. We wanted to call an ambulance, but she refused, so Dana called Barbara's doctor. He lives just a few blocks away, and he came right over. He said he's pretty sure she was having a reaction to a new medication. She's doing better now, though she's still very weak."

"Damn." Cody groaned and raked a hand through his hair. Wasn't this the way it always was for him? Dana had needed him, and he hadn't been here for her. He'd been running, pursued by his own old demons.

Could he have illustrated more clearly, for himself or for her, that she shouldn't start to depend on him?

"Where's Andy?" he asked abruptly.

"He's in the den, with Mr. Manningly. He'll be glad to see you."

Cody nodded. "I'll go on in. Let me know if there's anything I can do, okay?"

"Of course." Hilda turned to walk back in the direction of Barbara's bedroom.

Steeling himself, Cody went into the den.

The room was silent. Alan sat in a chair, staring at nothing in particular, occasionally clearing his throat. Andy was curled at one end of the couch, still wearing the jacket and tie he'd reluctantly donned for dinner, though the tie had been loosened and now hung crookedly. His huge, expressive eyes filled with tears when he saw Cody.

A moment later he was across the room, his face buried in Cody's chest.

Cody locked his arms around the boy, his heart aching. He wished he knew what to say.

Andy looked up at him, his lower lip quivering. "Mom got sick. She couldn't breathe."

"Hilda just told me. She said your mom's better now. The doctor thinks she was having a reaction to a new medicine."

Andy nodded glumly. "That's what Dana said."

Cody smoothed the boy's wildly disheveled red hair. He wanted very badly to tell Andy that everything would be okay, that his mother would be fine. But he couldn't say that. Everything wasn't okay, and Andy was much too bright to believe otherwise.

"Why don't you go change into something more comfortable?" he suggested instead. "No guy should have to wear a jacket and tie for longer than a couple of hours at a time," he added.

Andy managed a crooked smile. "I hate wearing a tie."

"Me, too, pal," Cody agreed fervently. "So go change into your pj's and wash your face, okay? You'll feel better."

Andy seemed reluctant to leave Cody's side. "Will you come talk to me later?"

Cody gave the boy a rough, affectionate hug. "You bet. I'll be in to say good-night."

Reassured by that promise, Andy left the room, though he looked back over his shoulder as he stepped through the doorway. Cody gave him a bracing thumbs-up, to which Andy responded with a slightly more natural smile.

"The kid likes you," Alan commented without getting up. "He hasn't said two words to me since we got home and found all the commotion going on."

"He needed a hug."

Alan shifted in his chair. "Yeah, well, I'm not very good at that sort of thing."

Cody bit back a sarcastic response, all too aware of the many things *he* wasn't good at.

He pushed his hands into the pockets of his jeans and paced the den, too restless to sit as he waited for Dana.

Would she blame him for leaving tonight to cope with a crisis alone? Would she be angry with him for the abrupt manner in which he'd left her, the way he'd almost pushed her out of his arms?

He certainly couldn't blame her if she was.

He didn't have to wait long. He heard a murmur of voices out in the foyer, the closing of the front door as the doctor left. A moment later, Lynette and Dana appeared in the doorway, both looking exhausted.

Lynette walked straight to a chair without pausing to touch or speak to her husband. Dana stood very still, looking at Cody.

Without hesitation, he held out his arms to her.

Without hesitation, she walked into them.

He let out a breath he hadn't realized he'd been holding as he folded his arms around her. He felt the fine trembles that coursed through her, and he pulled her closer.

"I'm sorry," he whispered, his mouth at her ear. "I shouldn't have left. I should have been here with you."

"It was awful," she murmured, her voice trembling. "She couldn't breathe. She was gasping and turning blue, but she refused to let us call an ambulance. She got so upset when we suggested it that it only made her worse. Thank God Dr. Levy was home, and so close. He was here within minutes of my call."

"Why wouldn't she let you call an ambulance?" Cody asked, genuinely puzzled. Barbara had seemed so levelheaded to him, so well prepared. He hadn't expected her to turn stubborn over her care.

"She said she didn't want to go into a hospital yet. She said...she was afraid she wouldn't come back out." Dana's voice broke on the explanation.

Cody held her tightly until she drew a deep breath and pushed away from him.

"Thanks," she said, avoiding his eyes as she tucked a stray hair behind her ear. "I needed that."

"Anytime," he murmured, suddenly aware that Lynette and Alan were watching them. He cleared his throat. "Is Hilda with Barbara now?"

Dana nodded. "We're going to take turns staying up with her tonight. Barbara's sleeping now, and Dr. Levy predicted that she would sleep soundly all night. He gave her a sedative."

"You need some rest yourself."

"I'll lie down soon. Hilda promised to wake me when she gets tired. Lynette's going to relieve me early in the morning."

"I'll sit with her for a while," Cody offered. "Whenever you need me to—tonight or tomorrow morning."

Dana gave him a tired smile of gratitude. "Thanks, but it would probably be better if you keep Andy entertained in the morning—maybe take him out to play basketball or something. You're good at keeping him diverted."

Ah, yes, Cody's true talent. Playing. He nodded. "Yeah, sure. Whatever you want me to do."

Dana frowned as though hearing something in his voice that puzzled her.

Alan distracted them when he rose suddenly from his chair. "I don't know about the rest of you, but I need a drink. Barbara still keeps the bar in here stocked, doesn't she?"

Dana turned away from Cody. "Yes. You know where everything is. Help yourself."

Alan had already moved to the small wet bar discreetly placed in one corner of the large room. "White wine, Lynette?"

She nodded. "Yes, please."

Alan set glasses and bottles on the mahogany bar. He poured wine for his wife, straight bourbon for himself. "Dana? Cody? What'll you have?"

"Nothing for me, thank you," Dana replied.

"Cody?"

Cody looked at the bottles on the bar and swallowed a bitter taste in his mouth. "No."

If his tone was curt, no one seemed to notice.

"God, what an evening," Lynette murmured, staring into her wineglass.

Dana moved to sit on the couch, and Cody took his place beside her. "I haven't had a chance to ask how your dinner with Andy went," Dana said to Lynette.

Lynette lifted one shoulder in a delicate shrug. "It was all right. Andy was rather quiet."

"He was probably a bit intimidated," Dana suggested. "He's not used to dining in such elegant restaurants. Since Barbara's been ill, his outings usually involve fast-food places with his friends."

"He seemed to have a great deal of fun on his outing with you and Cody the other night," Lynette said, a touch of resentment tinging her voice.

Dana didn't answer. Cody didn't know what to say, either. Truth was, he was sure Andy *had* had a better time with him and Dana. Lynette and Alan weren't exactly a fun couple—at least, not as far as he'd seen.

"Speaking of Andy," Cody said, breaking the awkward silence as he stood. "I promised I'd go up and tell him good-night."

"I'll go with you," Dana said quickly, standing with him.

Lynette sipped her wine, her eyes shadowed. "Tell him good-night for us, too, will you?"

"Of course," Dana agreed.

* * *

Dana and Cody parted outside of Andy's door. "You talk to him for a little while, okay?" Dana asked. "I want to go wash my face first."

Cody sensed that she needed a few minutes alone before putting on a cheery face for her little brother's benefit. He touched her cheek. "Are you okay?"

She gave a weary sigh. "Of course."

"Dana, I—"

"Go talk to Andy, Cody," she interrupted, as though afraid of what he might say. "He needs you."

She walked away before he could respond.

He glanced at Andy's closed door. *He needs you,* she'd said.

Grimacing at the ironies of life, Cody tapped on the door. "Andy? It's me."

A small voice bade him to come in.

Andy was sitting on the bed, dressed in pajamas decorated with a professional football team's logo. A hand-held video game lay beside him, turned off. A battered stuffed dog lay on the pillow beside Andy; the boy quickly pushed it away as though reluctant to be caught holding it.

Cody picked up the scruffy dog and smiled. "What's his name?"

Looking embarrassed, Andy shrugged. "I used to call him Tramp. Back when I was a little kid. I used to sleep with him. I'm too big for that now, of course."

"I had a stuffed monkey. You know, the kind with the plastic banana in one hand? I called him Jones. Slept with him until I was twelve."

"Yeah?"

"Yeah." Cody sat on the bed, still holding the toy. "Only reason I gave him up then was because he was falling apart.

I don't know what ever happened to him—I think maybe my mom had him bronzed."

Andy smiled. "Not really."

"No." Cody returned the smile. "Not really. She probably has him packed away somewhere with my baby clothes."

"Last time he was here for a visit, Alan said I should throw Tramp away. Said he looked grubby and was probably full of germs. He said I was too big to sleep with a doll."

Cody bit his tongue until he fancied he could taste blood. "I don't agree," he said after a moment. "Sometimes a guy needs an old friend in the middle of the night. To tell you the truth, there are still times when I wake up and miss Jones."

"Really?"

Cody ruffled the boy's hair. "Really. You keep ol' Tramp around as long as you want, you hear?"

And to hell with whatever Alan has to say about it, he thought recklessly.

Andy reached for the toy and set it carefully on the bed close beside him. "I will. Thanks."

"You bet."

Andy raised his knees, crossed his arms on them and rested his chin on his wrists. "Did you see Mom?" he asked.

"No. She's sleeping. The doctor left a little while ago."

"Is she going to be okay—for tonight, I mean?"

Cody rested a hand on the boy's back. "For tonight, yes. Hilda and Dana and Lynette are going to take turns sitting with her just to be sure."

Andy ducked his head so that his face was hidden in the crook of his elbow. His voice was muffled. "When we got home, and the doctor was here, and they said Mom couldn't breathe. . . ."

"You were scared?" Cody guessed when the boy's voice faded.

Andy nodded into his arm. "Yeah. I thought...I thought this was it. That she..."

Cody shifted closer. "It's okay to be afraid, Andy. And it's okay to get mad sometimes."

Andy lifted his head. His round cheeks were damp. "I do get mad," he whispered.

"I know. I don't blame you. It isn't—well, it just isn't fair." Cody thought of how Dana had used those very words when she was so angry with him for refusing to help her with her endeavor to get custody of Andy.

"Other kids have dads and moms," Andy mumbled, looking defiant and guilty at the same time. "My dad's already dead and now I'm losing my mom."

Cody had never felt more at a loss, less sure of himself. What if he said the wrong thing, did the wrong thing? Made Andy more miserable than he already was?

"I'm sorry, Andy," he said, feeling the uselessness of the words as they left him. Thinking again of how blessed he'd been to have his family all these years, how thoughtless he'd been not to fully comprehend his luck.

Needing to say something more, he cleared his throat. "You have your sisters, you know. They both love you very much."

Andy nodded and swiped at his cheek with one hand. "I'm sure lucky to have Dana. She's the best sister in the world."

"And Lynette?" Cody prodded carefully.

"Lynette's okay. When she's not around Alan she can be fun sometimes. Alan's boring. All he talked about at dinner was the stock market and stuff. He thought I should learn about it, he said."

"He didn't know what else to say," Cody said, forcing himself to be objective. "I'm sure he was trying to make conversation."

"*You* don't talk to me like I'm a stupid kid."

"I have a niece and nephew, remember? Alan doesn't spend much time with kids."

Andy shuddered. "Mom...Mom says I'll probably go live with them someday. I don't want to go to New York. I don't want to live with Alan and Lynette. I want to stay here. Or move in with Dana."

"Andy—" Cody groped helplessly for the right words. They didn't come to him.

Andy's breath was catching in quiet sobs now. His eyes were anguished. "I don't want to live with them, Cody. They don't want me."

Cody opened his mouth to assure him he was wrong, that Lynette and Alan did want him. The lie stuck in his throat.

Andy reached out to catch Cody's shirt in one small hand. "You're going to marry Dana. Can't you talk to them for me? Can't you tell them I want to stay with her?"

Oh, hell. Looked as if Cody was getting drawn into this no matter how hard he'd tried to stay out of it. He should have known all along that it was inevitable. "Andy, I—"

Andy suddenly winced and let his hand fall. "Maybe you'd rather I would go to New York," he muttered. "I guess when you and Dana get married, you're going to want to live by yourselves for a while. Have your own kids, maybe."

Cody reached out to take the boy's shoulders in his hands. He looked straight into Andy's tear-filled eyes when he spoke. "You're wrong, Andy. Dana would like nothing better than for you to live with her when you need another place to go. She loves you more than anything else in the world."

A flicker of hope lit the boy's eyes. "What about you?" he asked softly, shyly.

"I would be very proud to have you as a part of my family," Cody said evenly. "Trust me on that, okay? But you have to understand, this isn't my decision to make. It's up to your mom and your sisters. All of them love you, and all of them want the very best for you."

Andy swallowed. "I know."

"Besides, there's no need to worry about this now, okay? The doctor said your mom is doing okay now. He gave her something to help her get a good night's sleep. She'll wake up feeling much better tomorrow, I'm sure. She'll want to see you then, and you need to get some rest so you'll feel like visiting with her and cheering her up."

"Okay, Cody."

Cody moved the video game to the nightstand and pulled the covers back to let Andy crawl beneath them. He tucked the boy in carefully, making sure Tramp was close by.

"Good night, Andy," he said, forcing his voice past the uncomfortable lump in his throat. "See you in the morning, okay?"

Andy came off the pillow in a rush, locking his arms around Cody's neck. Cody pulled the boy into a tight hug.

It seemed to be his night to offer comfort to the Preston siblings. And he was stunned to realize he'd allowed himself to get very personally involved—with both of them.

A sound from the doorway made him look up, over the boy's head. Dana stood there watching him, one hand resting on the doorframe. Her eyes were warm, soft. He didn't know how long she'd been there, how much she'd overheard.

Oh, Dana, don't look at me like that. Don't make me into something I'm not.

She didn't seem to receive the mental message. Her expression didn't change as she came into the room, still looking at him in a way that made his stomach tighten.

"I just came to say good-night," she said as Andy settled back down into the pillows, his cheeks a bit flushed. She bent over to kiss her brother's forehead. "Sleep well, sweetie."

"'Night, Dana. Love you."

"I love you, Andy." She released him reluctantly, then smoothed the covers to his chin. "Good night. And good night to you, too, Tramp."

Andy giggled as Dana snapped off the bedside lamp. The sound was a welcome one to the adults who'd heard him cry.

"You'd better get some sleep if you're going to sit up with Barbara later tonight," Cody urged Dana when they stepped out of Andy's room, pulling the door closed behind them.

"Yes, I will. Are you going to bed?"

He glanced at his watch. Just after ten. He hadn't gone to bed this early in years. But since the alternative was to go downstairs and sit with Alan and Lynette, he nodded. "Yeah. I think I will turn in."

"All right. Good night."

"Good night, Dana. Sleep well."

She surprised him then by stepping closer and rising onto her tiptoes to press a warm, brief kiss on his cheek. "Thank you."

"For—for what?" he asked, after pausing to clear his throat.

"For being here for Andy. I'll never forget how kind you've been to him."

"Dana—"

Again, she forestalled his words by turning away. "Good night, Cody. See you in the morning."

And again, she slipped away before he could respond.

As he entered his own room and snapped on the light, Cody realized that he was still holding a hand to his cheek, where Dana had kissed him.

He dropped it with a weary curse.

This was all getting terribly complicated.

Chapter Nine

Monday morning, Labor Day, was warm, bright, cloudless. Cody imagined how many families were out boating, or picnicking, or barbecuing on their patios. His own, for example.

The Preston household was quiet, everyone tiptoeing around, careful not to disturb Barbara. Most of the occupants looked tired, as though sleep had not come easily to them.

Cody knew he didn't look any better than the others. He'd spent most of the night staring at the ceiling, wondering if the Fates were having a big laugh at his expense.

He put on a cheerful face for Andy's sake. Together, they polished off huge bowls of presweetened cereal for breakfast. Lynette and Alan, dining on fruit and yogurt, visibly shuddered at the sight. Afterward, Cody suggested going outside to work on Andy's free throws.

Andy politely invited Alan to join them. Alan actually looked tempted, until Lynette reminded him that he had said there was some paperwork he wanted to finish before noon.

"Think Alan could've hit the basket?" Andy asked as he dribbled the ball in preparation for his first shot.

"Oh, sure. Probably," Cody answered airily. *With a pole, maybe.*

"I don't know," Andy murmured, bending his knees the way Cody had taught him as he prepared to shoot. "I bet he'd need you to show him how."

He released the ball, held his breath as it arched near the basket, then let out a breath of disgust when it hit the rim and bounced away.

"Happens to everyone," Cody assured him. "Try again."

Approximately half an hour had passed when Dana joined them. Cody noted the faint signs of weariness on her face, then couldn't help thinking that they made no difference to her loveliness. She looked great in a dark green, short-sleeved tunic decorated with painted flowers, and matching, formfitting leggings. Her auburn hair was slightly tousled, as though she'd been running her fingers through it.

Cody curled his hands into fists, resisting the temptation to run his own fingers through her soft tresses.

"Hi, Dana. Watch," Andy said, and carefully aimed at the basket. He was delighted when the ball sailed neatly through the hoop.

"Very good, Andy. You're getting much better, I can tell."

"Thanks. You want to play with us?"

"I'll play with you for a little while. Cody, Barbara is asking to see you."

Cody stumbled in surprise. "Me?" he repeated. "She wants to see me?"

"Yes." Dana shrugged slightly to indicate that she was as much in the dark as he was. "She's waiting for you now."

Cody gulped. "Okay. I'll just, er, go on in, then."

He was aware that Dana watched him as he entered the house.

Cody tapped lightly on Barbara's bedroom door. Hilda opened it. She stepped aside with a smile. "She's waiting for you. I'll go wash up the breakfast dishes. Call if you need me."

Cody nodded and entered the room, his eyes on Barbara. She looked like hell, he thought. He could tell the difference in her condition just from the two previous days he'd spent with her.

"How are you feeling?" he asked, pulling a straight chair close to the bed and sitting on the edge of it.

She managed a smile. "Like hell," she said, eerily echoing his thoughts.

Cody was startled into a chuckle. "Yeah. That's about what I thought." And then he sobered. "Is there anything I can do?"

"I want to talk to you."

He waited patiently for her to begin.

She drew a deep breath. "Do you love Dana?" she asked without preface.

Cody swallowed. He held Barbara's gaze with his own, aware that his answer meant a great deal to her. "Yes," he said evenly, without even blinking. "I do."

The lie rolled off his tongue with an audible sincerity that rather surprised him.

Or had it been a lie?

That uncomfortable thought almost made him squirm on the chair. He told himself he was being foolish, carried away by the masquerade. Of course he wasn't in love.

He admired Dana, more as the weekend progressed. And, yeah, he was attracted to her. More each time he saw her.

He wanted her—but that didn't mean he loved her.

He wasn't ready for love. Didn't know if he would ever be ready for that.

Barbara smiled. "I was sure you loved her," she murmured in satisfaction. "I just wanted to hear you say it."

He smiled back at her, his conscience kicking him in the gut. "Do you feel better now?"

"Partly. There's something else."

Cody resisted an impulse to tug at his shirt collar. "What is it?"

"Your business in Arkansas—it's successful? You're making a good living with it?"

He lifted an eyebrow, a reaction of curiosity more than offense. "It's doing well enough. My partner and I haven't had any real complaints."

"I know you think I'm being vulgarly inquisitive," she said apologetically. "Please forgive me for being a prying old woman."

"Barbara," he said, reaching out to cover her frail hand with his own. "You aren't old."

She didn't smile. "I'm as old as I'm going to be," she said quietly.

There was nothing he could say in response to that.

"I didn't mean to make you uncomfortable," she apologized again. "But I don't have time for tactful prevarications now, Cody. I have to know—I have to be sure that I've done all I can to make my children happy. To know that they'll be all right when I'm gone."

"I wouldn't worry about your children. Any of them," Cody assured her. "You have a fine family, Barbara. You can be proud of the job you've done with them."

Her eyes glowed. "Thank you for saying that. It means a great deal to me."

"I'm just calling it the way I see it."

"I like you, Cody. I knew I would when I heard Dana talk about you. I'm so happy that you'll be here for her."

"For as long as she needs me," he said, and this time it was the absolute truth.

Barbara moistened her pale, chapped lips. "Andy came in to see me this morning before breakfast."

"Yes, I know. He told me. He said he thought you looked fine."

"Andy sees what he wants to see."

Cody nodded, knowing she was right.

"He's very fond of you, you know. You've become his new hero. He loves you like the big brother he's always longed for."

Cody felt his cheeks warm. "I'm no hero. But Andy's a great kid, Barbara. And I love him, too—as Dana's little brother and for his own sake."

"He told me about his dinner with Alan and Lynette last night. He didn't seem to enjoy it much."

"I don't think Andy's all that interested in the stock market right now," Cody replied lightly, afraid he knew now where the conversation was leading.

Barbara didn't seem to have heard him. "Andy loves his sister, of course. Both his sisters. But he and Dana have always had a special bond. Maybe because Dana was younger when he was born. Maybe because her father made sure to always include her in his new family."

She sighed. "God knows he tried to include Lynette, too, but she was so afraid of appearing disloyal to her own father. She never fully accepted my second husband, to my deep regret."

"The children of divorce often suffer from divided loyalties," Cody assured her. "I'm sure you did whatever you could to make it easier for her."

"I tried. Her father—well, he didn't help me much, I'm afraid. But that's not important now. What *is* important is Andy's happiness. He's going to need a lot of love, a great deal of understanding and patience."

Thinking of the similar conversation he'd had with Alan Manningly, Cody nodded.

Barbara sighed. "I know Lynette loves her little brother, in her own way. I've never quite understood Alan. I suppose he's always been kind enough to Andy. But as far as loving him . . . well, I'm just not sure."

Cody nodded again, his tongue between his teeth to keep him from speaking imprudently.

"Dana has asked me several times to consider changing my will to name her Andy's guardian. I suppose she's talked to you about that?"

"Yes," Cody admitted. "She has."

"And how do you feel about it?" Barbara asked, her too-intent eyes fixed on his face.

His throat tightened. He knew what she was asking—and why. She believed she was speaking to Dana's future husband.

He chose his words carefully. "I think Dana could provide Andy with the most loving and supportive home anyone could ever ask for him."

"I know that. I've always known it. But—" She made a rueful face. "Dana calls me old-fashioned. I am in many ways, especially when it comes to family. I hesitated to leave Andy to Dana because I wasn't sure a single young woman could provide a stable home for a spirited boy. And I knew she wouldn't be able to complete her education if she were solely responsible for her little brother.

"The money wouldn't be a problem for her—my estate is large enough to leave Andy well provided for, at least until he's grown and on his own. I'm leaving Dana enough to help her finish school. It's the very least I can do for her when she's been so good to me. But the responsibility of caring for him—for any child—is a full-time one. And Dana has always taken her responsibilities very seriously."

"Yes. She does," Cody agreed almost grimly.

He knew there were few people, if any, who would say the same about him. Jake, maybe. Certainly not Dana.

"I guess what I'm asking you, Cody, is can I count on you to help Dana if I entrust her with my son's future? It will mean a great sacrifice for you, as well. You'll be a newlywed with a ready-made family, a father before you've learned to be a husband. I want to know that you'll willingly accept that role, that neither Dana nor Andy will suffer because of my decision."

This was the very situation Cody had dreaded. Dana's happiness, Barbara's peace of mind—Andy's entire future—rested squarely on Cody's shoulders now. And God only knew he was no Atlas.

"Barbara—" he began.

She held up an unsteady hand. "I want you to know that I'll understand, whatever your decision might be. I won't think any less of you if you decide you aren't ready for a commitment of this magnitude, I promise you. Lynette and Alan will provide a good home for Andy, give him every possible advantage. I have faith that, in time, they will both learn to love him as deeply as Dana and I do. I'm not worried about leaving him with them—not really."

"Andy would have every material and cultural advantage with the Manninglys," Cody agreed. "But I'm not so sure he'd be completely happy with them. Not the way he'd be with Dana."

She watched him, a gleam of hope in her pain-faded eyes.

Cody pictured Dana's worried face. Andy's trusting smile. He drew a deep breath, and knew his own decision had been made. "If you choose to leave Andy with Dana, you won't have to worry about either of them, Barbara. I promise you that. Whatever I can do, whatever they need from me, they've got it. They're my family now—and I take care of my family. It's the way I was raised, you see."

Her smile was tremulous. "You won't regret this?" she asked.

"No," he said, conviction ringing in his voice. "I won't regret it. Dana and Andy should be together. It wouldn't be right for me—or for anyone else—to stand between them."

Barbara closed her eyes and drew a deep breath. "I knew you were right for Dana. Somehow I just knew it. Oh, Cody, thank you."

"Does this mean you've made your decision?"

She nodded against the pillow. "Yes. I'd like to see Dana now. Would you ask her to come in, please? Lynette, too."

Cody fought down a sudden surge of panic. Oh, hell, what had he done? What consequences would his rash actions have on these lives?

Why were they all acting as though they could depend on him to solve all their problems for them when it was all he could do to manage his own?

"I'll send them in," he said, hoping his turmoil wasn't visible on his expression.

She tugged at his hand, pulling him down to kiss his cheek. "My Dana has chosen wisely, Cody Carson. I always knew she would."

As Cody left the room, he found himself longing for his grandmother. How he could use Granny Fran's calm, practical, straightforward advice right now!

He rather guiltily suspected that she wouldn't entirely approve of his behavior this weekend, no matter how well intentioned his actions had been.

Cody was summoned back to Barbara's bedroom some time later that afternoon. Dana was alone with her stepmother when Cody entered the room. He noted that she looked faintly stunned when she met his eyes, her own huge and damp.

Barbara looked very tired, but satisfied. "I've told Lynette and Dana that I want to name Dana as Andy's guardian," she informed Cody, her voice weaker than it had been earlier. "I've already called my attorney and asked him to change my will and bring it by this evening for me to sign. He's a good friend. I know I can depend on him to take care of this for me."

Cody took Dana's hand and smiled at her. "Dana will take good care of your son, Barbara. I'm sure she will." He only hoped he hadn't ruined Dana's own future with his reluctant interference.

"Yes, I know," Barbara murmured. "She'll have you to help her, won't she?"

"Er, yes, of course."

Barbara nodded against her pillows. "I'm counting on you, Cody. Both of you. Please don't disappoint me. This is much too important."

Cody swallowed hard. The imagined weight on his shoulders doubled. He almost staggered beneath the burden. Instead, he held his chin high and said, "I won't fail you, Barbara." *God help me.*

Dana's fingers tightened convulsively in Cody's—whether from gratitude or distress, he couldn't tell.

Barbara's smile turned radiant. "I know you won't, dear. And now, if you'll forgive me, I have one favor left to ask you. And it's a big one."

Bigger than being responsible for her only son's future well-being? Cody wondered in near panic. Surely not.

A look of sympathy crossed Barbara's pale face. "You're probably wishing you'd stayed home in Percy this weekend, Cody. It would have been much simpler, wouldn't it?"

"Not at all," he lied airily. "What favor do you want, Barbara? You name it, you've got it," he assured her boldly.

"I want to see you and Dana married," she answered simply—devastatingly. "I would gladly give whatever time I have left to share that joy with you. Her father and I often talked of the day when we would see her married. He... he didn't live long enough to give her away."

Her voice broke, but she steadied it quickly. "Dana's father loved her very dearly, Cody. She was the joy of his life. I would give anything to be at your wedding, to represent him... and to bestow my blessing on my second daughter."

Dana's hand was trembling wildly now in Cody's, her fingers icy. Cody knew his own hand was not much steadier.

He really *should* have stayed in Percy, he thought dazedly. This was getting out of control fast.

The Fates must be laughing hysterically now.

"When—" He cleared his throat. "When did you have in mind?"

Before Barbara could answer, Dana spoke for the first time since Cody had entered the room. "Barbara, we really haven't discussed a date yet. I'm not sure we—"

Barbara held up a hand. "I can tell I've startled both of you with this. Obviously, you'll want to talk about it. I'll understand, of course, if you prefer to set your own timetable. I can't blame you. And yet..." She sighed wistfully.

"It's not that I'm not anxious to marry Dana, of course," Cody assured her. "But—"

"There's just so little time," Barbara murmured, lost in her own sad thoughts. "I'm sorry if I've embarrassed you."

Oh, damn. Cody could feel the guilt eating at him from inside out. A quick sideways glance let him know that Dana was sharing his misery.

"Barbara, you haven't embarrassed us. We understand," Cody said, aware that Dana was watching him with panic-stricken eyes, waiting for him to do something brilliant to get them out of this.

Unfortunately, he wasn't feeling particularly bright at the moment, much less brilliant.

"There's nothing either of us would like better than to have you with us at that special time," he continued, stumbling for words. "It's just that we haven't—we aren't—er—"

"I suppose it would be impossible to have the wedding this evening," Barbara murmured, as though she hadn't heard a word he'd said.

Dana's hand jumped at the same time Cody's heart stopped. "That might be pushing it a bit," Dana agreed hastily, breathlessly. "Maybe we should—"

"We have to think of the legal requirements—blood tests, license, a minister..." Cody couldn't think of any other excuses. Maybe the ones he'd given would be sufficient.

Barbara didn't seem fazed. "I could take care of the license and the officiate," she said confidently. "Judge Lawrence Herriman is my first cousin. I'm sure he could arrange something. As for blood tests, they're no longer required by the state of Tennessee. There's no waiting period now."

Cody swallowed a groan. *Oh, great.*

What had the legislators been thinking when they'd changed that requirement? What was wrong with requiring a waiting period? Didn't they understand that people shouldn't rush—or be rushed—into marriage? This was something that should be carefully planned...say for a couple of years or so.

"Lynette and Alan are staying through Wednesday. I know your club is closed tonight, Cody, so there's no need for you to go back this afternoon, is there?"

"Well, er—"

"We could probably arrange something for tomorrow afternoon. By the big fireplace in the den—that's where Dana's father and I were married. Did she tell you?"

"No, she didn't."

Barbara's smile was misty. "It was lovely. A small, private ceremony. Just us, and the girls and a few special friends. My cousin, the judge, married us. It was the happiest day of my life."

She suddenly stopped and raised a hand to her forehead, looking stricken. "Oh, would you listen to me? I can't believe I'm trying to railroad you into marriage. I'm so sorry. It's just...well, I suppose my little episode yesterday shook me more than I'd realized. I seem to be trying to tie up all my loose ends today. I'm so sorry."

Cody took Barbara's hand in his free one, without releasing Dana, whose fingers had gone ominously limp.

"Stop apologizing," he ordered Barbara compassionately. "We really do understand. We're both touched that you want to bless our marriage."

Somehow he said the M word without choking.

"Of course we are, Mom," Dana echoed, her voice a bit higher than usual. "There's nothing either of us would like better than to have you with us."

"I suppose you had a more elaborate ceremony planned."

"No," Cody said sincerely. "We hadn't."

Dana was shaking her head. "Absolutely not. I wouldn't even want a big, elaborate, expensive affair. I've always thought small, private ceremonies were the most touching and romantic. But—"

"I'm sure you'd want your family around you, Cody," Barbara went on. "And of course there would be no way to get them all together so quickly. It was a silly idea."

"It was no such thing," Cody heard himself arguing. "I agree with Dana, small ceremonies are the nicest. My sister Celia eloped—didn't have anyone from the family at her wedding. Everyone understood."

It occurred to him that if he didn't shut up, he was going to find himself a married man before he left Memphis.

Dana seemed to read his mind—and to agree with him. She tightened her hand around his until he winced.

"I think Cody and I should talk this over before we make any decisions, Barbara," she said gently. "You understand, of course?"

"Yes, dear, I do understand. Please, think carefully before you give me an answer. If you decide you want to wait, I'll understand. Of course, I would be delighted if you choose to be married tomorrow while the family is together," she couldn't resist adding.

"We'll talk about it," Dana repeated, her expression strained. "You look tired, Barbara. Why don't you get some rest now?"

"I am tired," Barbara said with a faint exhale. "It has been an eventful weekend."

Dana kissed her stepmother's cheek. "Get some sleep. I'll be back to check on you soon."

Barbara's eyes were already closing. She was still smiling faintly when Cody looked back at her as he and Dana left the room.

Chapter Ten

"I can't believe this." Dana paced Cody's bedroom, her hands clasping the sides of her head. Each time she turned, the diamond on her left hand glinted in the overhead light, catching Cody's attention. "I can*not* believe this is happening. How could I have gotten us into this mess?"

Sitting on the end of the bed, Cody sighed. "Dana, you've been pacing and muttering for the past ten minutes. Would you please sit down so we can talk rationally?"

"Rationally?" She spun to face him, her green eyes blazing in her blanched face. "*Rationally?* How can we possibly talk rationally about this...this disaster? This catastrophe? This complete fiasco? Oh, God." She clutched her hair again.

Cody stood, gripped her wrists and pulled them firmly to her sides. He guided her to the bed and all but shoved her down onto it. As soon as she was seated and he was convinced that she was going to stay there, he perched beside her. "Now," he said. "Calm down and let's discuss our options."

She exhaled deeply and shook her head. "We have no options. We're going to have to tell her the truth. And it's going to break her heart. Oh, why did I ever start this? I should have known it would never work."

"Dana," Cody said, resisting an impulse to shake her. "Stop it. Getting hysterical isn't going to do the least bit of good."

"I'm not hysterical," she muttered resentfully. "It's just that I wasn't prepared for this. I wasn't expecting it."

"You think I was?" he asked incredulously. "Damn it, Dana, she wants us to get married tomorrow! She's probably calling her cousin the judge right this minute."

"She wouldn't do that. Not without our permission."

Cody noticed that Dana didn't sound entirely confident. He took a deep breath. "Okay, first things first. She's already called her attorney, named you Andy's guardian."

Dana nodded. "Yes. She told me you helped convince her that it was the right thing to do."

She hesitated a moment, then added almost shyly, "Thank you, Cody. I know you were reluctant to get involved—and Barbara probably didn't give you much choice—but she said you told her you believed I could provide the best home for Andy. I know you wouldn't have said it if you didn't think it was true."

"No. I wouldn't have. If I'd thought the boy would be better off with Lynette and Alan, I'd have said so, for his sake. But now that I've met them, I know it isn't true. I can't help but believe he'd be miserable with them. From what I can see, they aren't all that delighted with each other."

"Andy wouldn't be at all happy with them."

Cody remembered the boy's tearful words from the evening before. "No. Not the way he'll be with you. How did Lynette take Barbara's decision?"

"She was relieved, I think. Oh, she made a token protest. Said she and Alan were both willing to give Andy a home. But she agreed that... that you and I would probably make better parents for him. She said it's obvious that Andy has bonded with you, and that you're very good with children, which she and Alan obviously aren't."

Dana pushed a strand of hair behind her ear. "She said Andy's made his choice clear. She asked that she be allowed to see him whenever she wants, and she wants me to stay in touch with her concerning Andy—but she won't fight my custody of him."

"That must have been quite a relief for you."

She drew a long, shuddering breath. "You just couldn't know how much," she admitted. "I've been so worried. So upset at the thought of sending him with them, knowing how unhappy he would be."

Cody touched Dana's hand. "Andy's very lucky to have you for a sister."

"I'll do my best for him."

Cody thought of all the sacrifices Dana was prepared to make for the boy. "I know you will."

"We have to tell Barbara the truth," Dana said after a heavy moment of silence. "About us, I mean."

Cody winced. "I don't think that's a good idea. She's too frail, too worried about the future. Telling her that you and I aren't really engaged would be too much of a shock for her. Do you really want to risk that?"

"Of course not," Dana whispered miserably. "But—"

"And besides," he cut in. "What about Andy? Barbara changed her mind about leaving him to you because she thinks you and I will be married, that we'll be raising the boy together. She still believes—whether you agree with her or not—that raising him would be too much for you alone. You tell her you're going to remain single, and she's likely to decide he'll be better off with Lynette and Alan, after all."

Dana's breath caught. "She—she wouldn't do that. Not now. Would she?"

"I don't know, Dana," Cody said honestly. "From what she has said to me during the weekend, I think it's entirely possible that she would. It isn't because she doesn't love you, or doesn't trust you. She just wants the best for you, and for Andy. She's terrified of ruining your future. She made me promise that no matter what happens, I'll encourage you to finish your education and pursue the career you've always wanted."

Dana buried her face in her hands. "Oh, Cody, I'm so sorry," she wailed, her voice muffled. "I never should have gotten you into this. It seemed like a good idea at the time, but it was just so stupid. So—"

"You didn't know what else to do," Cody cut in, laying his hand on the back of her bent head. "I understand, Dana. In your position, I might have done exactly the same thing."

She lifted her head a couple of inches, still not looking at him. "When did you change your mind? About me and Andy, I mean."

"When Andy cried in my arms last night," Cody admitted. "He and Alan had been sitting right there in the den without touching—or even talking—even though it was obvious the kid was terrified. All he wanted was a hug, some reassurance, and Alan couldn't even give him that. I knew then that sending him to live with the Manninglys would be a terrible mistake."

"Maybe—" Dana chewed her lip thoughtfully. "Maybe if you tell Barbara that. Explain to her that you think I could give Andy the best home even if I am single. Tell her—"

"Tell her that her daughter is an unfit guardian? That Lynette is spoiled and self-centered and her husband is a shallow, unfeeling money grubber? Do you really think that's going to make Barbara happy?"

Dana groaned. "No. She loves Lynette, of course, and she wants desperately to believe that Lynette and Alan are happy together. We can't say anything to disillusion her about them."

"It would be cruel. It would hurt her terribly."

"Yes. Oh, God, Cody, what are we going to do?"

"I, uh, I think we're going to have to get married," Cody said, and then wondered if he'd completely lost his mind.

Dana seemed to share the sentiment. Her head snapped up, her jaw dropping. "You . . . *what?*"

He was committed now, wisely or not. He drew a deep breath. "Let Barbara call her cousin. He can marry us tomorrow, in front of the fireplace in the den. And Barbara can be there to watch."

"You're kidding, right?" Dana asked with a touch of bitterness. "Your usual reaction to a tense situation—turn it into a big joke. Laugh it off."

Her words hurt. Cody's jaw tightened. "It's not a joke, Dana," he said quietly. "I am very serious."

She stared at him, nervously twisting the ring on her left hand. "You don't want to get married."

"Well—no," he admitted. "I hadn't really thought of marrying anyone, at least not for a long time. But it doesn't look as though we have a choice."

"But—"

"Look, I know it sounds crazy—hell, it is crazy. You and I have worked together for a year, but we hardly know each other in some ways. I know you haven't thought of me as anything other than an employer—and one you don't particularly like at times. Let's face it, I'm hardly the serious, dependable type. Just the opposite, in fact. I've let a lot of people down, and no one is more aware of that than I am. But this time, I give you my word. I won't let you down. For Barbara, for you—but mostly for Andy—I'm willing to do this."

Dana looked stunned. Cody thought wryly that this wasn't exactly the response he would have anticipated from his first proposal of marriage.

"We're talking about an old-fashioned marriage of convenience, Dana," he said when she remained silent, apparently unable to form coherent words. "They aren't exactly unheard of, even in this time."

She cleared her throat. "Yes, but...what about the future?"

He shrugged. "I've never thought about the future much. I've always pretty much taken it as it came. I guess that's what you and I should do now."

"You mean...get married."

"Yes. Together, we'll help Andy through the loss of his mother and give him a good start on a future. And then—well, then we'll decide what to do about the marriage."

Dana shook her head, her cinnamon hair swirling around her cheeks, which had gone from pale to flushed to pale again. "It won't work," she said flatly. "It's crazy. We'll just end up hurting someone—ourselves, probably, if not Andy. Not to mention your family."

"What *about* my family?"

"They'll be horrified."

Cody was startled into a genuine laugh, which surprised him almost as much as it seemed to surprise Dana. "You haven't been paying attention when I've talked about my family, have you?" he chided. "They will be thrilled. No one has to know that it isn't a real marriage—not Barbara, not Andy, no one."

"Jake will know."

"He won't say anything."

She searched his face. "You're actually willing to lie to your family? For my sake? For Andy's?"

"It seems to be the answer to both our problems," he said lightly, trying to convince her he knew what he was doing. Even though he wasn't at all sure that he did. "My family will get off my back about settling down, stop trying to throw me at every single woman in central Arkansas—and Barbara will know that you aren't alone, and that Andy will have two people who love him and want the best for him."

"But, Cody—" She moistened her lips, looking torn.

At least she no longer looked horrified, he thought ruefully.

"What about other women? What if you decide there's someone else you want to marry? Then what?"

He frowned. "I told you, I haven't thought about marriage. Didn't think anyone deserved me for a husband," he added, an attempt at humor that fell flat. Maybe because he hadn't really been joking. "But if you're worried that I'll humiliate you by running around on you—don't be. I've been raised to take marriage vows seriously. Even if the marriage is in name only."

"You mean—"

He shrugged, oddly embarrassed now. "Despite what you might think of me, I've never been one to sleep around, Dana. Sex is more than recreation to me, as it is to everyone in my family. I wouldn't make a vow to you that I'm not prepared to keep."

She drew a long, shaken breath, looking at him as though she'd never seen him before. "I don't—this is—I just—" She stopped, obviously disgusted with herself.

He smiled and gently squeezed her hand. "It's happening pretty fast, isn't it?"

"You could say that," she agreed dazedly.

"Think about it," he suggested. "Take your time. You might hate the very idea. Hate *me*, for that matter," he added with a strained laugh.

"I—" She swallowed. "I don't hate you, Cody. You've been very kind to me, and to my family, this weekend. I don't know how to thank you..."

He cut her off with a growl, deeply uncomfortable with the thought that she would feel obligated to him.

It wasn't gratitude he wanted from Dana. He no longer knew what, exactly, he did want from her—but he knew it wasn't that.

"Look," he said abruptly. "I think we can make this work. We can live together as good friends, and we can take care of Andy. He's going to need us."

"Andy's the only one who's ever really needed me," Dana said softly.

"And I've never been very good at being there when I was needed," Cody said. "But this time, I will be."

The words were a pledge, as solemnly given as any marriage vow.

Dana was still looking at him in that intense, discerning way that almost made him squirm. "Someday," she said, "you're going to tell me why you have such a low opinion of yourself."

He forced a laugh. "Trust me, it's a boring story."

"I'm beginning to wonder..." she murmured.

He abruptly changed the subject. "So what's your answer? Are we getting married? Do you want to think about it for a few hours? Want me to take a long walk off a short pier?"

She smiled, though it was a shaky attempt. "If you're absolutely sure this is the right thing to do..."

"I really think it is, Dana. I think it's the *only* thing to do."

She swallowed visibly. "All right, then. We'll do it. For Andy's sake."

"For Andy's sake," Cody repeated, his voice rather hollow.

Oh, God, what had he done?

Dana twisted the ring again, then seemed to realize what she was doing. She looked down at it. Cody followed her gaze. "Looks like Bob made a sale, after all," he murmured.

She looked startled. "You don't have to buy this ring. I don't need a diamond. Really."

"I like seeing it on you," Cody answered simply. "It looks nice. You do like it, don't you?"

"Yes, of course, but—"

"Then consider it my wedding gift to you. For luck."

She moistened her lips again. Cody thought incongruously that he wished she would stop doing that. Before he gave in to the urge to do it for her.

"Thank you," she said quietly. "I, um, I guess we should go tell Barbara what we've decided."

"I think she'll be pleased."

"Yes. Is there someone you want to call? I'm sure Rachel and Seth would drive over tomorrow afternoon, if you want them here."

"No," Cody said quickly. "I'll follow Celia's example and notify the family after the wedding."

He wasn't at all sure he could pull off the wedding with his family watching—especially not Rachel, who'd always seemed to read him too easily. She would take one look at him and know that he was a quivering, nervous wreck, terrified that he was doing the wrong thing.

She might even sense the strange, inexplicable excitement he'd been feeling ever since Dana had said yes.

"So—" Dana said slowly.

"So—" he repeated, smiling a little.

Their eyes met. Cody held out his hand. "We should probably shake or something," he suggested solemnly.

Hesitantly, she placed her hand in his. "Or something," she agreed, trying to smile back at him.

He leaned over and brushed his lips across hers. Once. Very lightly.

And then again. A little harder.

Dana's lips softened beneath his. Tasted as good as he remembered.

His lips settled firmly on hers, and he tugged at her hand, drawing her closer. He was all too aware that they were alone in the room. That they sat on his bed, thigh to thigh. That it would take only a nudge from him to have her lying beneath him, her lips open beneath his, her arms around him, her legs—

He pulled himself away from her with a start. A moment later he was on his feet, some distance away from her, one hand stabbing through his hair, the other shoved into the pocket of his jeans. "We'd, uh, we'd better go talk to Barbara," he said gruffly.

Dana started to speak, then stopped to clear her throat. "I'll be right with you," she said, her own voice husky. "I think I'll just go wash my face first."

That wasn't a bad idea, Cody thought as she left the room. It wouldn't hurt for him to splash some cold water on his face. Or on the rest of him, for that matter.

* * *

Thanks to Barbara's connections, the wedding was arranged to take place at one o'clock on Tuesday afternoon.

The anticipation of the nuptials seemed to give Barbara renewed energy; she insisted on getting up and dressing nicely. She wasn't strong enough to forego the wheelchair, but she made sure her hair and makeup were done, with Hilda's assistance. She also personally called her favorite florist, from whom she cajoled an immediate delivery of several baskets of white roses and baby's breath, which she demanded that Lynette arrange artistically in the den.

Hilda seemed almost as excited as Barbara. She worked all morning, cooking a large and sumptuous celebratory luncheon to be eaten after the ceremony. The judge and his wife had been invited to dine with them.

Andy was dazzled by the arrangements, all but bouncing with the excitement of gaining a new brother-in-law, particularly one who also happened to be his newest hero.

"Quite an occasion, isn't it?" Alan asked late that morning.

Having stepped out onto the front porch for a breath of fresh air, Cody hadn't realized anyone had joined him until Alan spoke. He nodded. "Yeah. Barbara and Hilda seem determined to turn it into a real party."

"Lyn and I weren't expecting to attend a wedding when we came down this weekend."

Cody smiled crookedly. "Neither was I."

"Yeah. I understand Barbara sort of railroaded you into this."

Feeling an urge to defend Dana's mother, Cody shrugged. "I don't mind. Dana and I were already engaged, after all."

"Mmm. Lyn tells me you and Dana will be taking the boy in, after Barbara's gone."

"Yes. Of course, we hope it won't be necessary anytime soon."

Alan chuckled. "Right. I'm sure you want your bride all to yourself for as long as possible."

Cody didn't smile. "No. We hope to keep Barbara around for as long as possible." Damn, but the guy was a jerk.

Alan had the grace to look embarrassed. "Oh, yeah. Of course. I, er—"

Cody shrugged and turned away.

"I have to admit, I'm relieved that Barbara's decided to make Dana the boy's guardian," Alan said after a moment. "I mean, we'd have taken him, of course, and given him a good home. But you and Dana seem to be better with the kid. Your jobs aren't all that demanding, and you don't have to worry about staying ahead in your career—all the stuff Lyn and I have to deal with in New York."

Cody bit his tongue. This wasn't the time to tell Alan exactly what he thought of him—or his fancy New York career.

"You realize, of course, that Lynette will still want to be a part of the boy's life. After all, he's her brother."

Cody nodded. "I would never keep Lynette from seeing Andy. We'll make sure they stay in contact."

"And she'll want to check the financial records occasionally, of course. Not that she wouldn't trust you or Dana, of course, but she has a responsibility to make sure that the boy's inheritance is managed correctly. You understand that, I'm sure."

Drawing himself up very straight, Cody turned to face the shorter man, who seemed to realize that he might have just stepped out of line.

"His name is Andy," Cody said precisely, evenly. "Andy. It's not so hard to remember, or to say. Stop calling him 'the boy,' as if his name doesn't matter.

"As for the money, I've told you before and I'll repeat it now—I have no intention of touching Andy's money. It will be held in trust for his education. Anything he needs in the meantime, he'll have. Whatever you think of my business, Manningly, I make enough to pay my way. I can support my wife, and her brother. Let's leave it at that, shall we?"

"Uh, yeah, sure," Alan said, quickly holding up his hands in conciliation. "I didn't mean to imply anything. Just making conversation, you know? Family business."

Cody nodded shortly. "Consider it settled."

"Yeah, sure. Uh, guess I'll go see if Lynette wants me to do anything for the party. You, er, need anything, Cody?"

"No. Thank you." It wasn't easy to sound civil, but Cody forced himself to do so. Alan was a member of Dana's family, and Cody wouldn't be the one to alienate him, if he could help it. But one more veiled warning about Andy's inheritance, and Alan would be lucky to return to New York with all his teeth!

The conversation had served to reinforce Cody's belief that this wedding was necessary to make certain that Andy was never forced to live with the Manninglys. If he hadn't already reached that conclusion, Alan's thoughtless lack of regard for Barbara's health would have settled it.

Only then did it occur to Cody how easily the words "my wife" had rolled off his tongue. And how he'd already come to think of Dana in those terms.

Shaken, he swallowed hard and slid his unsteady hands into his pockets.

It was a wonder that Dana hadn't paced a path right into the carpet of her bedroom. She must have paced for half the night, not to mention the past hour. She glanced at the clock on the nightstand and swallowed a groan. Twelve-thirty. Half an hour until her wedding.

Her wedding! She was actually going to marry Cody Carson!

She moaned and hid her face in her hands, cursing herself for daring this crazy scheme, cursing Jake for dreaming it up in the first place, even illogically cursing Cody for agreeing to it when she'd asked him.

She'd known something would go wrong—she just hadn't even imagined how very wrong things could go!

How could she have known that both Barbara and Andy would take one look at Cody and all but adopt him into the family? How could she have imagined that Barbara would have requested an immediate wedding? Or, even more astonishingly, that Cody would agree?

She felt as though she were on a roller coaster that just kept going faster and faster, wilder and wilder. She'd gotten on willingly, but she'd quickly discovered it wasn't nearly as safe a diversion as she'd anticipated—and there seemed to be no getting off until the ride ended. She just hoped she wasn't in for a spectacular and disastrous crash.

There was a tap on the door, and then Lynette stuck her head in. "Dana? You need any help getting ready?" She took one look at her stepsister and closed the bedroom door behind her. "Yes, I can see that you do."

Dana looked down to find that she was still wearing the jeans and T-shirt she'd thrown on that morning. Her hair was tousled and straight, her makeup sketchy. She felt very plain compared to Lynette, who was wearing a beautifully tailored garnet-and-navy-print silk dress, her hair and face immaculately done.

"I guess I'd better hurry, hadn't I?"

Lynette nodded, her smile surprisingly understanding. "Yes. I suppose you'd better. Your wedding starts in half an hour."

Dana groaned.

Lynette laughed and moved to the closet. "I understand, you know. I was a nervous wreck before my wedding. Don't you remember?"

Lynette had married during the August before Dana's senior year in high school. Dana had been included very little in the wedding preparations, Lynette having surrounded herself with her friends. Dana's only function had been to sit behind the guest register in the church lobby and make sure everyone remembered to sign with the fluffy feather-tipped ballpoint that matched the ornately covered guest book.

"No," she said. "I don't remember your being nervous."

"Well, I was. I cried because my hair wouldn't hold a curl, because I got a run in my hose and had to change, because I couldn't get my makeup straight—and then because crying streaked my mascara. Mother almost lost all patience with me. We had four hundred guests waiting while I had hysterics over a missing tube of lipstick."

Dana managed a shaky smile. "Then I'm glad Cody and I decided to be married so privately. The thought of four hundred people watching me today is almost enough to make me faint."

Lynette nodded. "This is much nicer," she agreed. "Just family. What were you planning to wear?" she asked, flipping rapidly through the few outfits Dana kept at her stepmother's house.

"I don't know," Dana admitted. "I didn't have time to buy anything special...."

"How about this?" Lynette drew a cream-colored suit from the closet and held it up for inspection. "Dana, this is lovely. It even looks bridal."

Dana had almost forgotten that suit. She'd worn it to a fancy tea Barbara had talked her into attending a couple of years ago. Barbara had bought the suit for her, surprising her with it on the morning of the tea. Dana had worn it only once since; she didn't often have occasion to wear expensive suits, especially in Percy.

"That will be fine," she said, wondering if Cody had even brought a jacket with him. Her groom was more likely to show up in jeans and a western-cut shirt. Not that it mattered, of course, she reminded herself. It wasn't as if this were a real wedding, exactly.

Lynette insisted on helping Dana get dressed. "It's tradition," she explained. "Brides always have help. It's probably bad luck to get dressed alone on your wedding day."

"I've never heard that one."

"I just made it up. I'll plug in the curling iron and let it heat while you do your makeup."

Dana realized that Lynette wasn't going to be satisfied until she was properly primped and powdered. She sighed and surrendered rather than risk a quarrel. To be honest, she found her stepsister's attentions a bit touching—probably because they were so rare.

Twenty minutes later, Lynette stood back to appraise the results of her efforts. "You look beautiful," she said at length. "Really beautiful."

Dana was surprised to feel a wave of heat warm her cheeks. "Thank you."

Lynette frowned at her stepsister's bare ears. "You need pearls. Do you have any?"

"No. The only earrings I brought with me are the small gold hoops I've been wearing this weekend. If you think I need earrings, I'll wear them."

"Wait right here."

"But—"

Lynette had already hurried out of the room.

Dana sighed, shook her head and turned to the mirror, trying to study her reflection dispassionately. The cream-colored suit fit her nicely, emphasizing her slender waist and hips. She'd dug out the cream heels that matched, which added a couple of inches to her height and made her legs look long and curvaceous.

Under Lynette's critical supervision, she'd taken great care with her makeup, applying smoky eyeshadow, softly blended eyeliner, dark mascara, delicately tinted blusher, glossy mauve lipstick. It was more makeup than she usually wore, but it looked good, she decided. Not overdone.

Lynette had personally taken over the hairstyling. She'd softened and fluffed Dana's usual bob with the curling iron and a styling comb, brushing her bangs away from her face to emphasize her cosmetically enhanced eyes. The woman in the mirror looked calm, sophisticated, confident.

Only Dana knew what a misleading illusion that reflection was. Inside, she was a mess.

Lynette returned in a rush. "Here," she said, holding out her hand. "Wear these."

Dana looked at the tasteful pearl earrings on her stepsister's palm. Even their soft glow looked expensive.

"I can't wear those," she said nervously, putting her hands behind her back. "What if I lose one? Or both?"

"You won't lose them. Hurry and put them on, Dana, we don't have much time. Besides, it's good luck to wear something borrowed, remember?"

"I never realized you were so superstitious," Dana said, reluctantly donning the earrings with exaggerated care, thinking ruefully about Lynette's insistence that Dana wear pale blue panties. For luck, of course.

"I'm only superstitious about weddings. And ladders—I simply can't walk beneath one."

Earrings in place, Dana turned to her stepsister. "I didn't know that, either."

"There's a lot we don't know about each other," Lynette agreed with a touch of regret. "And I know it's my fault. I'm sorry I haven't been more of a sister to you, Dana."

Caught off-guard, Dana stammered, "I, um, it's okay, Lynette. I—"

Visibly uncomfortable, Lynette waved a manicured hand. "This isn't the time to get into that. I just want to say again that I truly appreciate what you've done for Mother these past few months. And for Andy. Whatever you might think of me, I do love them. And I'm very grateful that you've been here for them."

"Thank you, Lynette. That means a great deal to me."

"Now don't start crying," Lynette said brusquely, her voice a bit husky. "You'll streak your mascara and then we'd just have to start all over. Wait here and I'll go see if things are ready downstairs. Don't move a muscle, you hear? I don't want you to disturb one hair. I've worked too hard to make you presentable."

Dana smiled faintly, still stunned at her stepsister's kind words.

This was turning out to be one incredibly unpredictable weekend, she thought in a near daze.

Chapter Eleven

"There you are, Cody. Oh, my, don't you look nice?"

Cody tugged self-consciously at his tie as Barbara looked at him in open admiration from her wheelchair in the flower-bedecked den. Across the room, Alan stood in conversation with a man and woman who Cody assumed to be Judge Herriman and his wife. Dana, Lynette, Andy and Hilda hadn't come in yet.

"Thanks, Barbara. I'm glad I thought to throw a jacket and tie into my bag for this weekend. Of course, had I known I'd be getting married, I'd have brought a nice suit." He would have even bought one for the occasion.

"You look very handsome," Barbara assured him. "I'm glad I had a new roll of film for my camera. Alan's volunteered to take pictures for us. He's an excellent photographer."

Cody bit the inside of his lip as he thought of how Alan had probably been sweetly coerced to "volunteer." Barbara had a way of gently getting what she wanted—this wedding, for example. "That's very thoughtful of him," he said.

"Yes, isn't it? I know you and Dana will treasure the photographs, and I'm sure your family will want to see them."

Cody pulled at the tight knot in his tie. "Yes, I'm sure they'll enjoy seeing pictures of my wedding," he agreed, thinking of his cousin Adam's certain wicked delight in finally seeing Cody shackled.

Cody had taken such pleasure in teasing Adam over unexpectedly tumbling into love with a woman and her tiny infant, both of whom Adam now claimed as his own. Adam wouldn't miss the chance to have his revenge.

Barbara took Cody's free hand. "I hope you aren't having second thoughts," she fretted. "I've been so worried that I've rushed you into this."

"I'm not having second thoughts," he assured her, gently squeezing her fingers. "I'm absolutely certain that I'm doing the right thing," he added sincerely.

And he was. For the most part.

Barbara searched his face for a moment, then visibly relaxed, apparently convinced. "I'm so glad. I have something for you. For Dana, actually."

She held out her hand to him. "I know you didn't have a chance to get Dana a wedding band. Her father put this on my hand in this very room. I'd like you to put it on Dana's today."

Cody took the small gold band with unsteady fingers. "This is going to mean a great deal to her," he said.

Barbara nodded and touched her own bare left hand. "I want her to have it," she murmured.

The guilt gremlin took another gleeful bite out of Cody's insides. He wished fleetingly for an antacid—though he suspected the medication would do nothing to alleviate his discomfort.

Granny Fran would probably take him behind the nearest woodshed if she knew of the lies he'd told this weekend, he thought wryly.

Andy skipped into the room, wearing the same jacket and tie he'd worn for dinner with Lynette and Alan. He looked much happier to have it on this time, Cody noted.

"Is it time for the wedding?" he asked eagerly. "Can I throw rice when it's over?"

Barbara laughed and motioned her son to her side. "We'll discuss that later," she told him fondly. "Oh, look, Alan's going to take our picture. Smile, Andy."

Lynette glided in a moment later. "Dana's ready," she announced. "Shall we begin?"

Cody's tie immediately tightened itself around his throat. He tugged at it again.

Judge Herriman stepped forward to introduce himself to Cody with a warm handshake. "We'll wait for your bride in front of the fireplace," he said.

"Okay. Sure," Cody said, grateful his voice didn't come out a squeak. He put a hand on Andy's shoulder. "Where does my best man stand?"

Andy beamed. "I'm your best man?"

"You bet."

Smiling, the judge instructed Andy to stand at Cody's right side.

Hilda rushed in, flapping a paper tissue. "Music!" she cried. "We have to have music."

She did something with the stereo system in the entertainment cabinet and a moment later piano music drifted softly out of concealed speakers. Sniffling into her tissue, Hilda moved to perch on the edge of the couch, smoothing what was probably her best dress around her thick knees.

Yanni, Cody thought, recognizing the music. Could this ceremony possibly get any schmaltzier? One more touching addition and *he* was liable to burst into tears.

Mrs. Herriman took a seat beside Barbara's wheelchair. Alan made a production of positioning himself with the camera.

The music swelled.

Cody wondered absently if anyone would notice if he slunk out of the room.

Lynette reappeared in the doorway with Dana beside her. She hurried across the room to take the position of matron of honor, opposite Andy, who stood so proudly.

Cody's tie promptly went into strangling mode again.

God, he thought dazedly, staring at his bride. She looked . . . beautiful.

Dana met his eyes with a brave little smile that he knew must hide a panic at least as great as his own. And then she started toward him. The single white rose she held—Lynette's touch, he was sure—quivered as though being shaken by a strong breeze.

Barbara detained Dana as she would have passed her on the way to Cody's side. Dana bent over the wheelchair for a moment. Cody couldn't hear their murmured conversation, though he saw Barbara press something into Dana's hand. Blinking rapidly, Dana pressed a tender kiss to Barbara's cheek, and Cody suspected that he wasn't the only one powerfully affected by the visible affection between the two.

Dana straightened, smiled one more time at Barbara and then turned to face Cody. She was pale beneath her skillfully applied makeup, but her steps never wavered as she moved to stand beside him.

Judge Herriman began to speak. Cody hardly heard anything the man said. He thought there were scriptures read, a few words of wisdom imparted. He couldn't be sure.

He heard the question the judge directed at him. Clearing his throat, Cody managed a reasonably coherent, "I do."

The judge turned to Dana. Her own response was only a whisper, but it was the appropriate one.

Satisfied, Judge Herriman turned back to Cody. "You have a ring?" he asked.

Cody nodded and groped in his jacket pocket for the ring Barbara had given him. Aware that Dana was watching him in surprise, he turned to face her. "It was Barbara's," he murmured, showing the ring to her. "From your father. She wanted you to have it."

Dana's eyes filled with tears.

"Please repeat after me," the judge intoned. "With this ring, I thee wed. . . ."

Cody parroted those words and the ones that followed in a voice he hardly recognized as his own. He slid the ring on Dana's finger, relieved when it fit perfectly.

"Dana, do you have a ring for Cody?" the judge asked.

Moving almost in slow motion, Dana nodded. She opened her hand, displaying the plain gold band she'd been holding so tightly it had furrowed into her palm.

"It was Daddy's," she whispered, looking at Cody. "Barbara just gave it to me."

"Do you want me to wear it?" he asked, ignoring the others for a moment, his expression demanding that she answer him truthfully.

"Yes," she murmured, reaching for his hand. "I want you to wear it. It—it will please Barbara," she added in a hasty whisper meant only for his hearing.

An inexplicable pang went through him, but Cody ignored it. He allowed her to place the ring on his hand, hardly hearing the words she repeated after the judge. The ring was a little big, but not so much that it wouldn't stay in place.

The judge spoke again, saying something about a long and happy life together, about the gravity of the vows they'd just taken, about the commitment they had just made. And then he officially pronounced them husband and wife.

Cody was greatly relieved that his knees didn't buckle. *Married!* The joke was most definitely on him this time.

"You may kiss your bride," Judge Herriman urged, sounding amused—probably at the stunned, deer-in-the-headlights look on the groom's face.

His gaze locked with Dana's, Cody leaned over to brush his mouth across hers. He couldn't help thinking of the kiss they'd shared the day before, alone in his bedroom. Sitting on his bed.

And he couldn't help thinking that the next time they were alone in a bedroom together, they would be legally married.

Dana's cheeks were flaming when the chaste kiss ended. Cody hoped she hadn't read his mind.

Andy was the one to break the solemn spell of the ceremony. He gave a whoop and wrapped his arms around Cody's waist. "All right!" he said. "You're my brother-in-law now, Cody! That is so cool."

Cody laughed and hugged the boy, promptly reminded of the reason for this whole charade. How could he possibly regret his actions when this child's future was at stake?

The rest of the family started forward to offer their own congratulations. The flashbulb on the camera popped dizzyingly as Alan recorded the scene for posterity.

Barbara's cheeks were wet when Cody leaned down to kiss her. "You can't know," she said brokenly, "how happy I am. You can't imagine how great a burden has been lifted from me."

He didn't understand, exactly, but he only smiled and kissed her again.

Lunch was a cheery affair. Hilda had outdone herself on preparations, providing a menu any professional caterer would have been proud to claim. Judge Herriman was a naturally talkative man who kept the conversation moving. His wife gossiped happily with Lynette; Alan made the occasional pompously irrelevant comment; Andy chattered; Barbara smiled and contentedly watched everyone.

Cody and Dana were both uncharacteristically quiet. They ate mechanically, seated side by side, hardly glancing at each other during the meal.

Cody was trying to keep up the charade, but it was becoming more difficult as the afternoon progressed. Dana's smile was growing a bit strained around the edges.

They had coffee and wedding cake afterward in the den. Sensing that Barbara was beginning to watch them closely, Cody forced himself to talk and laugh with the others as naturally as he had before the wedding.

He put his arm around Dana's waist, as though wanting to keep his new bride close to him. She gave him a bright, glittering, affectionate and completely fake smile. Cody wondered if he was the only one who saw the truth in her eyes.

"Are you lovebirds staying the night here?" the judge inquired as the festivities drew to an end.

Cody managed a rueful smile. "I'm afraid not, sir. Actually, I have to work. I'm expected at my club this evening."

"And so am I," Dana explained with a slight laugh. "The boss hasn't given me permission to take the evening off."

Smiling perfunctorily, Cody sensed that Dana was operating solely on nerves, and that they were stretched close to the breaking point. He only hoped she could hold herself together for another hour or so, at least until they were alone.

"I can't believe you're actually going to wait tables on your wedding night," Lynette said, shaking her head in implied disapproval.

"Dana knows she can have the evening off if she wants," Cody replied quietly.

"It's Kasey's night off," Dana reminded him. "I won't neglect my job."

"Don't you think going to college and taking care of your new husband will be enough responsibility for you?" Mrs. Herriman inquired a bit archly. "Should you be tending bar, as well?"

Cody hadn't cared for Judge Herriman's wife at first impression, though he'd forced himself to reserve judgment. Now he decided that he really didn't like her. She had embarrassed Dana.

"My wife is free to do whatever she likes, as far as her job is concerned," he said evenly. "I would like her to devote as much time as possible to her studies, and I'll do anything I can to help her. If that means quitting work, it's fine with me. As for me, I'm perfectly capable of taking care of myself."

"And my husband knows that I will continue to help him with his business as much as I can," Dana added. "I like working with him at the restaurant." She emphasized the final word, making it clear that Country Straight was not merely a bar.

The judge's wife arched a thin brow.

Barbara hid a smile behind her hand.

Cody put an arm around Dana's shoulders and pulled her close. "Speaking of work," he said, judging the time to be right, "we should probably get ready to go. By the time we pack and change into traveling clothes, it will be time to leave."

Dana gave him a grateful look. "You're right," she said quickly. "I'll start packing."

"Would you like for me to help you?" Lynette offered.

"No, thank you." Dana nodded toward Barbara, who was beginning to droop a bit in her chair. "Why don't you take Mom back to rest for a while? She looks tired."

The Herrimans said their farewells and repeated their congratulations to the newlyweds. The judge refused any payment for his services, assuring Cody and Dana that he considered it a privilege to perform a favor for his favorite cousin.

Together, Dana and Cody walked up the stairs to their rooms. They hesitated outside her door.

"Shall we plan to leave in an hour?" Cody suggested.

She nodded. "Fine. I'll be ready."

"Need any help?"

"No. Thank you," she added belatedly.

He nodded and turned toward his own room.

"Cody?" Dana's voice sounded very small.

He turned to find her watching him, her eyes large and vulnerable. "Tell me we've done the right thing," she whispered.

He cupped her cheek in his hand. Her skin felt chilled. "We've done the right thing," he said obediently. And then he managed a smile. "I hope."

She drew a shaky breath. "Thanks," she said dryly. "I needed that reassurance."

He chuckled. "That's what husbands are for, isn't it?"

She groaned and closed her eyes. "Oh, my God. You're my *husband.*"

"And you're my wife." The word didn't sound as disturbing as it probably should have. "Who'd have believed it, hmm?"

She sighed and opened her eyes. "You know, of course, that the next few days are going to be dreadful. We'll have to tell everyone. Can you imagine how they're going to react?"

Cody shuddered. "We'll manage," he assured her with more confidence than he felt. "If we can survive that wedding, we can handle anything."

She gave him a wan smile. "I guess you have a point. See you in an hour, Cody."

One hour, he thought as he entered his own room. In only one more hour, he'd be taking his wife home.

He sank onto the end of the bed, his knees finally giving out.

It was just over an hour later when Cody and Dana finally got away. They spent several minutes alone with Barbara before they left.

"It was a beautiful wedding," she told them from her bed. "Thank you for indulging me with this. You've made me very happy today."

Dana smiled tenderly at her stepmother. "Then I wouldn't change a thing," she said sincerely, knowing she would have married Cody a dozen times over just to see the happiness in Barbara's expressive eyes.

"I've given Hilda my home telephone number and my sister Rachel's number," Cody told Barbara. "If Dana or I can't be reached at home or the club, either my partner or my sister will know where to contact us at any time."

Home. Dana gulped silently. Was Cody implying that she would be moving in with him when they returned to Percy?

She hadn't really thought that far ahead...but she supposed it was a reasonable assumption. They were married, after all, and for Andy's sake, they had agreed to make everyone believe it was a real marriage.

They could hardly live in separate places, nor could she imagine Cody moving into her tiny studio apartment fifteen miles from his club, when she knew he owned a house only a few blocks from Country Straight. She'd seen it when he and Jake had thrown a Fourth of July barbecue party on Cody's patio for the Country Straight staff. She hadn't even imagined then that she would actually be moving into that house with him only two months later.

"You and Dana will be living at your place?" Barbara asked Cody with interest.

He looked questioningly at Dana. "We haven't actually had time to talk about it," he admitted. "I have a small, three-bedroom house close to both my club and her college, so I'm assuming we'll live there, at least for now."

Dana managed a smile. "Cody has a lovely house," she assured Barbara. "It's a red brick bungalow with white shutters and a big, fenced yard. He has a patio in back that's perfect for casual entertaining."

"It sounds nice," Barbara approved. "How long have you lived there, Cody?"

"I bought the house two years ago, not long after Jake and I opened the club. I got a good deal on it, and I thought it was a good investment."

"The nesting instinct," Barbara murmured with a smile. "You were preparing a home for your future family."

"Of course," Cody agreed easily, his smile so natural that only Dana knew what a big lie he'd just told.

"It sounds as though there's plenty of room for Andy."

Cody patted Barbara's hand. "Always room for Andy. And for you, too. I hope you'll be able to visit us there soon."

"I would love to see it," Barbara said wistfully. "Maybe..."

"We'd better be going," Dana said, reluctant to leave, but knowing it was time. "I'll probably drive back over to spend Sunday afternoon with you."

"We both will," Cody promised.

"You mustn't feel you have to spend every free moment here with me," Barbara chided them. "You'll want to spend some time together. After all, you should be starting your honeymoon."

"Dana and I will take care of the honeymoon," Cody said with one of his wicked grins.

Barbara giggled. "I'm sure you will, at that."

Dana felt her cheeks warm. She avoided Cody's eyes as she kissed her stepmother. She was already moving toward the door when Cody bent to kiss Barbara's cheek.

Dana looked back from the doorway. Barbara lay against the pillows, looking pale and so very fragile. And yet she was smiling, the excitement of the afternoon still glowing in her eyes.

Cody took Dana's hand. "Ready?"

She nodded, blew her stepmother a kiss and turned away.

Andy, Hilda, Lynette and Alan were waiting outside by Cody's Jeep. They showered the newlyweds with handfuls of ecologically correct bird seed, to Andy's noisy delight.

While Cody chased Andy down and teasingly trickled bird seed down the back of the boy's shirt, Dana took her leave of Lynette.

"We'll be going back to New York first thing in the morning," Lynette said. "We'll try to get back in a few weeks. Or at least I will—I don't know if Alan can get away again so soon. Of course, if...if anything happens, he and I will both be here immediately."

"Of course. I'll keep you informed."

"Thank you. I'll try to call Hilda every day. I really didn't know Mother had gotten so bad, Dana."

"I know you didn't," Dana answered gently. "It has happened so quickly. Even though you and I have talked, you really had to see her to understand."

Lynette drew a deep breath. "She's determined to stay out of the hospital for as long as possible. A part-time nurse will be helping Hilda, starting next week. I know Andy wants to stay here as long as he can, but..."

"Cody and I are prepared to take him as soon as it becomes necessary," Dana cut in. "We'll be checking out schools in Percy and talking to his teachers here about his academic standing."

Watching her little brother tussling with Cody, Lynette nodded. "I know he'll have a good home with you. He'll be happy...after a while."

"Yes," Dana murmured sadly. "After a while."

Both of them were silent for a moment. And then Dana forced a smile and held out her closed hand to Lynette. "I almost forgot. Here are your earrings. Thank you again for letting me borrow them for the wedding."

"I want you to have them. A wedding gift, from me."

Dana's eyes widened. "Oh, but—"

"I bought those earrings myself, with one of my first paychecks from the ad agency. Now I want to give them to you. A memento of your wedding day. Please let me do this, Dana."

Lynette looked so sincere that Dana found herself unable to refuse. Touched, she swallowed and nodded, her fingers closing protectively around the expensive pearls. "Thank you. I'll treasure them."

Characteristically, Lynette quickly brushed off Dana's thanks.

After swapping hugs and kisses with Andy, it was time to go.

Dana looked over her shoulder as Cody drove away from the house. Andy and Lynette were standing side by side, Lynette's hand resting a bit awkwardly on Andy's shoulder. Alan stood behind them, looking distant and detached.

Her family, Dana thought with a sigh. What a complex word that was.

And speaking of family...

She looked at her husband.

Cody's hair was tousled from his roughhousing with Andy. Dana smiled when she spotted a grain of seed among the heavy golden strands. She started to reach out to remove it, paused, then casually brushed at his hair. The grain fell away.

Cody glanced sideways at her.

"Bird seed in your hair," she explained.

He smiled. "You'd better check your own."

Self-consciously, she fluffed her hair. "Are we going straight to the club? It'll be after five when we get there as it is."

"I'll call Jake, let him know we're running late. We can stop by your place on the way so you can pick up a few things for tomorrow."

She moistened her lips. "You, uh, want me to move into your house tonight?"

"You might as well, don't you think? We've agreed we should make this marriage look as real as possible, for Andy's sake. And, to be honest, for our own. I really don't want to make complicated explanations about our personal business, do you?"

"No," Dana agreed. "I don't."

It would be easier all around if she and Cody just let everyone believe they'd married for love—quietly, privately. Their acquaintances would be surprised, but accepting.

Dana admitted to herself that she would find it very embarrassing if everyone knew Cody had married her as a charitable gesture. Was he aware of that?

Was his insistence on making the marriage look real another favor he was doing for her?

"You're sure you don't want to tell your family the truth?" she asked, wondering if he'd be able to pull the charade off in front of those people who knew him so well.

"Not yet, anyway," Cody said after a momentary pause. "My family will take you and Andy in without reservation, regardless of the circumstances, but I don't want Andy to have any reason to feel he doesn't fully belong. He won't be an outsider... and I don't want him to feel like one."

Dana twisted her hands in her lap, thinking of Cody's family... and the true outsider who would be among them. Her.

"I promise that Andy will never have to deal with the burden of knowing that you and I married just for his sake," Cody added. "Whatever happens in the future, you have my word that I'll be a good husband to you. I know it's happened fast, and that circumstances moved beyond our control in some ways, but I went into this marriage willingly and with every intention of making it work. I, uh, I just thought you should know that."

Dana was inexplicably touched by the note of sincerity in Cody's voice. His expression was uncharacteristically serious, and she knew instinctively that he was being perfectly honest with her. She owed him honesty in return.

"I'll be a good wife to you, Cody," she repeated, feeling that the vows they were making now were even more binding than the ones they'd swapped in front of witnesses that afternoon. "It's true that I married you for my little brother's sake, and I can't help feeling rather guilty about it. Even though I know it was your choice, I feel that I've taken terrible advantage of you, but I will never give you reason to feel used. I won't ask anything more of you than to help me provide a good home for Andy, and if there comes a time when you need your freedom, I won't cause you any problems. I'll always be grateful to you for what you've done for me today."

She'd thought to set Cody's mind at ease, to let him know how much she truly appreciated what he'd sacrificed for her sake, and for Andy's. She couldn't imagine why he looked as though she'd just said something he found extremely distasteful. His hands gripped the steering wheel so tightly his knuckles gleamed white. His brow was creased with a frown.

"I said I knew what I was doing," he said rather curtly. "I don't want either guilt or gratitude from you in return. Just let me help you take care of Andy."

She wished she knew what she'd said to offend him. She wished she understood this man who was now her husband, who'd just promised so much to her.

She wished...

She shook off that line of thinking, knowing she was straying close to dangerous emotions she wasn't prepared to examine too closely at the moment.

"Why don't you turn on some music?" Cody said abruptly, bringing the conversation to an end. "There are CDs in the console, if you can't find a radio station you like. Choose whatever you like."

Watching him surreptitiously from beneath her lashes, Dana reached for the radio controls, wondering if she would ever fully understand Cody Carson.

Chapter Twelve

Dana gave Cody directions to her apartment. She hesitated before inviting him in, and once inside he saw why. The place was tiny, plain, almost Spartan. "I don't spend a lot of time here," she explained.

He nodded and offered to help her pack. Refusing his assistance, she waved him to the couch while she threw some things into a bag.

"We'll come back for the rest tomorrow," Cody said as they left. "Do you have a lease commitment?"

"Only until the end of the month, but—"

"Good. Then you can talk to your landlord tomorrow, find out what your responsibilities are."

"You, uh, want me to give the apartment up completely?"

Cody lifted an eyebrow. "There's no need to keep paying rent on a place you won't be using, is there?"

"No," she said slowly. "I suppose not."

He doubted she could be emotionally attached to the apartment, austere as it was. He suspected that she was more attached to the idea of a place of her own, and reluctant to sacrifice her independence to move in with him. He could understand—but that was the choice she'd made when she'd said, "I do."

It was almost seven by the time they reached Country Straight. The parking lot was moderately well filled, indicating business was about as usual for a Tuesday evening. Cody parked by Dana's car, which, of course, was still sitting where they'd left it Saturday morning—back when he'd been a single man.

He sat for a moment looking at the front doors, steeling himself for what was to come. Dana didn't seem to be in any greater hurry to go in.

After a moment, he chuckled wryly. "Might as well get it over with," he said, turning to look at her.

She swallowed and nodded. "You're right. They'll be wondering where we are."

Cody's smile deepened. "Actually, this could be fun."

Dana rolled her eyes. "You have a very bizarre sense of humor."

"So I've been told. Let's go, Mrs. Carson."

Dana groaned, hid her face in her hands for a moment, then bravely opened her door.

Cody almost groaned himself when the first people he saw inside the club were his sister Rachel and her husband, Seth, sitting at a table close to the bar, plates of barbecue in front of them. Jake stood beside the table, chatting with Seth as the rest of the staff bustled around waiting on other customers.

Tonight, of all nights, his sister and brother-in-law had to choose to dine at his place, Cody thought in resignation.

The way his luck had been running for the past few days, he should have expected this.

Dana clutched Cody's arm. "It's Rachel," she whispered urgently, as though Cody hadn't already seen them for himself. "What are you going to tell her?"

Cody shook off her hand, then wrapped an arm around her shoulders. "Come say hi to your new sister-in-law, darlin'."

"Cody, please don't—"

But Cody was already propelling her forward. "Rachel! Seth! How's it going? Where are the kids?"

Rachel looked at him in surprise, her dark eyes lingering on the arm he had around Dana's shoulders. Cody knew she hadn't missed the fiery blush on Dana's cheeks. Seth, too, looked surprised and curious.

Jake was grinning. Cody suspected Jake thought they were setting up the practical joke he'd suggested.

Little did his partner know how the joke had turned.

Rachel spoke first. "The children are at the skating rink for a birthday party. Seth and I are taking advantage of a free couple of hours to eat out."

Cody had always admired his older sister's tact. She was obviously curious about where he'd been, why he and Dana had come in together, why Dana looked so flustered, why Cody had his arm around her...but Rachel would never be so indelicate as to pry.

Seth had no such reservations. His sandy hair tumbling onto his forehead, green eyes alight with curiosity, he tilted his head and asked, "Where've you been the past few days, Cody?"

Rachel sighed faintly.

Cody smiled. "Dana and I spent the long weekend with her family in Memphis."

"Did you?" Seth was almost vibrating now with questions. Jake grinned and winked at Cody.

Dana cleared her throat. "I'd better get to work," she murmured. "Everyone looks busy."

"Wait a minute, darlin'. Don't you want to tell them our news first?" Cody asked in a lazy drawl.

Dana gave him a look that warned him of dire retribution.

"News?" Seth asked eagerly. "What news?"

In answer, Cody held up his left hand and wiggled the ring finger, on which glinted the gold band Dana had placed there only hours earlier.

Jake's grin faded. "Is that...?"

"Show them your rings, Dana," Cody urged.

Her silent warnings grew more lethal, but she managed a creditable smile as she held out her left hand.

Cody noticed the unsteadiness in her fingers, and knew the others would, too. He hoped they would mark her nervousness down to shyness.

"Those are...wedding rings," Rachel said after a stunned moment of silence.

"We were married at one o'clock this afternoon," Cody proclaimed, thoroughly enjoying the moment now that it was upon him. "Congratulate me, Seth. I've joined the ranks of shackled men."

He couldn't have asked for a more dramatic response to his announcement.

Rachel sat frozen, her lovely oval face expressionless, only her widened eyes reflecting her shock. Seth was open-mouthed in astonishment. Jake looked as though he'd been poleaxed.

Rachel recovered first. She rose to her feet. "This is such a surprise," she said, moving to Cody's side. "I didn't even know you and Dana were... But where are my manners? Let me be the first to welcome you to our family, Dana."

Dana smiled tremulously. "Thank you, Rachel. I hope you aren't hurt that we sprang this on you this way. It all happened rather quickly."

"We seem to have a family record of swift courtships," Rachel replied. "Celia only knew Reed for two weeks before they were married. The rest of us didn't have a chance to meet him until they were already married. At least you and Cody have known each other awhile."

Seth wasn't as quick to accept the news. Standing, he planted his fists on his hips and looked suspiciously at his longtime friend. "All right, Cody, give it to us straight. Is this another one of your jokes? Because if it is..."

"It's no joke," Cody cut in good-naturedly. "Would you like to see our marriage license? I have it out in the Jeep. All legally signed and everything."

"You've really gotten married?"

"Seth," Rachel murmured, nodding toward Dana. "Wouldn't you like to give your best wishes to the bride?"

Seth had the grace to look abashed. "Uh, yeah, sorry, Dana." With natural charm, he leaned over to kiss Dana's pale cheek. "It isn't that we disapprove of Cody's choice," he assured her. "Just the opposite, in fact. To be honest, we're wondering what you see in the big lug."

Dana smiled. "He has his odd charms," she murmured.

Seth laughed. "Yeah. I guess that's close enough."

Jake had moved close to Cody's side. He nudged him with his elbow. "Uh, Cody..."

Cody gave his partner a warning glance. "Aren't you going to congratulate me, Jake?"

"You bet," Jake replied with admirable aplomb, though Cody knew he was in for an intensive grilling later. "Congratulations, Cody. You've got yourself a beautiful bride."

Following Seth's example, he kissed Dana's cheek. "Didn't I tell you this would be a great match?" he asked her with an impish grin.

Dana's color heightened, but she responded easily enough. "Yes, you did, Jake. You could almost say you're the one who brought us together. And now I'd better get my apron...."

Jake looked scandalized. "You'll do no such thing. Don't even think about working tonight. This calls for a celebration. Hey, Angela!" he yelled, turning toward the waitress who was watching them with open curiosity from across the half-filled room. "Break out the champagne we keep for special occasions. We have a wedding to toast. Dana and Cody were married today!"

Cody made a solemn vow right then that someday, somewhere, somehow, he would find a way to utterly mortify Jake Dennehy in front of as many people as possible.

Most of the diners in the restaurant that evening knew Cody, and were familiar with Dana through her job there. A wave of excitement surged through the room, and before long Cody and Dana found themselves surrounded by well-wishers. Bottles of champagne were opened, poured and served.

Jake pressed a glass of mineral water into Cody's hand. "A toast!" he shouted. "To Cody and Dana Carson. May their marriage be long, happy...and fruitful!"

Cody choked on his water. Dana groaned heartily, looking as though she would love to crawl into the nearest hole.

Jake looked smugly satisfied with himself as he drained his champagne, then grinned at Cody.

Rachel managed to catch Cody alone in his office for a few moments before she and Seth left. "I have to admit I'm staggered," she said honestly. "I had no idea you were thinking of marriage."

It had been fun watching the various reactions of shock and disbelief; now Cody felt the familiar nibblings of guilt at the deception he was pulling. He'd known his family would be the real test for him, especially Rachel. As for Granny Fran . . . he couldn't even think about talking to her yet.

"We hadn't actually planned to be married this weekend," he confessed, choosing his words carefully. "Dana's stepmother is very ill—terminally ill—and she wanted us to be married while she was well enough to be a witness. Since we'd already announced our engagement to her family, there didn't seem to be any reason to wait. I knew my family would understand."

Rachel immediately looked sympathetic. "Of course. Is Dana close to her stepmother?"

"Very close. It meant a great deal to her to have her stepmother there with us."

"I'm sure it did. I'm so sorry for her. Is there anything I can do?"

Cody shook his head. "Not now. Dana and I will be spending most of our spare time in Memphis for the next few months . . . if her stepmother lasts that long. There's a lot of family business to take care of, and Dana has a ten-year-old half brother who needs her right now."

"It sounds as though you've taken on a lot of responsibility with this marriage," his sister commented, watching him closely.

Cody swallowed, wondering if Rachel was asking herself if her formerly reckless, notoriously incorrigible little brother could handle the challenge. "I know what I've done," he said evenly. "Dana and I both know what's ahead for us."

She nodded, as though satisfied with his response.

"No wonder you've been so distant from our family lately," Rachel said after another moment, as though a great puzzle had just been solved for her. "We've all been wondering—now I know. You've been courting Dana. You always have valued your privacy when it came to something that important to you."

Cody murmured something noncommittal. What could he say? How could he explain that he'd been avoiding the family because he *didn't* want to get married—only to end up married almost by accident?

"Anyway, I want you to know that I'm very happy for you," Rachel said, reaching up to kiss his cheek. "I've always liked Dana. I'm looking forward to getting to know her better. I hope you and she are as blissfully happy as Seth and I have been."

Cody's throat tightened. "Thanks, Rachel. Um, you're feeling okay?" he asked, anxious to change the subject. "No morning sickness or anything like that?"

"I feel wonderful," she answered, her smile deepening. "Seth and I are so excited about the baby, and so are the kids."

"That's great, Rachel. You deserve to be happy."

There was a tap on the door, and then Dana peeked in. "Rachel? Seth says you're going to be late picking up the children if you don't hurry."

"I'm on my way." Rachel stopped impulsively to hug Dana on her way out. "It's so nice to have another sister," she said warmly. "I can't wait to sit down and have a long, cozy chat with you. I'll have you over for dinner soon, okay?"

"That would be very nice," Dana said. "Thank you."

Rachel discreetly closed the office door behind her as she left.

Dana released a long, gusty breath and collapsed into a chair. "Why," she asked Cody forcefully, "didn't you throw me out of here when I came in to ask you to go along with this crazy scheme? Why didn't you just fire me or something?"

He ran a hand through his hair and grimaced. "Neither of us could have foreseen this, Dana. Not in our wildest dreams."

"Or nightmares," she muttered.

He frowned. Was it really necessary for her to keep harping on how reluctant she'd been to marry him?

"How did it go with Rachel?" she asked after a moment. "Are you okay?"

He was a bit surprised by the question. "I'm fine. And Rachel accepted our story without question. There's nothing to worry about."

She nodded. "One member of your family down—a couple of hundred to go."

Cody smiled. "Not quite that many."

Dana tossed her hair back from her face. She looked tired, Cody thought. A bit dazed.

He knew exactly how she felt.

"Jake and the others refuse to allow me to work tonight," she said. "They think we should go home now. They're all, er, concerned about us working on our wedding night."

"How thoughtful of them."

Dana's smile was a weak effort. "Should we stay and argue with them?"

"Let's not," he said on a sudden decision. "Business is slow tonight, they can get along without us. Let's go home."

Dana's eyes widened at his words. "Home," she murmured, almost to herself. "That sounds...odd."

"Get used to it," he advised her, more grimly than he'd intended.

Jake tried to detain Cody on his way out. "You want to tell me what happened?" he inquired pleasantly.

"No," Cody answered bluntly. "I'm going to let you stew about it awhile. Just keep in mind that I *am* married— legally married—and it was all your idea!"

He left Jake looking curious, frustrated—and thoroughly entertained.

Dana followed Cody home in her own car, which started promptly this time, to her obvious relief. Though she had seen his house before, she looked around when they entered as though it was a strange and rather intimidating place. Cody supposed it looked different to someone moving in than it would to an afternoon guest.

He tried to see his house through Dana's eyes. It certainly wasn't anything fancy—mostly secondhand furniture and hand-me-down decorations. Rachel and Celia had helped him arrange everything when he'd moved in; they'd selected paints and wallpapers and the few knickknacks that made the place look like a home. He was sure it could use a lot more work, but it wasn't bad. And, thank God, it was reasonably clean—he'd had someone in to clean it only last week.

Dana turned to him with a forced smile. "Well," she said. "This is awkward."

He nodded. "I want you to be comfortable here, Dana. This is your home now, so feel free to do anything you want to it. Uh, with the exception of purple satin or red velvet, of course," he added, trying to lighten the moment with a joke.

Her smile was merely perfunctory. "Where am I going to sleep?" she asked bluntly.

Cody swallowed. He was instantly assailed with memories of kissing her in his bedroom at her stepmother's house. Of the way their thighs had pressed so closely together, their hands seeking, lips clinging. Of the big, soft bed that had stretched so invitingly behind them before he'd forced himself away from her.

He couldn't help thinking that he had another big, soft bed in his room here—and no one to interrupt them should they kiss again. Or anything else that might follow.

She was his wife, Cody thought dazedly. He wanted her to sleep in his bed. With him. He wanted to make love to her, to watch her sleep, to wake her up with tickles and kisses and morning lovemaking.

He wanted to see Dana's face when she finally lost that careful control she held over her emotions.

He must have been staring at her for longer than he'd realized. She cleared her throat and shuffled her feet, looking uncomfortable. "Cody?" Her voice was unsteady.

"If there comes a time when you need your freedom, I won't cause you any problems. I'll always be grateful to you for what you've done for me today."

He could hear her saying the words again, almost as clearly as he'd heard them the first time, in his car. And he reacted to them the same way now, with immediate, powerful resentment—and more than a little hurt.

He didn't want Dana's gratitude. He didn't want her to politely offer him his freedom. He didn't want her treating him like a pal to whom she owed a rather sizable favor.

She was his wife. And if she came to his bed, he didn't want it to be out of gratitude.

Oh, man, he thought with a mental groan. *Going through that ceremony must have addled your brains, old son.*

"There are three bedrooms," he said abruptly. "They're all furnished. Take your pick."

Looking at him oddly, Dana went off to explore. Cody tagged behind her. "That's mine," he said when she opened the first door she came to. "But you're welcome to it if you want. I can move into one of the others."

"I won't put you out of your own bed," Dana replied, stepping away without looking in. She moved across the hall, looked into one empty bedroom and then the other. "I'll take this one," she said, motioning toward the room closest to Cody's. "The other room is a bit larger—Andy can have that one when he comes to us."

Cody wondered if Dana planned to maintain separate bedrooms even after her brother joined them. He decided to worry about that then.

He was sure that, like him, Dana fervently hoped it would be a long time before unhappy circumstances brought her beloved little brother into her care.

"I'm really tired," Dana said then, her eyes shadowed. "It's been a long day, and I have an early class tomorrow. I think I'll turn in early."

"Yeah. Me, too. Call out if you need anything, okay?"

"I'm sure I'll be fine. But thank you."

She was being so polite he wanted to snarl at her. Or grab her and kiss her until her bland, courteous facade cracked and he found the real Dana Marie Preston—Dana Marie Preston Carson, he reminded himself glumly. Instead, he merely nodded, turned and walked into his bedroom, closing the door behind him with a peevish snap.

He threw himself onto the bed and lay on his back, staring angrily at the ceiling.

It wasn't quite 10:00 p.m. And it was his wedding night. He was sure a lot of his friends—Jake, for instance—would find this whole situation hysterically funny.

For once, Cody couldn't share the joke. He wasn't at all amused.

* * *

Dana didn't allow herself to fall apart until she was safely alone in her own bedroom, two closed doors between her and the man who'd become her husband that afternoon. Only then did she start to tremble, so hard it was all she could do to sink onto the bed without falling face first into the pillows.

God, what a day! It was a wonder she'd survived it with her sanity. Or *had* she?

She couldn't stop thinking of the way Cody had looked at her when she'd asked him where she would sleep. Something had blazed in his usually laughing blue eyes then, something she'd never seen there before. And she'd found herself fighting the temptation to run...along with an equally strong compulsion to move closer to him and find out exactly what that expression had meant.

Funny. She'd thought, after a year of working for him, that she'd known Cody Carson pretty well. She'd had him pegged—or so she'd believed.

She'd been wrong.

The man she'd met this weekend hadn't been the shallow, unreliable joker she'd thought she'd known before. The man she'd imagined him to be wouldn't have immediately bonded with a little boy who'd desperately needed a new hero. Wouldn't have been so kind to, or so patient with, a frightened, dying woman. Wouldn't have sacrificed the freedom and irresponsibility he'd seemed to treasure so greatly for the sake of a casual acquaintance and her little brother. Wouldn't have held her when she cried, or kissed her until her tears had almost turned to steam.

Cody had changed his entire life for her—and as far as she could tell, he was asking for absolutely nothing in return. Not even her gratitude, which he'd rejected instantly and irritably.

The magnitude of his generosity staggered her.

But what was even more astonishing to her was the realization that it wasn't just gratitude she felt for him. Her eyes had been opened in many ways during the past few days. And one of the things she'd seen was that Cody Carson—her husband—was a fascinating and extremely attractive man.

A man who had looked at her as though he wanted her.

A man she could want in return—except that she was utterly terrified of falling in love with him.

What if she did, only to find out that he wasn't really the man she now believed him to be?

Or—even worse—what if he *was* everything she'd ever wanted in a man? A man who'd married her only because circumstances had compelled him to, who didn't—couldn't—love her in return?

What if she gave him her heart, only to find that he didn't really want it? He would shatter it.

She buried her face in her hands. The future loomed ahead of her, grim and frightening. And she wanted nothing more than to bury her head in Cody's shoulder and rediscover that surprising sense of security she'd found there once before.

The telephone woke Cody the next morning, after a restless night of too much thought and too little sleep. He groped drowsily for the extension on his nightstand, knocking off an empty soda can as he did so. "H'lo?"

"Oops. You were still sleeping. Did I inconveniently disturb you and your new bride, I hope?"

Cody rubbed the grit from his eyes with his free hand. "Celia?"

His younger sister laughed, sounding as though she were just across town instead of halfway across the country.

"You are out of it this morning, aren't you? Must have been an . . . mmm . . . interesting night."

His mind was clearing just enough to allow his memory to return. Cody grimaced. "Rachel called you."

"Yeah. Last night. I wanted to call you then, but Reed wouldn't let me. He said no man wanted to talk to his sister on his wedding night."

Cody muttered something incomprehensible and shifted to sit up in the bed, running his hand through his tousled hair, wishing for a cup of coffee. He really shouldn't have to deal with Celia before his morning caffeine fix.

He glanced at the clock. It was after nine. The house was silent; he sensed that he was alone in it. He remembered Dana telling him that she had an early class this morning. He wondered if she'd gotten any more sleep than he had last night.

Realizing Celia was still talking, he tried to pay attention. "So, anyway, having eloped myself, I told Rachel I understood perfectly," she chattered. "It really isn't important to have all that pomp and ceremony, is it? Reed and I didn't want to wait long enough to arrange a formal wedding with all the trimmings, and I guess you and Dana didn't, either."

"Uh, no, we—"

"I couldn't believe it when Rachel called. Especially when she said you'd married *Dana!*"

Cody frowned. "What's wrong with Dana?"

"Stop being so defensive. Nothing's wrong with Dana. I've always liked her. I just didn't know you were dating her. To be honest, I thought you were interested in her for a while when she first started working with you, but nothing seemed to come of it, so . . . Anyway, I think this is terrific and I can't *wait* to see the two of you next month. It's so hard to believe you're really married!"

"Yeah," Cody murmured. "I know the feeling."

"I'm sure your new bride is getting impatient for your attention again, so I'll let you go. Be happy, Cody. I love you."

"Love you, too, Celia. Er, thanks for calling."

He hung up and crawled out of bed, knowing he was in for a long morning of telephone calls. He was right. The phone was ringing again before he'd even finished brushing his teeth.

His grandmother called late in the morning, just as Cody had decided he could face food. He'd gathered the ingredients for a sandwich-and-chips lunch; he resignedly set them aside and answered the phone in the kitchen, wishing he'd turned on the answering machine.

At the sound of his grandmother's voice, he winced and immediately started shifting his weight, just as he'd done when he was a boy caught in some mischief. He hadn't reacted this way even when his bewildered mother had called earlier, demanding to know all the details of her only son's impulsive marriage.

"Hi, Gran," he said.

"Is it true?" she demanded. "Have you gotten married?"

"Yes, it's true. Dana and I were married yesterday. You remember Dana, don't you? The pretty redhead who waited on you last time you ate at my club?"

"I remember her. If *you'll* remember, I told you then that I liked her, and that I thought you should ask her out. You told me to mind my own business."

"I did no such thing."

"Well, perhaps not quite so bluntly, but the message was the same. You said you and Dana were just friends."

"We were. Then."

"So this romance is a recent development?"

"Very."

"Cody...is there anything you'd like to talk to me about?"

Cody was tempted then to pour out the entire story. His grandmother was the one person who'd always understood him, who'd always listened without judgment, who'd always known just what to say to make him feel better about himself. She fussed over him, fussed *at* him, at times—but she loved him. Unconditionally. And he loved her deeply in return.

But this was one thing he found he couldn't talk to her about. Especially not over the telephone. "I know it happened fast, Gran, but don't worry. Everything's fine."

"I can't believe you let me go on about introducing you to my friends' granddaughters when you were planning this all along," she said good-naturedly. "You really do love to get the last laugh on us, don't you, darling?"

Cody was glad she couldn't see his sorry excuse for a smile. She would know then that things weren't at all as they seemed—that the last laugh this time was most definitely on *him*.

Granny Fran asked him to bring Dana for dinner on Sunday. Cody explained about Dana's stepmother. "We'll be spending most of our free time in Memphis with Barbara and Andy," he concluded. "But I'm still planning to attend the family gathering next month if everything goes well. We'll certainly see you then, if not before."

His grandmother expressed her sympathy about Dana's family troubles, and her understanding that Cody would be very busy for the next few months. "You take care of your wife," she added. "She's going to need you."

"Yes." And Cody had made a vow to come through, this time. Whatever he had to do.

He and his grandmother talked a few more minutes, and then concluded the call with I-love-yous and see-you-soons.

Cody felt emotionally drained when he hung up the phone—and it wasn't even noon yet.

He reached for the mustard, trying to regain his appetite. Before he could open the bread, the doorbell rang.

Sighing heavily, he went to answer it.

His wife stood on the doorstep, her arms loaded with textbooks, her eyes nervous.

"Dana, you don't have to ring the bell," Cody chided, stepping aside to let her in. The stressful telephone calls on top of a restless night had left him irritable. He tried to lighten up when he added, "This is your home now."

"Yes," she answered quietly. "But I don't have a key."

He winced. "Oh. Sorry. I forgot. I've got a spare in the kitchen. Have you had lunch?"

"No."

"I was just about to have a ham sandwich and some chips. Want to join me?"

She managed a smile. "Sure. Just let me put these books in my room and wash my hands."

Cody walked back into the kitchen and poured himself a soda, briefly wishing for the first time in years that it was something stronger.

Chapter Thirteen

It wasn't an easy first week of marriage. Not only did they have to contend with the well-intentioned congratulatory calls and conversations with their friends and acquaintances, but they had to adjust to living together and suiting their schedules accordingly. They got along surprisingly well, on the whole. Maybe because they were both trying so very hard.

Cody unintentionally initiated the first conflict. It was Saturday afternoon, only a couple of hours before he and Dana were expected at the club. He'd been out in the driveway for the past hour and a half, his head stuck under the hood of Dana's old car. Dirty, sweaty, shirtless and thirsty, he headed for the kitchen for a cold drink before his shower.

He found Dana sitting at the kitchen table, her head propped on her hand, textbooks and notebooks spread in front of her. Her eyes were closed. Unless he was mistaken, she was asleep sitting up.

He shook his head. She was doing too much, he thought grimly. A full class load at college, six hours or more at the club every evening. Worrying about whether her car would start every morning, the constant dread of a frantic phone call from Memphis, not to mention the tension of her new living arrangements. He hadn't liked seeing the lines developing around her mouth this past week, or the purple smudges beneath her eyes.

He was her husband, damn it. He'd promised to take care of her. It looked as though now was the time to start.

He touched her shoulder. "Dana."

She jumped half a foot out of the chair.

Flustered, she tried desperately to regain her composure. "I, uh, sorry, you startled me," she stammered, her hand over her heart. "I was just, um, thinking about my schoolwork."

"You were asleep," Cody said flatly. "You're exhausted. You can't keep this up, Dana."

Her expression turned stubborn. "I don't know what you're talking about."

"Then let me spell it out for you. I want you to quit your job at the club."

Her mouth opened. "You want me to do *what?*"

"You heard me," he said. He turned to the refrigerator, pulled out a canned soda and opened it. He took several long, appreciative swallows before he carried it over to the table and took a chair across from Dana, who still looked as though he'd goosed her or something.

"I'm not quitting my job, Cody," she said.

He decided to try reasoning with her. "Why?"

"I need the money."

"No. You don't."

Her hands flew up in exasperation. "How can you say that? Of course I do!"

"Your tuition is paid for this semester, isn't it?"

"Yes, but—"

"You've bought all your books and supplies?"

"Well, yes, but—"

"You gave up your apartment, so there's no rent for you to worry about—and don't start in again about paying part of my house payment," he warned her quickly when she opened her mouth to speak. She closed it, confirming that he'd guessed correctly about her intentions.

"You think I don't know you've been trying to study in the middle of the night when you should be getting some sleep?" he asked irritably. "You think I haven't seen how tired you get at work, running from table to table after a long day of classes? Well, I do. And I don't like it."

"Cody, I can't quit working. I have a car payment, insurance, other miscellaneous expenses of going to school. If nothing else, I need money for everyday expenses—toothpaste, shampoo, all the things people need money for. If you think I'm going to let you buy those things for me—"

"I'm your husband, Dana."

She flushed. "That—that's not relevant right now."

Sometimes it amazed him how an obviously bright young woman could be so dense. "Not relevant?" he repeated in disbelief. "What the hell does that mean?"

"You married me to help me with Andy, not to support me while I finish school," she insisted, not quite meeting his eyes. "I wouldn't let Barbara support me before, and I won't let you do so now."

"And how the hell are you going to take care of Andy with the schedule you've got now?" he demanded. "You've got—what?—an hour free a day? And you've been using that up doing housework around here, even though I've told you it isn't necessary."

"I want to pull my weight around here," she said. "As for Andy, I'll manage."

"How?"

She swallowed. "I'll manage," she repeated. "Somehow. When it's necessary."

"Honey, we both know it isn't going to be too long before it's necessary. Neither of us wants to face it, but we have to. Barbara doesn't have much longer. And you can't take care of Andy if you keep this schedule up."

"Then I'll quit school. At least for a while."

So much for reasoning. He slammed his fist down on the table, startling her into jumping again. "The hell you will!"

"Cody, I—"

"Look, the reason we got married was to reassure Barbara that you wouldn't have to sacrifice your education if you took Andy in. I promised her I would help you with him so you wouldn't have to quit school, and damn it, I'm not breaking that promise. You can attend classes in the mornings, while Andy's in school, and then you can be home with him in the evenings. You can do your homework and your studying together. You won't waste your time waiting tables in the evenings. We've had a few applications at the club lately. I'll hire someone else to take your place there."

He saw the angry glitter in her eyes, the obstinate set to her chin, but he pressed on without giving her a chance to argue. "Jake and I have worked hard to make that club a success and we're earning a good living there," he said. "His wife works part-time at a dress shop, and that's only because she wants something to do while their kids are in school. Jake is capable of supporting his family—and I'm damned well capable of taking care of mine."

Dana shook her head. "I can't let you do that," she whispered. "You shouldn't have to support me in addition to everything else."

He'd worked himself up into a genuine state of wrath now. He scowled at her.

"I make my own choices," he informed her coldly. "It was my decision to go into this marriage, and I fully intend to uphold my part of it. Barbara's counting on me to help you—and I'm going to do it right. Is that clear?"

Dana sighed. "I don't understand you," she admitted helplessly. "Why are you so angry about this? Why is it so important to you?"

"Let's just say I'm trying to prove something—to you, and maybe to myself," he said, his tone curt. "Just as you're trying to prove something by insisting on trying to do it all."

She looked at him without speaking for a long time.

He met her gaze evenly. "I could always fire you," he suggested after a moment.

She exhaled wearily, her anger seeming to slip away. "And I could always find another job," she replied.

"But you won't." It wasn't a question.

"No," she conceded reluctantly. "I won't."

Satisfied, he nodded. "Good. Then you can concentrate on your schoolwork in the evenings while I'm at the club, and get some sleep at night."

"Fine," she said a bit shortly. "But I'm taking on more of the housework around here if you're going to be the only one working full-time."

"You'll still be putting in as many hours away from the house as I am," he stated. "Earning a degree is every bit as demanding as running a business."

"I mean it, Cody. Either let me take over the housework, or I won't agree to this. I have to feel that I'm pulling my weight."

"I'll still help out." He had always been in the habit of picking up after himself, anyway. He didn't intend to change that because Dana had decided housework would assuage her conscience about leaving her job at the club.

She nodded, looking a bit sulky. Cody knew she was aware that she had lost that battle; he only hoped she'd realize eventually that he'd fought her for her own sake.

"We'll go to the bank Monday, add your name to my checking account," he said, daring her to argue. "Anything you need—toothpaste, shampoo, whatever those other expenses you named—you get it, you hear? I'll add you to my insurance. It'll probably be cheaper that way than to insure us separately. As for your car payment, well, I hope it isn't much, because to be honest, that piece of junk isn't worth it. But we'll discuss that later," he said quickly, seeing the renewed spark of battle light in her eyes.

He had every intention of replacing her car as soon as he got the chance, but maybe he'd better concentrate on one skirmish at a time.

This marriage bit could be very stressful, he was learning. Hadn't he always suspected it would be?

He noticed then that Dana was surreptitiously looking at his bare chest. Suddenly aware of how dirty and sweaty he was, he cleared his throat and stood. "I'm going to take a shower."

"I'm going with you to the club tonight," she called after him, a note of challenge in her voice. "I'm not quitting until you find someone to replace me."

He only nodded and kept walking, deciding to retreat while he was ahead.

They spent Sunday in Memphis. Andy was as delighted to see them as though it had been months since they'd left, rather than a few days.

Barbara seemed equally pleased. Her condition was unchanged from the last time they were there; she was in pain, and tired easily, but she was still able to be up for a while each day. There was no reason for them to remain past the time they'd agreed to start back for home, after assuring Barbara that they were blissfully happy newlyweds and available to her at a moment's notice should she need them.

Dana was quiet during the drive back to Percy. After a while, Cody reached out and took her hand. He didn't say anything, just folded his fingers warmly around hers.

She clung to him gratefully, drawing strength from his silent support.

Dana pulled into the driveway at just after one o'clock on Tuesday afternoon, classes finished for the day. A wave of heat assailed her as she climbed out of her car. Though it was the second week in September, summer was still hanging on with a vengeance, the temperature still in the low nineties. She plucked at the bright red T-shirt she wore with faded jeans, shaking her head when the soft cotton stuck to her skin. The air conditioner in her car had died months ago.

Bundling her books under one arm, she climbed the steps to the front door and stuck her key in the lock. It didn't feel quite as strange now to enter so casually, though she still couldn't think of it as anything other than Cody's house.

His Jeep had been parked in the driveway, so she knew he was home. "Cody?" she called.

"In here," he called from the direction of the kitchen. "Have you had lunch?"

"No. Let me put my books away and I'll join you."

She'd expected to find him still in the kitchen when she came out of her room. He was waiting for her in the living room instead. Wearing a striped T-shirt and a pair of denim cutoffs, his golden hair tousled around his handsome, tanned face, he looked as though he'd stepped off "Baywatch." All he needed was a lifeguard's whistle.

She had to clear her throat before she could speak normally. "Have you already eaten?" she asked.

"No. I was waiting for you. Come on." He motioned toward the door.

She lifted a questioning eyebrow. "We're going out?"

He grinned. "Yeah. Consider yourself kidnapped."

"Why are you kidnapping me?" she asked politely.

His smile deepening, he took her arm and led her unresistingly toward the door. "It's our one-week wedding anniversary. We're going to celebrate it by having some fun."

"Fun?" she repeated as he closed and locked the front door behind them.

"Fun. You remember the word?"

"Vaguely."

He held open the passenger door of the Jeep for her, then climbed behind the wheel. "Buckle up," he said cheerfully. "It's playtime!"

Intrigued despite herself, Dana snapped her seat belt and waited to see what Cody had in store for her.

What Cody had in mind was a picnic. He parked at a secluded spot by a nearby wooded lake and produced a picnic basket out of the back of the Jeep with all the flourish of a magician conjuring a rabbit.

"Just how long have you been planning this?" Dana asked in bemusement, watching as he spread a blanket on the grass and proceeded to cover it with containers of food.

"I thought of it in the shower this morning," he admitted. "It's been years since I was on a picnic. I thought it might be fun to share one with you."

Curling her legs beneath her on the blanket, Dana propped her chin in her hands and watched as he filled paper plates with food. Sandwiches, raw vegetables and dip, sweet pickles, cheese cubes, deviled eggs, fruit...

"Do you really expect me to eat all that?"

He grinned and nodded. "We've got brownies for dessert. Made 'em myself. From a mix, I'm afraid, but I added fresh pecans."

"I'm impressed."

"So you should be." He reached over to plop a juicy cherry tomato in her mouth. "Isn't this fun?"

She chewed and swallowed. "It's a pleasant change of routine," she agreed.

Cody groaned. "A pleasant change of routine?" he repeated. "That's all you can say about it?"

"We just got here," she reminded him. "Give me a chance to unwind a little, okay?"

"Here. Have a carrot stick. That should relax you."

She didn't even try to follow his reasoning. She only smiled and began to eat. Funny. She hadn't realized quite how hungry she was. She couldn't remember when simple food had tasted so good.

Dana had never denied that Cody could be a charming and very entertaining companion. He'd set out to make this picnic fun—and he succeeded. He soon had her laughing at his silliness, the tensions of her day forgotten—or at least set aside—if only for this brief interlude.

She drained the last drop of a chilled canned cola and shook her head when Cody offered more food. "I can't eat another bite now," she said.

"Not even dessert?" He looked absurdly crestfallen.

"Not yet, anyway," she amended, oddly reluctant to disappoint him, though she couldn't tell if he was teasing her or not.

"What you need to do is work off your lunch," he informed her, jumping agilely to his feet. "A little healthy exercise."

She groaned. "Cody, it's still at least ninety degrees. If you think I'm going to run around after a Frisbee or something in this heat..."

"I was thinking of a nice, cool swim," he said, motioning toward the small, sparkling lake. "Wouldn't that feel good?"

Wiping beads of perspiration from her upper lip, Dana looked longingly at the water. "Yes, it would," she admitted. "But I didn't bring a swimsuit."

"No problem. Swim naked," he suggested with a grin.

She gave him a cutting look. "I think not."

"Come on, darlin'. We're married. We can legally skinny-dip together."

She still wasn't quite sure if he were serious, but there was no way she was swimming nude with him, especially not in the middle of the day when just anyone could happen upon them. "I'll sit this one out," she said, refusing to let him see that he'd embarrassed her. "But you go ahead if you like. I'll just watch."

His grin turned wicked. "You'd like that, wouldn't you?"

"I've been told it's an awe-inspiring sight," she replied without a pause.

He laughed and reached down to haul her unceremoniously to her feet. "Why, Dana Carson," he said. "I believe there is a sense of humor lurking inside that serious head of yours, after all."

She still couldn't get used to being called Dana Carson. She opened her mouth to tell him she would continue to use her maiden name, but somehow his lips got in the way. She hadn't even realized his intention to kiss her until she found herself pressed against him, her mouth being thoroughly, lazily, savoringly explored by his.

By the time he released her, the heat inside her had nothing to do with the warm weather. "Your swimsuit's in the back of the Jeep," he murmured, his lips moving against hers. "You can change in the bushes, if you want. I'll swim in my cutoffs."

With that, he broke away from her, stripped off his shirt and shoes and dove neatly into the lake, leaving Dana to stare openmouthed after him.

He'd brought her swimsuit? She opened the back of the Jeep and found the royal blue maillot lying neatly folded on a beach towel. She blushed to the roots of her hair, remembering that she'd put the suit in her lingerie drawer. Had Cody noticed that she had a decided preference for delicate little bits of lace beneath her more practical jeans and T-shirts?

Something told her he'd noticed.

She thought of yelling at him for going into her room, pawing uninvited through her things. And then she remembered the look in his eyes when he'd served her picnic lunch, and thought of the time he must have spent preparing the simple meal. He'd wanted her to have fun, she thought, touched despite herself by the gesture.

And she found she couldn't spoil the outing he'd planned for her.

Carrying the towel over her arm, she headed for the thickest clump of bushes she could find. She hadn't undressed outdoors in years, not since she was a kid on family camping trips, but there seemed to be no other choice at the moment. Not if she wanted to get into that lovely, cool water.

She changed in record time. Tossing her clothing in a pile beside Cody's shirt and shoes, she waded into the water, gasping when it lapped against her calves. "It's cold," she said, looking at Cody, who watched her from several yards away.

"Feels great once you get in," he assured her.

A bit self-conscious beneath his scrutiny, she minced deeper, shivering. And then she caught her breath in a strangled cry when her foot came down on a slippery rock and shot out from beneath her.

The water closed over her head as she fell backward, arms flailing.

Cody was there in an instant, his strong arms pulling her upward, supporting her as she regained her balance. "Are you all right?"

Swiping at her streaming face, she coughed from the mouthful of lake water she'd swallowed and nodded. "Fine," she managed. "I slipped."

He smiled, relieved. "That's one way of getting into the water, I guess. Most people dive face forward, of course, but my wife seems to have her own style of doing things."

She wondered if he was making a deliberate attempt to remind her of their marital status that afternoon. That made the third or fourth time he'd mentioned it.

Did he really think she'd forget?

She pushed away from him. "The water does feel good once you get used to it," she said casually. "I haven't been swimming in ages."

"Are you having fun now?" he asked, idly splashing water at her.

She smiled and splashed him back. "Yes," she admitted. "I'm having fun now."

His grin was almost blinding. "Glad to hear it," he said, and then initiated a no-holds-barred water fight that almost drowned both of them.

* * *

By the time they dried off, packed up their picnic supplies and went home to shower and change, Cody was late leaving for the club that evening.

"Jake's going to dissolve your partnership if you keep showing up late like this," Dana commented, watching as he collected his wallet and keys and prepared to leave.

"Jake understands that I'm a man who's still basically on his honeymoon," Cody replied with a shrug. "And he knows that I'll fill in for him whenever he needs me to. That's why we make such good partners. Neither of us likes to be rigidly tied to a schedule."

Dana had gulped at his mention of the word *honeymoon.* She wasn't at all sure that term applied to their present circumstances—but she supposed it was close enough for lack of a better word.

"You'll be home at the usual time?" she asked unnecessarily, finding herself oddly reluctant to see him go.

"Yeah. Around midnight, I guess. Don't wait up, you have an early class tomorrow."

"I know. I guess I'll spend the evening studying. I have a test tomorrow."

"Good luck with it."

"Thanks."

Cody swept a hand through his hair, which was still slightly damp from his shower. He wore a black western shirt with white mother-of-pearl snaps, and tight black jeans that were sure to attract more than a bit of feminine attention during the evening. Dana frowned, suddenly aware that she didn't at all like the idea of other women drooling over Cody while she sat at home alone!

"Guess I'd better be going," he said, moving toward the door.

She detained him by putting a hand on his arm. "Thank you for the picnic," she said, looking up at him. "I really had a good time."

"You're welcome," he murmured, touching her cheek. "And I had a good time, too."

She waited for him to kiss her. When he didn't, she was flooded with disappointment. He started to move away. She thought of those women waiting at the club and tightened her grip on his arm. "Cody?"

He looked at her, and she saw the hunger in his eyes. It gave her the courage to stand on tiptoe and press her mouth shyly to his. "See you later," she murmured as she stepped away.

He swept her into a hard embrace that threatened to crush her ribs. His mouth slammed against hers in a kiss that made the first one seem like nothing more than a friendly peck. They were both gasping for air when they broke apart.

"See you later," Cody said, his voice ragged.

And then he was gone, leaving Dana alone in his house, fanning her flaming face with one unsteady hand.

Chapter Fourteen

Three more weeks passed, so quickly Dana was amazed. Though her schoolwork had grown more difficult as the semester progressed, she hadn't felt so well rested in months.

She couldn't believe what a difference it made not having to study in snatches between class time and after work hours. Having time to eat regular meals, to get enough sleep—even to do her nails occasionally. It had been months since she'd had time for a decent manicure.

Barbara was still holding her own, her condition basically unchanged. The doctor told Dana the situation could worsen at any time, but Dana refused to dwell on the possibilities, choosing to enjoy the respite instead. She and Cody still made the drive to Memphis once a week, and it pleased her to see that Cody and Andy grew closer with each visit.

They spent a little time with Cody's sister Rachel and her family, and Dana was surprised at how warmly she'd been accepted into their midst. Cody's family seemed to understand the necessity for them to spend most of their spare time in Memphis, but Dana had talked to several of them on the telephone and they had all expressed their personal welcome to the clan.

She'd been touched by their willingness to accept her without question, merely because Cody had chosen her to be his wife. She thought it said a great deal about their love for Cody.

As for Cody, he had been going out of his way to make Dana comfortable. He was inexhaustibly cheerful, conscientious at helping with housework, never failed to ask if there was anything she needed or wanted. He was trying so hard to be the perfect husband that it set Dana's teeth on edge at times.

She found that she wanted him to be himself, not a mild-mannered clone of the exasperating and fascinating Cody Carson she'd married.

She wanted him to kiss her again. He hadn't since the night of the picnic, the night he'd left for work after kissing her until her ears had buzzed and her head had spun.

She wasn't quite sure why he was keeping such a distance between them now. There were times when she caught him looking at her, and she was sure she saw that familiar hunger in his bright blue eyes. But each time she spotted it, he quickly looked away, pulling an invisible barrier between them.

What was holding him back? An understandable reluctance to further complicate this already complex situation? A fear of making an even more lasting commitment than he'd already stumbled into?

Or was he keeping his distance out of deference to her, uncertain that she would welcome his advances when she'd made it clear that she'd married him only as a necessary convenience?

Puzzled by his behavior, Dana found herself hiding her own emotions from him, pasting on smiles as bright and artificial as his own, laughing politely at his jokes, pretending she was perfectly content the way things were.

Only during the long evenings at home by herself, while Cody was at the club and Dana had nothing but her textbooks and a radio for company, did she allow herself to privately acknowledge that she missed him when he wasn't with her. That she'd grown to like having him around. That she wanted more from this marriage than an amiable roommate.

She wanted Cody. When had *that* happened?

And what was she going to do about it?

She was waiting for Cody in the living room on Tuesday evening, her hands clasped nervously in front of her, the tip of her tongue darting out to moisten her dry lips. She heard his car pull into the driveway, heard his door slam, heard his footsteps on the porch as he hurried toward the front door.

It was 8:00 p.m., exactly the time Jake had promised to send Cody home. She sent Cody's partner a mental thank-you, then followed it with a silent prayer that nothing would go wrong this evening.

"Dana?" Cody came through the front door in a rush, his expression worried. "What is it? Jake said you needed me to come home—is it Barbara?"

She managed a reassuring smile. "Jake was supposed to tell you that it wasn't an emergency."

Cody looked only marginally relieved by her composure. "He told me not to worry, but I couldn't help it. Why did you need me to come home? Is something wrong here?"

"Nothing's wrong. I have a surprise for you."

He cocked his head, looking confused and intrigued. "A surprise?"

She smiled and motioned for him to follow her into the dining room. "Jake promised he wouldn't give you a chance to eat this evening," she said, her throat tight with nerves. "I hope you didn't fill up on barbecue or anything behind his back."

Cody paused in the doorway, studying the beautifully set table, the crystal and silver and candles and flowers.

Unable to read his expression, Dana twined her fingers together so tightly they ached. "It's our one-month wedding anniversary," she reminded him. "I wanted to surprise *you* with a celebration this time."

He looked at her then, and he began to smile. And Dana felt her muscles slowly relax. "Consider me surprised," he said gravely.

"I had to borrow some things from Rachel," she said, motioning toward the table. "We're a little short on fancy table service."

"Then we should see about getting some," he replied easily.

She saw that he was as aware as she was of their use of the word *we.* Oddly enough, it felt as though they'd just strengthened their commitment to each other by the seemingly casual decision to buy more tableware.

Dana smiled. "I hope you're hungry."

"I'm starving," he assured her, his voice deep. Husky.

A tremor ran through her in response, and something warm and liquid began to bubble deep inside her. It felt surprisingly like... happiness.

"Sit down," she said, her own voice a bit unsteady. "I'll serve dinner."

The meal was delicious, each dish prepared with exquisite care. Cody wouldn't have minded if she'd served him sawdust with a side order of scrap metal.

Nothing had ever touched him more deeply than Dana's shy smile when she'd told him why she'd summoned him home tonight.

"You must have worked on this dinner all day," he said in awe when she set dessert in front of him, a rich, fruit-and-cream-filled, chocolate-drizzled confection she must have known would appeal to his well-documented sweet tooth.

"I started most of it after you left for the club this afternoon," she replied. "It took only a couple of hours."

"It's the nicest thing anyone has ever done for me," he told her sincerely.

He was rather amused when she blushed to the roots of her hair. Had she been standing, he suspected she would have scuffed her toe on the carpet like an embarrassed schoolboy. "It wasn't all that much," she murmured, toying with her own dessert. "I just made dinner."

And then her eyes suddenly widened. She clapped her hand over her mouth. "Oh, no! I forgot something."

What could she have possibly forgotten? Cody wondered as she leapt to her feet and bolted from the room. He couldn't have eaten another bite—it had been all he could do to manage dessert. As far as he could tell, absolutely nothing had been missing.

Dana came back into the room wearing a sheepish expression and carrying a bottle of chilled champagne.

Cody's heart sank to his shoes.

"I meant to have you open this before we ate, so we could make a toast to our anniversary," she said. "I got so flustered, I forgot. Sorry."

"Dana—"

She produced two delicate champagne flutes and set them on the table in front of him. "These didn't come from Rachel," she explained. "They were my mother's. I've had them packed in a box for years, but this seemed like a nice time to get them out and put them to use."

"Dana," Cody said again, covering her hand with his when she would have opened the champagne. "Wait."

She looked at him in question. "Would you like to open it?"

He sighed. "I can't."

She frowned, not understanding. "Why can't you?"

"The champagne—I can't drink it. I guess I should have told you this before, but... I'm an alcoholic."

He made the admission with a set jaw and steady eyes, the words bitter in his mouth. It was the first time he'd said them—to anyone—in years.

Dana's eyes widened. Her face paled.

"Oh, Cody, I'm so sorry," she whispered. "I... I didn't know."

"I should have told you before," he repeated, hating himself for spoiling her lovely evening. "This wasn't the way for you to find out."

She set the bottle on the table with a thump. "I should have known," she said, her voice heavy with self-recrimination. "I've noticed that you usually drink juice or cola when everyone else has beer or whatever, but I didn't realize... and when we had champagne at the club the night we were married..."

"I had mineral water," he explained. "Jake poured it into a champagne glass for me. I guess you didn't notice."

"So Jake knows."

"Yes."

"I'm so sorry," she repeated, looking stricken.

Standing close in front of her, Cody placed his hands on her shoulders. "No. Don't apologize. You couldn't have known. I don't exactly publicize it. I haven't even told my family. Only my dad. The others—well, they just think I grew up and quit drinking after an accident I had on my twenty-first birthday. They don't know how hard it was for me to quit, or how many times I've had to fight the desire in the years since," he added bitterly. "Jake's the only one I've talked to about that—and only because he recognized the symptoms."

"Tell me about it," she urged, looking up at him in encouragement.

He searched her eyes for the distaste or condemnation he might have expected. He saw only sympathy.

He swallowed hard. "I started drinking when I was in high school. You know, hanging out with the guys after football games or whatever. It was our way of showing off, having a good time, proving our manhood. It was stupid. I was in college when I realized that I couldn't get through a day without it. I tried a few times then to quit, but I always let myself get pulled back into it by my fraternity buddies who didn't think a party was a real party without booze."

"Seth was one of your friends in college, wasn't he?" Dana asked, obviously wondering if the upstanding young attorney was one of the ones who'd encouraged Cody's weakness.

"Yeah, but he was younger and more ambitious than the rest of my crowd. He managed to pull back before he got in too deeply, to his credit. I flunked out. He went on and got his degree. I've always admired him for that."

"You admitted your weakness and conquered it," Dana said, loyally defending him. "You own a successful business, live a very productive life. I find that just as admirable as getting a law degree."

Cody winced and dropped his hands, unable to accept her rationalization. She didn't know the whole story. And, as his wife, she had a right to hear it.

"I didn't just wake up one morning and decide to straighten out my life," he said heavily, turning away from her. "A man and a woman and their two small children almost had to die before I came to my senses."

"What . . . what do you mean?"

She sounded shocked. And so she should be, Cody thought grimly. "I celebrated my twenty-first birthday with a group of friends and a fifth of whiskey," he said, his words curt, unembellished. "And then I got behind the wheel of a car. I hit a van that was carrying a nice young family of four. It was only by the grace of God that no one was killed. They were all badly hurt—I'm sure some of them still carry the scars."

"You were hurt, too."

He shrugged. "A broken leg, a shattered arm. Not much punishment, considering the crime. The court gave me probation, since it was my first offense and I had a loyal, loving family to vouch for me. I got off easy."

Dana touched his arm. "And you've been punishing yourself ever since. Wearing the guilt like a crown of thorns. I don't think you got off so easy, at all."

"It wasn't enough," he said, his voice barely audible, even to him.

"Have you had a drink since?"

"No."

"Will you ever drink again?"

"I—no," he said, his fists clenched at his sides. "No."

"You've paid for your mistakes, Cody. Let it go."

"It isn't that easy."

"I didn't say it was easy," she corrected him. "I know it isn't. But it's time."

He looked at her then, his jaw aching from holding it so tightly, his chest tight with guilt.

"I didn't want to spoil your party," he said regretfully. "I guess you know the man you've married is no bargain. But I swear to you, Dana, I'll never give you cause to regret it. I'll take care of you, and of Andy. I—"

"Cody." She put a hand over his mouth, firmly, her eyes glinting with what might have been temper. "Stop it," she said fiercely. "Stop apologizing for being who you are. Don't you know you don't have to apologize to me, of all people? After all you've done for me, all you still plan to do, how could you possibly imagine I could think any less of you because you aren't perfect?"

He gripped her forearms so tightly he knew he must be hurting her, but he couldn't seem to ease up. "I don't want your gratitude, damn it!"

"And I don't want you using me or Andy to assuage your guilt about your past!" she shouted back at him.

His grip loosened then, in shock. "You think that's why I married you?"

"Isn't it?" she challenged him.

"No!"

"Then why?"

"*This* is why." He crushed her mouth beneath his.

Dana melted into his arms like the warm chocolate she'd served him for dessert. Her arms locked around his neck, her slender body pressing tightly to his. Her lips parted eagerly beneath his, an invitation he didn't even try to resist.

He'd tried to back off the past few weeks, tried to control the hunger for her—the *need* for her—that had only grown stronger with each passing day. He hadn't wanted her to come to him out of gratitude, or a sense of obligation, or for any other reason than a desire that equaled his own.

And now she was kissing him like she meant it. Like she wanted him. Like she needed him almost as much as he needed her. And he found he didn't have the strength to question her reasons. Didn't have the willpower to draw back and give her a chance to change her mind.

"Dana," he muttered against her lips, his hands gripping her waist, holding her close to the arousal he couldn't have concealed from her if he'd tried. "I want you. Damn it, I've wanted you for more than a year, since the first day you walked into the club and told me your name."

Her smile was sweet, a little shy. "I wasn't sure—"

"I wouldn't admit it, even to myself. You always seemed so distant, so unapproachable. So far away."

She tightened her arms around his neck. "I'm here now," she murmured against his mouth. "And I want you, too."

A shudder went through him. "Are you sure?" he asked rawly.

Her lips curved into a tiny smile. "Do you really think I'd have gone to all this trouble just to feed you dinner? Don't you even know a staged seduction when you see one, Cody Carson?"

It no longer mattered why she'd reached out to him—only that she had. Cody kissed her again, until they were both gasping for oxygen. And then he drew away and held out his hand, his eyes locked with hers.

Though her smile trembled, Dana placed her palm in his without hesitation.

They walked into his bedroom together for the first time. Cody reached for the lamp on the nightstand; Dana stopped him with a hand on his arm. "Don't," she whispered. "Not this time."

He smiled and turned to take her in his arms. "Are you going to be shy?"

"Maybe a little." She drew a deep breath. "There's something you should know."

Straining to see her through the dim light that filtered in from outside, he smoothed a strand of hair away from her face. "What is it, darlin'?"

She seemed to choose her words with care. "This, um, this is our wedding night, in a way."

He smiled in anticipation. "Yes. Our first night together."

"A first for me in more ways than one."

He blinked as her meaning hit him. "You mean—?"

"I was a virgin bride, Cody. I know it's terribly old-fashioned of me, but that's the way it is. Do you mind?"

"Mind?" he repeated, cupping her face in trembling hands. "No, of course not. I'm honored beyond words. It's just that I didn't realize... I thought..."

"I said I'd dated someone before you," she reminded him quietly. "I never said I went to bed with him."

"Dana." Her name was a reverent whisper. He brushed his lips across her face, his heart breaking with the beauty of her gift to him. "I won't hurt you," he promised. "Not tonight. Not ever."

"I know you won't, Cody," she murmured, rising on tiptoes to slip her arms trustingly around his neck. "You gave me your word when you made me your wife."

She believed in him in a way no one had before her, Cody realized as he pressed his lips to hers and bore her gently down to the bed. He'd never been more determined to prove himself worthy of anyone's trust.

Starting now.

He made love to her slowly, tenderly, painstakingly. He undressed her with reverent hands, stopping often to explore and caress. He found a patience within himself he hadn't known he possessed.

Dana responded eagerly, urging him on when he paused a bit too long, her breath catching in ragged little cries when he did something she particularly liked.

She tried to return the pleasure, but he held her still. This time, he told her gently, was for her.

There would be plenty of other times for him.

"I like the sound of that," she whispered, stroking his perspiration-damp cheek.

"So do I," he murmured, lowering his head to kiss her again. "Oh, Dana—so do I."

He loved her until she was incapable of coherent speech, until she clung to him and writhed beneath him with a hunger so great that there was no room for apprehension or inhibition. He'd reined his own needs so tightly that he was trembling, drenched in sweat, every muscle rigid, but still he held back. Still he gave. And she accepted his ministrations with gratifying delight.

He told her she was beautiful, told her she was perfect, told her he wanted her as he'd never wanted before. He meant every word.

And when he finally slipped carefully, lingeringly inside her, he felt as though he'd found something he'd been looking for all his life.

Dana. His wife.

He managed to restrain himself until he'd brought her to a shattering, gasping climax in his arms, his name on her lips as she convulsed delicately beneath him. He'd never heard anything more beautiful.

Only then did he allow himself the freedom to let go, to give in to the needs that had been threatening to rip him apart. Only then did he give himself permission to fly.

* * *

It felt like a very long time before he slowly, reluctantly returned to earth. Holding Dana close to his heart, he rolled to his side, tucking her tenderly next to him.

"We'll move your things in here tomorrow," he murmured as his eyes closed, and he was aware of the new note of possessiveness in his voice. "From now on, you sleep here. With me. Where you belong."

Dana went very still, and he was prepared for her to protest his arrogant presumption. He was relieved when she only nodded against his shoulder. "Fine," she murmured. "If that's what you want."

It wasn't exactly what he'd hoped she would say, but he was suddenly too tired to pursue it. The strain of the past weeks seemed to weigh heavily on him then, the shattering release of tension leaving him sated and lethargic. He nestled her closer, his cheek on her soft hair.

"Rest now," he whispered, his lips moving against her temple. "We have plenty of time to talk later."

She murmured an unintelligible agreement and rested her hand on his chest, just over his still-pounding heart. They fell asleep without moving again.

Over the next few days, Dana discovered the true meaning of the term "conflicting emotions." Her moods swung wildly between happiness and doubt, sadness and joy, fear and anticipation.

She was relieved that Barbara's condition hadn't worsened, but sadly resigned to the inevitable outcome of the disease.

She was pleased that Andy's guardianship had been settled, but she didn't want to have to lose her stepmother in order to have her little brother with her.

She was satisfied with her progress in her classes, but growing bored with the time she now had on her hands in the evenings alone.

She was wholeheartedly, head-over-heels, crazy in love with her husband, but she didn't have the courage to tell him so. Probably because he'd never said the words to her.

If there'd ever been a more complex, puzzling, utterly bewildering man than Cody Carson, Dana had never encountered one. One minute he was making love to her so beautifully, so passionately, she thought she'd shatter with pleasure. The next minute he'd pull back, his expressive eyes shuttered, his flashing smile forced. And she would have no idea what she'd done, what she'd said, to cause him to withdraw from her.

He was still trying so hard, so obviously, to please her. He'd cut out the wisecracks, the irreverent jokes, the exasperating teasing. No woman could have asked for a more attentive, more thoughtful, more considerate husband.

And it was driving Dana slowly insane.

Cody was trying so hard to be perfect that he hardly resembled the man she'd married. The man she'd fallen in love with.

She tried to approach the subject a time or two. Suggested that it wasn't necessary for him to spend every free minute catering to her. That she didn't need constant attention, or a puppylike eagerness to please. She just wanted him to be himself. Cody. The clown. The dreamer. The lover.

The man—flaws and all.

He didn't seem to hear a word she said.

It was almost time for the Carson family gathering she'd first heard about six weeks ago—the day Jake had come up with the brilliant idea of having Cody and Dana pose as a couple. Dana and Cody made tentative plans to go—depending, of course, on her stepmother's condition.

Dana called Memphis every day, only to be assured by Hilda that Barbara was no better, but no worse, either. There was no reason Cody and Dana shouldn't take one weekend off for his family, Hilda insisted, seconded vehemently by Barbara. Dana gave Hilda emergency numbers and a long list of instructions, which the longtime retainer accepted with patient understanding.

And finally the designated Saturday morning arrived, and it was time to go. And Dana was a nervous wreck.

"Relax," Cody insisted as he drove the last few miles toward his grandmother's house in Malvern, where the family had agreed to gather in honor of her eightieth birthday. "Nothing's going to go wrong in Memphis. And if it does, I can have you there in three and a half hours if I break a few speed limits."

Dana tucked her hair behind her ear. "I know. I talked to Barbara just before we left home. She sounded fine."

"Then why are you so nervous? Surely you aren't worried about spending the day with my family."

"I'm not?" Dana asked wryly.

"Of course not," he assured her firmly. "They're very nice people, Dana. You've already met most of them. They like you. They love me. What more could you ask?"

She made a face at him. "Don't tell me this is going to be easy for you. It's the first time you've seen any of them but Rachel since we were married. You know they're all going to make a big deal of it."

"I would hope so," he said with teasing indignance. "Being married *is* a big deal. I expect my family to treat me with the new respect I deserve as a mature, married man."

"I'll agree with the married part," Dana murmured. "As for the maturity..."

He chuckled and changed the subject. Dana thought wistfully that there would have been a time when he'd have shouted in overstated outrage, and then have immediately retaliated. Outrageously, most likely.

She missed the old Cody.

Chapter Fifteen

Granny Fran met them at her door, visibly quivering with excitement at welcoming her grandson and his new bride.

"Cody," she cried, opening her arms to him. "Oh, it's so good to see you!"

Cody gathered his petite, gray-haired grandmother close, his expression so tender that Dana felt a lump form in her throat. He had so much love to give—would he ever feel free to love *her?*

Frances Carson turned to Dana then, studying her in satisfaction. "Dana," she said, holding out steady, age-spotted hands. "Welcome to my home—and to our family."

Touched by the simple words, Dana took the woman's hands in her own and pressed a shy kiss against her soft, lined cheek. "Thank you," she said. "Happy birthday, Granny Fran."

"Thank you, dear. Come in. Everyone else is already here and they're eager to see you."

Dana silently gulped. As though sensing her sudden surge of panic, Cody slipped an arm around her waist.

Frances led them through her small, neat house to the back lawn where the family had gathered with picnic tables and lawn chairs. "It's a good thing the weather is still so nice," Frances commented. "This mob fills my house from rafter to rafter when they all try to get inside."

Had Dana not met most of Cody's family at one time or another, she would never have been able to learn all their names that day. There seemed to be dozens of them, milling, chattering and laughing on Frances's tiny back lawn.

"Cody!" someone squealed. A dark-haired figure in brightly colored clothing broke away from the mob to throw herself on Cody's chest.

Laughing, he caught her and lifted her for an enthusiastic hug. "Hi, Celia," he said. "You look great."

"Must be that maternal glow everyone's always talking about. I'm pregnant, Cody. We just found out for sure yesterday."

"You're kidding! Celia, that's great. Oh, God, you're going to be a mother. That poor, helpless baby."

"Hey," his sister protested with a laugh. "I resent that."

"So do I," said a tall, dark-haired man who'd approached more sedately behind Celia. "The baby won't be entirely helpless—he'll have me to protect him from her."

"Reed!" Celia wailed, tossing her head and planting her hands on her slender hips. "What a rotten thing to say. Besides, it's going to be a girl. I have a very strong feeling about that."

Her husband groaned and held out a hand to his brother-in-law. "Good to see you, Cody. And congratulations on your marriage."

Celia had already turned to Dana. Dana had always considered Cody's younger sister to be one of the most beautiful women she'd ever known. Her flawless oval face framed in clouds of dark hair, her eyes the same bright blue as Cody's, Celia had been turning heads since she was a teenager. Cody had explained that his sister hadn't lost her own head until she'd met Reed Hollander. And then she'd fallen hard.

"Dana," Celia said, startling her with an eager hug. "I'm so happy for you. You always were the best waitress at Country Straight."

Dana couldn't help laughing. "Is that why you approve of me as a sister-in-law?"

"No. I approve of you because Cody chose you—and because you had the good sense to see behind that smart-aleck exterior of his to the pretty decent guy inside. But it doesn't hurt that you never let my hamburgers get cold before you served them to me," she added impudently.

Dana smiled. "It's wonderful news about your baby. When is it due?"

"Late in June—a couple of months after Rachel's. The family's growing fast, isn't it?"

Celia's husband greeted Dana politely. She'd met him only once before, but she'd been impressed then by the government agent's quiet strength and aura of command. She might have found him a bit intimidating had it not been for the utter adoration in his eyes when he looked at his lovely wife.

"You remember Adam and Jenny, don't you, Dana?" Cody asked, having already greeted his cousin and his wife. "And the little imp in Adam's arms is their daughter, Melissa."

Dr. Adam Stone was a prominent plastic surgeon in Little Rock. Many people considered him arrogant and brusque. He'd always been very polite to Dana, though they'd met only briefly at the club. He was an attractive man, but of course, not as handsome as her own husband, she privately decided.

His wife, Jenny, was a serene-looking woman with a cap of dark brown curls and beautiful golden-brown eyes. Their curly-haired daughter was adorable, her chubby cheeks creased with deep dimples, her dark brown eyes flashing with intelligence and lively curiosity.

Cody had explained that Melissa was born nine months ago when Jenny had been stranded in a secluded cabin with Adam—a stranger to her, then—during a dangerous ice storm. Adam had delivered the baby, and had then fallen in love with both mother and child. They were married a few short months later, and Adam had legally adopted Melissa.

They seemed to be a very happy family, Dana thought with a touch of wistfulness.

Rachel and Seth waved a greeting, and Rachel's children, Paige and Aaron, rushed up to Cody for hugs and tickles, which he obligingly provided. They'd already accepted Dana as their favorite uncle's wife; they greeted her with sweet kisses and a touch of smugness that they'd already spent time with the woman the others were just getting to know.

The only member of the family Dana had never met was Cody's aunt, Arlene—Adam's widowed mother. Cody had mentioned that his aunt was a rather self-centered and demanding woman with a healthy dose of snobbishness thrown in, so Dana was a bit nervous about meeting her.

Immaculately groomed and a bit overdressed for a family potluck on the lawn, Arlene was quite gracious when introduced to her nephew's wife, much to Dana's relief.

Cody's parents had held back while the others came forward. When it was their turn, they hugged and kissed Cody and then Dana. They had already expressed their approval of the marriage over the telephone; they took the opportunity now to do so in person.

"How is your stepmother, dear?" Cody's mother, Evelyn, asked, her kind face creased with sympathy and concern.

"She's about the same," Dana replied, knowing Cody had kept his parents informed. "I'm afraid it's just a matter of time now."

Evelyn squeezed her hands. "I'm so sorry. If there's anything Bill and I can do, I hope you won't hesitate to call on us."

Dana had to blink back a film of tears as she thanked her.

"Come sit down and talk to us, Dana," Granny Fran urged, taking Dana's arm and leading her toward a group of chairs that the women had claimed. "The boys are going to start the grill soon. That's why we wanted to cook out—it's the only time men think they're supposed to do the cooking. That macho thing, you know."

Dana giggled.

Cody gave her a smile of approval as he joined the men who'd gathered around the grill to ponder the most efficient arrangement of charcoal briquettes.

It was a hectic, yet delightful, day. Dana enjoyed it immensely—or she would have, if Cody hadn't been trying so hard to make sure she had a good time.

"Honestly," Celia grumbled at one point, shaking her head in bewilderment at her brother's uncharacteristically solicitous behavior after sending him off on a trumped-up errand. "One would think you were made of spun glass, Dana. Doesn't he ever relax and let you just enjoy yourself?"

Dana forced a smile. "I think he's worried that I won't feel a part of the family. I keep telling him that everyone's made me very welcome, but he wants to make sure I'm having a good time."

"It's very sweet of him, I suppose," Celia conceded. "But weird."

Dana smiled, but privately agreed.

Even Cody's family was noticing that he wasn't acting like himself, she thought in regret. They would obviously decide it had been marriage that had changed him.

Would their initial approval fade when they realized that the Cody they all loved so dearly had somehow changed since he'd donned that gold band?

Late that afternoon, Granny Fran drew Dana inside for a chat alone. Since no one followed them in, Dana assumed the older woman had let the others know she wanted her new granddaughter-in-law to herself. She steeled herself for what was to come.

Frances sat on the sofa in her living room and patted the cushion beside her. "Come sit beside me."

Dana perched carefully on the overstuffed sofa. "Did you want to talk to me, Granny Fran?" she asked, having been specifically requested to use the affectionate nickname the others called her.

"Yes, dear." Frances rested a hand on Dana's arm. "I know about your family problems. Cody said you've been almost single-handedly holding your family together for quite a while now."

Dana squirmed, uncomfortable at that image. Was that really how Cody saw it? "I've only done what was necessary," she explained.

"Cody tells me you are a young woman who takes her commitments and her responsibilities very seriously. He's told me how hard you've worked to earn your degree, how devoted you've been to your stepmother and your little brother. It's obvious that he admires you very much."

Dana looked down at her lap. Admiration was one thing—love something else, entirely. And she found that she very much wanted both from Cody. "It's very kind of him to say so," she said mechanically.

"He wasn't being kind, dear. He was being a very proud husband. He wanted me to know what a fine young woman he has married."

Dana swallowed hard.

"I think it's been a long time since you've had anyone to turn to with your own problems," Frances said gently. "I just want you to know that I'm here for you now, if you'd like to talk. Something seems to be bothering you, and if there's anything I can do, anything at all..."

"Thank you," Dana choked out, blinking rapidly. "But I don't—"

"I'm not trying to pry, Dana. It's just that I consider you one of my own now, and my grandchildren have always been able to come to me with their problems. I want you to feel free to do so, as well."

Dana was so tempted. Frances Carson was such a kind and obviously caring woman. But it had been so long since Dana had felt free to burden anyone else with her own problems. So long that she'd been the one who had to find her own answers. Until Cody had made her problems his own, and had offered to help her shoulder them.

Had he sacrificed his own needs in the process? Was that why he'd changed—why he'd seemed so anxious lately? So grimly determined to be the perfect mate?

Dana didn't know what set her off. One minute she was shaking her head, telling Granny Fran she had no problems—and in the next minute she heard herself spilling the whole story, from start to finish. From Jake's impulsive suggestion of a practical joke on the Carson family, to Dana's own adaptation of the charade for her stepmother's benefit. From her fears for Andy's future to Cody's unselfish offer to help her raise him.

She told Granny Fran the circumstances of their hasty wedding. The promises Cody had made to Barbara—and to Dana. The promises Dana had made in return.

And Frances listened to the whole complicated tale without saying a word, though she couldn't help shaking her head a few times.

When Dana had finished, she waited apprehensively for a reaction.

She didn't expect Cody's grandmother to place an arm around her, hug her warmly and say, "Oh, you poor dear. What a difficult time you've had. It's no wonder you're so confused. Or Cody, either."

Dana dashed at her wet eyes with an impatient hand. "Cody's trying so hard," she whispered. "He's taking his promises very seriously."

"He's trying *too* hard, isn't he, dear?"

Dana nodded miserably. "I don't think he's very happy. He acts as though he's terrified of making a mistake, doing or saying the wrong thing. How can he be happy in this marriage if he's afraid to be himself?"

Frances sighed and sat for a moment in silence, Dana's hands in hers. And then she smiled ruefully. "Most people who know my grandson would never believe that he has a terrible problem with insecurity. That he's been fighting a battle with low self-esteem for more years than I like to think about."

Dana's head lifted. She knew about Cody's problems—at least, some of them—but she'd understood that his family had been kept in the dark. Just how much *did* his grandmother know?

"I suspect you are aware that Cody once had a problem with drinking," Frances said, almost as though she'd read Dana's mind.

Dana gulped. "Well, yes, he told me, but—"

"But he thinks I don't know," Frances completed wryly. "He's wrong, of course. The family knows. We just didn't accept it until it was almost too late. His parents and I told ourselves that he was simply going through that wild stage many young men have to travel on their paths to maturity. We underestimated the problem. We were terribly wrong not to get involved sooner. Cody blames himself. Bill and Evelyn and I blame ourselves."

"I told Cody that it's time to let the past—and the guilt—go," Dana murmured. "I've tried to tell him that he paid for his mistakes and that he's done a wonderful job of turning his life around. He seems to find it hard to accept."

Frances nodded sadly. "That car accident almost killed him, in more ways than one. He was so wracked with self-recrimination that it broke my heart. There was a time when I wondered if I would ever hear him laugh again. After that, he seemed to shrug everything off with a laugh and a wisecrack, as though nothing mattered very deeply to him. I knew, of course, that just the opposite was true."

"He had me fooled," Dana admitted. "For a while, I thought he was little more than a good-looking clown. There were times when I thought I saw something more behind the facade, but he was so very good at hiding it. Now that he's convinced himself that he has to be serious and responsible—for my sake and Andy's—I miss his teasing and his laughter. And I don't want to be guarded and protected by him, Granny Fran. Not from a misplaced sense of obligation or a determination to prove that he's competent and dependable. I want to be..."

"Loved?" the older woman gently supplied when Dana hesitated.

Dana nodded mutely.

"My dear, do you really think Cody would be trying this hard if he *didn't* love you? Do you really think earning your approval would matter so very much to him if he didn't care very deeply?"

Dana's eyes widened. "But—"

Frances smiled. "Let me tell you a little more about my Cody, dear. As his wife, there are several things I think you should know."

Leaving Bill, Evelyn and Arlene to stay the night in Frances's two spare bedrooms, the second generation of Carsons spent the night in an aging, but immaculately clean little motel a couple of miles away. They parted outside their rooms, Adam carrying his sleeping daughter, Seth holding a groggy Aaron, Rachel guiding Paige, who was so tired she was almost sleepwalking.

Celia pointed out happily that next year she and Reed would have a baby to put to bed. Dana found herself picturing a little boy with Cody's blue eyes and heartbreaking smile, and wondered if their marriage would ever have a foundation solid enough for them to start a real family.

She told herself that she would know soon. She couldn't live in this limbo much longer.

Carrying their bags, Dana and Cody entered their own room after promising to meet the others for breakfast the next morning. Cody dropped his bag at the foot of the bed and shook his head in dismay at the room's color scheme. "Orange carpet with a peach-and-green floral spread?" He shuddered. "I might not be a decorator, but even *I* know that's a fashion mistake."

Dana smiled. "It goes rather nicely with the pink-and-white Degas print over the bed, don't you think?"

"Is that what that is?" Cody studied the faded, gracefully posed ballerina for a moment, then shrugged. "Okay, so it's a classy place. Genuine reproduction art on the walls."

Dana laughed. "It's clean. I'm not complaining."

"No, you aren't, are you? Do you ever complain, Dana?" he asked, only half joking.

"Only when there's something I don't like," she replied. "I'm having a good time this weekend, Cody. It's nice to be away from everything for a couple of days, isn't it?"

"Did you really enjoy today?" he asked, looking a bit anxious. "Everyone treated you okay? No one made you feel uncomfortable? Aunt Arlene, maybe?"

"You have a very nice family," she told him firmly. "And your Aunt Arlene was quite pleasant. After spending three days with Lynette and Alan, how could you possibly imagine that I would complain about *your* relatives?"

He seemed satisfied, at least for the moment. "I think I'll take a shower," he said. "Er, unless you want to take one first?"

"No, go ahead," she said with a suppressed sigh.

He pulled a few things out of his suitcase and disappeared into the tiny bathroom, closing the door behind him.

Dana dropped onto the end of the bed and groaned. God, she couldn't stand this much longer, she thought. Cody was being so thoughtful and polite that she was very close to biting him.

She heard the shower running in the bathroom, and she stared glumly at the bathroom door. And then she cocked her head and bit her lower lip as a mischievous thought occurred to her.

She tiptoed quietly to the bathroom door and tested the knob. It wasn't locked. She peeked inside.

The old bathtub-shower combination was concealed by a heavy plastic curtain. Steam rose from behind it, and she could hear Cody lathering up. Her mouth went dry as she pictured him. She shook the erotic images off, telling herself there would be time for that later. She hoped.

His clean briefs and pajama bottoms lay neatly on the counter, waiting for him to step into them. She tucked them beneath her arm, adding the discarded pair as an afterthought. And then, moving silently and swiftly, she gathered every towel from the room and carried them into the bedroom.

Stepping back into the bathroom, she looked around reflectively, wondering if there was anything else she could do to get her husband's full attention. He hadn't noticed her intrusion yet, but she knew it wouldn't be long before cool air would warn him that the door was open.

She tugged at her lip, wondering if the plumbing in this motel was as antiquated as the decor.

She turned on the hot water in the sink, full strength.

A startled yelp came from behind the shower curtain as Cody was undoubtedly hit by a blast of icy cold water. "Dana?" he called out curiously.

She smiled and left the room, closing the door firmly behind her.

She sat on the end of the bed, her chin in her hands, the towels and Cody's clothing beside her. Waiting.

She heard him turn off the water, heard the shower curtain rings scraping against their metal bar. Heard Cody stumbling around—groping, probably, for a towel.

"Dana?" he said again, sounding confused. "Hey, Dana?"

She didn't move.

A moment later the bathroom door opened and Cody stuck his dripping head around it, blinking water from his eyelashes. "Dana?"

"Yes, Cody?" she asked sweetly, keeping her seat.

"Did you take the towels?"

"Yes, Cody."

"And my clothes?"

"Yes, Cody."

"Er, you want to tell me why?"

"No," she said consideringly. "I don't think so."

He paused a moment. And then he opened the door and stepped through it in all his naked, wet glory.

"You know," she said on a sigh. "You were right. It really *is* an awe-inspiring sight."

Cody planted his fists on his hips. "You want to tell me what's going on?"

She sighed in exasperation. "It's a joke, Cody. Remember them? Remember fun?"

"Oh." He seemed genuinely taken aback. "I see. Yeah, that was funny."

She rolled her eyes. "I can tell you're just rolling with laughter. Honestly. Jake was right. You *have* gotten staid. And it's a real shame."

"I really don't know what... damn it, hand me a towel, will you? I'm getting goose bumps."

"And lovely goose bumps they are, too," she assured him.

Staring at her, he snatched a towel and wrapped it around his waist. She would have sworn he was very close to blushing.

"Are you trying to tell me something?" he asked finally.

She sighed again, more expressively this time. "Staid *and* slow," she muttered. "Yes, Cody, I'm trying to tell you something. I'm trying to tell you that you've changed, and

I don't like it. I want you to laugh again. To crack silly jokes. To play practical jokes on me and make me want to strangle you again. I want the old Cody back, damn it. Not this... this Stepford husband you've been trying to be for the past few weeks."

"I don't know what you're talking about."

She summed up her reaction to that in one succinct word. Cody blinked in surprise, having never heard her curse like that before.

"Stop it," she said then, fiercely. "Stop trying so hard. You're making yourself miserable—you're making *me* miserable. You don't have to prove to me that you're a paragon, or a hero, or a model of perfection. I know you're human. I know you have flaws. And I don't care. I love you, anyway."

Cody almost dropped the towel. He made a hasty grab for it, holding it up with one white-knuckled fist. "You...Dana, do you know what you're saying?"

She threw up her hands. "Yes! I know what I'm saying. I'm not an idiot. Would you please stop treating me like one!"

He looked stricken as he moved to perch carefully beside her. "I never meant to treat you like an idiot," he said sincerely. "If I've hurt you, if I've done anything to upset you, I want you to tell me. I'll make it up to you, I promise."

"You're hurting me now, Cody," she whispered, her eyes burning. "Can't you see? I love you. But I can't seem to reach you. And it's breaking my heart."

His eyes were tortured, his jaw so tight she could see the muscles clenched in his cheek. "We've talked about this before. You're feeling grateful to me, and you're very vulnerable right now. You need time to—"

She hit him. Doubled up her fist and smacked him right on his bare, wet shoulder.

"Damn you, Cody. Don't you dare tell me what I'm feeling," she said heatedly. "I am perfectly capable of taking care of myself—*and* my little brother—without your help, if I have to. I've told you that from the beginning, and I haven't changed my opinion. I married you for a lot of reasons, some of them the wrong reasons, I'm aware. But mostly I married you because I loved you, even then. I just couldn't admit it until now."

"Dana—"

She held her chin proudly. "I've learned during the past month that I don't want a marriage of convenience. I don't want you staying with me because you think I need you, or because you've made a promise you feel obliged to keep. I want a marriage—a *real* marriage, like your sisters and your cousin have—or I'd rather be alone."

"Dana, I love you. I've probably loved you from the day I met you," Cody said quietly.

Her eyes narrowed. "You love me?"

"Desperately." His voice was husky. "I'll never give you cause to doubt it again."

"Then why have you been acting so strangely?" she demanded, afraid to give in to the hope that had suddenly blossomed inside her. "Why have you been so serious—so unhappy?"

"I haven't been unhappy," he assured her. "I've been . . . scared."

She frowned. "Scared? Of what?"

"That you'd realize what a mistake you'd made in marrying me," he admitted quietly. "I knew you could take care of yourself and Andy. I've always known. You've never really needed me, not like that. But I thought if I could convince you that I can help you with him, that I can be a good husband to you, a responsible and dependable role model for Andy, maybe you would give me a chance to earn your love."

"You don't earn love. It isn't something you acquire with so many points for good behavior. Look at your family."

"What about my family?"

"They adore you," she said simply. "They see you exactly as you are, flaws and all, and they love you even more for it. You haven't had to earn their love—they've given it freely and gladly."

He looked away. "They see me the way they want to see me, because I'm part of the family. Because they've always loved me. They don't know—"

"Don't they?" Dana asked gently. "You're underestimating them as well as me. They know you. Much better than you think."

He looked at her questioningly.

"I talked to your grandmother for a long time today," she said. "She knows about your history of drinking, Cody. She knows what happened the night of your accident. They were devastated for you, because it was hurting you. Yet they always believed in you. Your father and Adam spent a long time talking to the police and the courts while you were in the hospital, convincing them that you knew the magnitude of your mistake and that they fully believed you would never drink and drive again."

Cody winced. "I didn't know Adam got involved then."

"Did you know that Adam called your bank in Percy and personally guaranteed the loan on your club?" Dana asked, hoping and praying she was doing the right thing by telling him this.

He choked. "No."

"Well, he did. He didn't tell you because he didn't want you being grateful to him—I'm sure you can understand that feeling," she added dryly. "Gratitude, as you know, is a very pale substitute for real love."

"I can't believe he did that."

"He trusted you," she said simply. "He knew it would be hard for two young men with little credit history to get a loan on a risky endeavor like Country Straight, but he knew you would do everything you could to make your business a success. He knew you wouldn't let him down. And you haven't. Granny Fran said Adam's been very proud of you, as all of them have."

"I'll have to thank him—"

"You'll do no such thing," Dana told him curtly. "He didn't want you to know, and I want you to promise you won't embarrass him, or me, or Granny Fran by breaking this confidence."

"But—"

"Granny Fran thinks you're worried that you disappointed your father by dropping out of college, and by getting into the trouble with your accident. She says you're wrong. Your father brags about you all the time, she said. He says he was never much of a businessman himself, and he admires anyone who can successfully run a restaurant and handle all the paperwork and everything that goes along with being a business owner. They all know that you carry most of that responsibility at the club, that Jake concentrates more on hiring and supervising the employees.

"Your family loves you, Cody. They admire you very much. They trust you. And so do I."

He turned to her then, his hands unsteady as they settled on her shoulders. "I'll never give you reason to regret loving me, Dana," he said fervently. "I'll never let you down."

"Yes," she whispered. "You will."

He flinched as though she'd hit him, but she swept on without giving him a chance to say anything, trying desperately to make him understand.

"Of course you'll make me angry. You'll hurt me with a careless word or action. You're human, damn it, not a robot. Do you honestly believe I'll never make a mistake in our marriage, that I'll never accidentally hurt you or disappoint you? I hope you don't expect that of me. I'm human, too. I make mistakes. And I'd hate to think you would stop loving me just because I can't be perfect."

She could almost see her point sink into him. His eyes widened. "I never expected you to be perfect," he said slowly. "I don't care about that. I love you."

The heady relief made her sag against him. He understood, she thought. He finally, really understood what she'd been trying to tell him.

"Say it again," she demanded, lifting her face to his.

"I love you," he murmured against her lips. "Oh, God, Dana, I love you so much."

He kissed her then, and she wound her arms around his neck, her fingers buried in his dripping hair, her breasts crushed against his damp chest. He felt warm and wonderful and oh, so very human. And she loved him so much it hurt.

She knew there were painful, difficult times ahead for them. But they'd get through them. The love they'd found together would give them strength and comfort. Just as it would bring laughter, and joy, and contentment in the happier days.

"Dana?" Cody murmured as he pressed her down onto the bed.

She had already reached for his towel. "Mmm?" she asked as she tossed the scrap of terry cloth aside.

"Next time you take a shower...brace yourself," he warned wickedly. "I *will* have my revenge."

She laughed. "Sounds like fun," she assured him.

"I'll show you real fun," he promised, a piratical grin creasing his handsome face.

She threw herself wholeheartedly into the celebration of their love.

And found that Cody was right. It really *was* fun.

Epilogue

Frances Carson sat on the sofa in her living room, a thick stack of photographs in her hands. The pictures had been taken two weeks earlier, at Christmas, when the family had gathered at Adam's house for a noisy, love-filled celebration of the season.

A clatter from the kitchen made Frances look up for a moment, but she quickly turned her attention back to the photographs. The full-time, live-in housekeeper Adam had insisted on hiring just before his grandmother's eighty-fifth birthday was a nice lady, but she certainly could make a racket when she fixed dinner.

Frances didn't complain. The housekeeper had been a compromise: Frances remained in the little house where she'd lived with her husband and children for so many happy years, and Adam could rest easy, knowing she had someone looking out for her welfare.

The photographs were wonderful. They brought back so many happy feelings and memories. There was one of Celia and Reed and their precious four-year-old son, Joshua Damien Hollander, named after a good friend of theirs.

Celia looked lovely, as always, even round with pregnancy again. They were hoping for a little girl this time, though Frances knew they would gladly welcome a son, if that's what they'd been given.

There was a shot of Seth and Rachel, still looking blissfully happy after six years of marriage, and Paige and Aaron and little Lisa. Paige was getting so grown up, Frances thought with a faint sigh. A teenager now. And Aaron wasn't far behind her. They were bright and very well-behaved; Frances was extremely proud of them, as she was of all her grandchildren and great-grandchildren.

The next photograph was of Arlene, surrounded by her own grandchildren—Melissa, Kevin and Emily. Proud parents Adam and Jenny stood in the background, his arm around her waist. Adam looked content, Frances thought in satisfaction. Happy.

And then she laughed when she turned to a photo of Cody and Dana and Andy, a tall, handsome young teenager now. Dana was holding the new baby, Barbara Lynn, who slept soundly, unaware of the festivities around her. Cody stood behind his wife and young brother-in-law, grinning and making bunny ears behind their heads with his fingers.

Her grandson was such a joker, Frances thought with an indulgent smile. She hardly ever saw him without a smile on his face. But they were real smiles now, not a disguise to conceal his insecurities. Dana had helped him become aware of his own self-worth; Frances would love her for that, even if she didn't love Dana for her own sweet personality.

She'd worried about them at first. Their marriage had certainly gotten off to a shaky start, based on a very tentative foundation. But Frances had long since been reassured that the marriage had quickly become a real one, a partnership that would last a lifetime. Cody was happy and fulfilled; Dana had learned to relax more, especially once she obtained her degree and found a job teaching elementary students, a career she seemed to love.

They'd done a wonderful job thus far raising young Andy, who adored both of them. She knew it hadn't been easy for them at first. Andy had been grief stricken when his mother passed away only a few months after Dana and Cody married, and it had taken time for him adjust to his new home, and his new life. But the love he'd found with them had given him strength and peace, and he was on his way now to becoming a very fine young man.

Frances loved him as though he'd always been a part of her family, and she knew he was equally fond of his Granny Fran—as all her children were.

"Dinner's ready, Miz Fran," Mary, the housekeeper, said from the doorway. "You want to look at the rest of your pictures after you eat?"

Frances set the photographs reluctantly aside. "Yes. Perhaps you'd like to look at them with me."

"That would be nice," Mary agreed with a smile. "I always like hearing about that big, happy family of yours."

Frances's own smile was proud, and satisfied. She'd done her job well, she thought in contentment. Her family *was* a happy one.

They had all been blessed with love.

* * * * *

Dear Reader,

It is a great honor for me to have this chance to participate in Silhouette Special Edition's Celebration 1000! As a longtime romance reader, I've been a fan of Special Edition since the beginning, and have many, many "keepers" in my own personal library. As a romance writer, I feel it's a special privilege for me to be associated with a line that continually strives for freshness and excellence.

Cody's Fiancée is my fourteenth Special Edition. In these books, I have often explored the dynamics of family relationships—all types of families. With the Family Way series, I wanted to study an "average" family—people tied together by blood and a common background, yet each individual with special needs and dreams. In the future, I hope to explore other types of interpersonal relationships and interesting characters who find romance in fresh new ways. I have several unrelated ideas brewing now, and perhaps I'll start a new series when another set of characters present themselves to me.

It's a great pleasure for me to know that the editors and staff of Special Edition will be there to encourage me with those ideas. It's also a special treat to hear from readers who have enjoyed my books and tell me they look forward to more. It is my goal to make each book better than the one before—and always, of course, to provide a happy, satisfying ending for readers like myself, who love to escape into the pages of a good romance.

Congratulations, Special Edition!

Gina Ferris Wilkins

COMING NEXT MONTH

#1009 THE COWBOY AND HIS BABY—Sherryl Woods
That's My Baby!/And Baby Makes Three
Forgetting Melissa Horton had never been easy for Cody Adams. And now that he'd discovered she was the mother of his baby, he had even more reason to reconcile with his one true love....

#1010 THE MAN, THE MOON AND THE MARRIAGE VOW—Christine Rimmer
The Jones Gang
Evie Jones had been waiting all her life for love to conquer all. Single father Erik Riggins had given up on love, but once he'd laid eyes on Evie, nothing would stop him from proposing matrimony!

#1011 FRIENDS, LOVERS...AND BABIES!—Joan Elliott Pickart
The Baby Bet
Ryan MacAllister and Deedee Hamilton never expected that their status as friends would change to lovers. But then Deedee's pregnancy changed all the rules–and Ryan had to face his true feelings for her....

#1012 BUCHANAN'S BRIDE—Pamela Toth
Buckles & Broncos
She was just what he needed, but tall, silent cowboy Taylor Buchanan would never let his guard down around Ashley Gray. It was up to Ashley to lasso his heart and show him how to love again....

#1013 CHILD OF MIDNIGHT—Sharon De Vita
If renegade cop Michael Tyler had a soft spot, it was for kids in trouble This time the child came complete with hotshot Alexandria Kent–the one woman who set his heart on fire and whom he'd sworn he'd stay away from....

#1014 THE WEDDING CONTRACT—Kelly Jamison
If Laura Halstead accepted Jake McClennon's generous offer of marriage, she could keep custody of her daughter. While Jake stressed a union in name only, Laura was hoping this marriage of convenience would be interrupted by love....